CONSUMING REDEMPTION

LOVE IN THE NORTH

J S GREY

Copyright © 2021 by J S Grey. All Rights Reserved.

No part of this publication may be reproduced, distributed, or transmitted in any form or by any means, including photocopying, recording, or other electronic or mechanical methods, or by any information storage and retrieval system without the prior written permission of the publisher, except in the case of very brief quotations embodied in critical reviews and certain other noncommercial uses permitted by copyright law.

Consuming Redemption: Love in the north

This book was published thanks to free support and training from:

TCKPublishing.com

Beta Readers:

Nadia Mack

Nicole Peck

Yann-Shern Keh

Contents

Chapter 1 – Tyler

Chapter 2 – Tyler

Chapter 3 – Lukas

Chapter 4 – Tyler

Chapter 5 – Tyler

Chapter 6 – Tyler

Chapter 7 – Lukas

Chapter 8 – Tyler

Chapter 9 – Tyler

Chapter 10 – Lukas

Chapter 11 – Tyler

Chapter 12 - Tyler

Chapter 13 - Lukas

Chapter 14 - Lukas

Chapter 15 - Tyler

Chapter 16 - Lukas

Chapter 17 - Tyler

Chapter 18 - Lukas

Chapter 19 - Tyler

Chapter 20 - Lukas

Chapter 21 - Tyler

Chapter 22 - Lukas

Chapter 23 - Tyler

Chapter 24 - Lukas

Chapter 25 - Tyler

Chapter 26 - Lukas

Chapter 27 - Tyler

Chapter 28 - Lukas

Chapter 29 - Tyler

Chapter 30 - Lukas

Chapter 31 - Lukas

Epilogue -

ACKNOWLEDGEMENTS

This being my first full length-ish book is kind of a big deal for me. Writing is something that I have ALWAYS dreamed of doing. It's like I had a thousand stories in my head and never really possessed the dedication to put pen to paper **(hands to keyboard – it *ain't the 1920's up in here*)** and actually do it. For the push that I needed and all the support I could hope for I have to thank my amazing husband. Between your own busy career, raising our son together and listening to my crazy ramblings when writing this story, you somehow managed to find the time to proofread the entire book numerous times and edit all my typos **(There were lots).** Lots of love always. *This book is dedicated to you.*

Also, I have to thank an amazing friend and sounding board Nadia Mack. I don't think I would have been able to navigate this crazy author world without her constant support and harsh slaps of reality. I love you! :P

Chapter 1.

Tyler

2001

The shrill sound of my alarm screeches next to my bed. The sharp chill of winter bites in the air; my mother, always trying to be as green as possible shuts off the heating last thing at night. The covers, still pulled over my head, only dull the sound slightly. I know I have moments before my mother, in her booming voice, starts telling me to shut the damn thing off.

I reach out from underneath the blankets, the frigid air raising goosebumps along the length of my arm. As I now have this practiced down to a fine art, I'm able to take one quick swipe at the gold-coloured bell alarm that adorns my bedside table, knocking the thing under my bed and silencing the demon device. The quiet gives me the moments of peace I need to fall back into dreamless sleep. I pull the blankets back over my head and snuggle into their delicious warmth.

"Don't even think of going back to sleep Tyler!" my mother calls from the next room.

"I'm not!" I yell back through the wall.

"Then why are the covers back over your head?" I pull down my duvet looking around to see if somehow she has managed to creep into my room unnoticed. Seeing I'm alone in my room, I frown at the wall.

"That's better," she calls. My eyes widen as I stare at the adjoining wall.

"Gotta be a witch," I mutter to myself. Swinging my legs off the side of the bed I give myself a moment to contemplate existence as I stare into the middle distance, my brain now fully awake.

Suddenly the realisation hits me: "It's not Saturday, it's Friday!" I groan, falling back onto the bed. Another day at that god-damned place before the sweet precious release of the weekend.

The weekend is a place of solitude and peace where I can be whoever the hell I want to be without the constant worry that I'm going to run into *him*. School would actually be fairly enjoyable if it wasn't for *him*. I get along well with most of my teachers, and when I am given the time and space to concentrate during class I actually get good grades. All of that changed though the day Lukas Ford came into my life.

Forcing myself to stand, I stumble past the discarded clothes I had left on the floor the night before and head towards my bathroom. I stop along the way to open the dark wooden slats currently blocking the rising sun's rays from entering my room. Flicking on the bathroom light, I rub away the remnants of slumber from my eyes and gaze at myself in the mirror. The thick blonde neck-length hair that normally falls quite nicely and frames my face has rearranged itself into quite a decent-looking bird's nest on top of my head. I run my long fingers through the messy mop, before resigning myself to the fact that I'm going to have to wash and dry it into some type of style. I give myself an appraising once-over. My light blue eyes stare back at me tiredly, the threat of dark circles under my eyes trying to make themselves known on my slightly tanned complexion.

There were times when my self esteem was affected not only by *him*, but by what I perceived to be the shallowness of my own thoughts. I had looked at myself in this very mirror previously and thought to myself, *But I'm actually quite hot, shouldn't I be popular?*, before giving myself an internal bitch slap for sounding like a dick. Shallow me wasn't wrong though, I am not a bad guy to look at: nice full lips, a dimpled chin that reminded me of Clark Kent from old Superman comics, sunkissed skin that gave the impression that I had either spent a lot of dedicated hours at the beach, or had made regular visits to the sunbed, when in fact I had my mother's Italian heritage to thank for my naturally olive skin.

Whilst our surname might be Dane through my father's side, my mother's original surname had been Fiorentino, which I thought was just awesome. She had not been convinced when I had begun high school to let me use her maiden name instead of my father's name. So I'm just plain old Tyler Dane.

After taking a quick shower and pulling on what I think will be acceptable wallflower attire I make my way downstairs. My mother has beaten me to it; she's standing at the stovetop pouring pancake batter and blueberries into a skillet.

"I'm going out on a limb and saying I think it's a pancake kind of morning," she says, craning her neck around the corner to give me a small wink.

I hand her a small dish and nod. "Load me up please; that bacon as well," I say, pointing to the stack of crispy streaky bacon piled on a greasy kitchen towel next to her. Letting out a small breathy chuckle she nods and puts a few rashers on the plate. "Syrup?" I ask in a more accusatory tone. She purses her lips and reaches onto the shelf next to the stovetop, pulling down a small white jar of maple syrup. Pouring on what could arguably be called a drip onto my plate, she hands it to me. I move across to a small dining nook on the far side of the room and take a seat at our old country style farm table.

"Your teeth are going to fall out you know?" she tells me matter-of-factly, "Also it's really not fair how you can eat that much food and still stay in shape."

"Curse of all this beauty," I say, gesturing from my face down my body with a flourish of my hand. My mother smiles wide and nods.

"So what's the plan for today?" she asks.

My mood sours almost immediately. She picks the paper up from the worktop and comes to join me at the table, taking a seat on the bench opposite me. The gleam in her eye fills me with a morose sadness, she is likely hoping against hope that I've sprung some kind of social life overnight and that I'll tell her I'm going to a party or meeting some friends and getting drunk in a park somewhere.

"Just school then home." I try for a bright smile, but from the look she gives me I can see she isn't buying whatever it is I'm trying to sell her.

"My handsome boy, I know things aren't great right now, but I promise you, just hold on and things will get better." She reaches across the old wooden table and rests her hand over mine.

"They have to," I smile. She bites her bottom lip and looks down at the paper, the pain tangible on her face. "I'll be ok, but only if I get going now otherwise I'm going to be late," I say, glancing down at my watch. My mother loves me, of this I am very sure, but part of me hates myself for making her worry about me. I wish I could be normal like everyone else and not weigh her down with the burden of having me for a son. Running back up to my room, I grab the last of my things and head out the door towards school.

Six hours after I arrive at school I stare out of the classroom window, watching the icy rain pelt against the windowpane. The clouds were already dark, growing thicker with each passing hour. The noise of the water hitting the glass distracts me from listening to our History teacher trying desperately to make the

Industrial Revolution interesting to a group of 16-year-old high schoolers on a Friday afternoon. The battle had been lost before it had begun; she knows it, the students know it, but pretenses must be kept up. So, on the lesson goes.

"Can anyone tell me firstly, what a Spinning Jenny is, and secondly, how its invention is mirrored in automation today?" Miss Allen stares out at the sea of blank faces, I glance around at the looks of confusion on the faces of the other students as they suddenly realise that they have been asked a direct question. "Does anyone need me to repeat the question?"

I stare around the classroom, looking from person to person in hopes that one of them had the answer stored somewhere in their subconscious. I know from experience that if someone doesn't come up with an answer fast then Miss Allen will 'call upon someone at random', *meaning she will ask me directly,* for the answer. Gazes avert to the floor, the ceiling, out of the window, staring desperately at the person's head in front of them... anywhere but directly at Miss Allen.

"Any takers?" I can already feel her eyes searching the classroom for me before she finishes asking her last question. "Ah, Mr. Dane, would you care to enlighten us as to the use of the Spinning Jenny?"

I can feel the tension leave the rest of the students around me, and the clear joy at not being asked the dreaded 'gotcha' question. Their lizard brains seem to wake up though, noticing that the socially weakest among them has been highlighted for the kill. Whispers shoot up around the classroom.

My brain quickly tries to access the stored knowledge that I know is hidden somewhere in there. We had talked about this in the last session. Something about....GAH! The correct answer hovers on the periphery of my brain but refuses to come clearly into the light of day. Each time I think of the phrase 'Spinning Jenny', my brain becomes very adolescent and thinks of most perverse answers. I look to Miss Allen desperately, my eyes pleading for a reprieve, one which I know will not come. Miss Allen smiles at me, waiting for my response to her ridiculous question posed at 2pm Friday. Does she not know school finishes in two hours? What is the reason for this torture... education, that's it.

Suddenly the fog lifts, and my brain lights up and has a *eureka* moment. "I think the Spinning Jenny was a multi-spindle spinning frame?" My eyes shoot down to the table immediately, hoping to miss the disappointment on my History teacher's face or the looks of vicarious embarrassment surely plastered on my classmates' faces. The answer suddenly seems not so correct in my head.

"Thank god one of you actually pays attention. You all could learn something from Mr. Dane here. You don't have to go out partying every weekend to have a good time, sometimes the quest for knowledge can be just as exhilarating!" I wonder how long it would take for me to will myself to burst into a ball of flames to destroy all evidence of my body and my shame. My face is surely hot enough to make this happen.

I feel the heated glare of people staring at me with a mixture of pity and hatred. I am by no stretch of the imagination popular. Actually, that's incorrect; if by being the go-to guy for someone to beat up, or dump their lunch or drink over, or shove into the bushes, then I am definitely very popular. Being the only confirmed gay guy in a high school in the North of England will generally have that effect.

I have never openly admitted to my classmates that I was gay, but it's clear for the world to see. My thin frame, clad in skinny jeans and colorful graphic t-shirts confirms everyone's suspicions. Given that every other male 16-year-old in the school wears solely track suits and sneakers, the one kid daring to wear something other than the socially approved attire means only one thing to these guys... gay.

I've known I was different from the first time I watched Interview with the Vampire and Brad Pitt had exploded my world. The feast of flesh on screen from the many beautiful female actors had not once prized my view from Louis the Vampire: his long dirty blonde hair, the full pouting lips and those broad perfect pecs. Maybe the term gay hadn't felt right at that point, but I had known then that something was different about me.

"Would you like to inform your classmates why the Spinning Jenny mirrors the issues with automation and workforce issues today?" She asks the question with a certain smugness to her voice. It is the type of smugness that comes from being sure that later in the day, you will not get your ass kicked. I can make myself no such promises.

Teachers have been my armour since I came to realise that I am at the very bottom rung of the social hierarchy in high school. Scratch that, I'm one of the little plastic things at the bottom of the stubby legs of the ladder. Teachers have provided a type of safe haven for my mind when my thoughts turn dark to the fact that my classmates are basically unaware of my existence, and when they become aware it is only to brush past me, shove me out their way or to kick my ass for daring to exist in their presence. I can tell myself that at least the teachers see me, that they value me as a human being and that I am worth more than the others lead me to believe. This time however I wish Miss Allen had also glossed over my existence.

Part of me at that moment hates her, but my conscience will not allow that to happen for long. A crushing guilt settles into the pit of my stomach as I see the look of pride on her face as I realise how much she enjoys having me there. She deserves to have at least one person in the class give an actual fuck rather than some mumbled response designed to placate her and move her along to the next topic.

"At the time of its invention, it enabled fibers to be spun at the same rate of eight workers, which allowed for the faster production of coarse fiber materials. Also, as the invention became more popular, cloth was imported at a much cheaper price than that produced more locally in England. So not only had the machine cut the workforce requirement, but the labor was being outsourced to India and China." I barely take a breath as I speak, to get the word vomit out as quickly as possible. No sooner has the answer left my mouth than a voice sounds from the back of class, sending a thrill snaking down my spine, exciting and terrifying me in equal measure.

"Of course, teacher's little faggot got the answer right, probably spent last night having a sleepover with Teach, huh Tyler?" I know that voice like I know my own. It is *him*.

I turn to face Lukas Ford like some kind of homing pigeon: I hear his voice and my eyes gravitate towards him. This pigeon however is like a bird with a crack habit - no matter how much I know making myself visible to him makes me his target, I can't seem to help myself.

I think back to that first day when Lukas Ford moved to our town and my high school.

I had been lost in my own thoughts running a paintbrush across a canvas on the easel in front of me, trying to find a way to alter a classical piece of artwork into something more contemporary and coming up blank. I had hoped that if I just started working, inspiration would strike. I hadn't looked up when the classroom door had opened, or even when Mrs. Woods, the Art teacher, introduced the new student Lukas to the entire class. Lost in my thoughts, my head snapped up when I heard her voice speak to me directly.

"Did you hear what I said Tyler? Can you please show Lukas where to get an easel, canvas and supplies?" She looked at me the same way a quizzical Labrador would look at its master doing a handstand, with a tilted head and furrowed brow. I only saw Mrs. Woods however.

"Who?" She motioned her head to the side with a nod to her right. There is no one standing next to her.

She frowned and threw up her hands. "To your left Tyler, I swear it's like you live on a different planet sometimes."

I suddenly became aware of a presence beside me. My head snapped to the side and I gave a startled yelp. A quick laugh escaped the boy standing next to me. My eyes struggled to process him. He was a LOT! I allowed myself a precious second for my eyes to roam over the Greek god in front of me, or what passed for a Greek god to the eyes of a kid who was twelve years old.

The first thing I noticed were the honey coloured eyes giving me a curious stare, as if I'd asked a question he was struggling to answer. I took in his dark brown hair, thick and shiny, cropped short at the sides but with a mess of curls on the top that you could only get away with if you knew you were cool. I fisted my hands at my sides to stop myself from running my fingers through his hair. My eyes settled on Lukas's full mouth with (oh god) a full, pouty bottom lip...

"Erm....hello? Aaaaaanybody home?" I suddenly realised that like a creeper, I had been staring and obviously perusing the new kid in class in full view of the rest of my classmates, while he was waving his hand in front of my face and biting back a smile. *"I think you are supposed to be helping me here man. I don't know where anything is."*

My brain sputtered back to life and I finally drew in a sharp breath. I knew I had to say something, anything. But nothing seemed to be coming out of my mouth. I prayed something would come out – anything would be better than this dead air currently crackling around us. Suddenly I had it! "You're new." Well done, genius. I squinted my eyes and thought that I probably shouldn't have said anything.

"Yep, that's right, like I said I don't know where anything is, could you show me where to get set up?" Again this was a normal request which should have elicited a normal response, but there was nothing normal about what was happening to my brain right now. Under normal circumstances I would have assumed I was suffering from some form of obscure neurological disorder that removed IQ points from the victim at a rapid pace.

My breathing started to pick up, I was inhaling way too much air, and a full blown panic attack was definitely on the horizon. Before I had a chance to mutter back a half-assed response, which was what I was sure what was coming next, my world came crashing down around me.

"Hey check it out, gay boy is popping a boner over the new kid!" I looked around wondering who the hell was shouting and who they were shouting about. I saw Caleb Irwin was pointing directly at me and laughing, tears streaming down his face. I looked down at myself and sure enough I was starting to tent inside my trousers. The protrusion was pointing directly at the new kid as if to blame him for daring to awaken it. Heat filled my cheeks once more and I moved to cover myself. I looked up at him in hopes that I wouldn't see the disgust that I ultimately expected to see there. His face twisted into a mean scowl as he looked around the room as if to let everyone else know that he was not a part of this.

Caleb stalked up behind me and whispered into his ear, "I don't think he wants what you're offering, faggot." The sneering tone of his words dripped into my mind and settled down in my stomach making it churn to the point where I felt as if I would *throw up the contents of my lunch. Caleb reached around me and patted Lukas on the shoulder. "Come on man, I'll show you where to get set up. I think if this homo takes you into the store room he might try to suck your dick or something."*

Lukas chuckled at Caleb and moved quickly away from me. The simple move felt like a sword piercing my stomach, letting all the shame pool on the floor for all to see. Each and every person in the room was reacting to the sight in their own way. Some were laughing directly in my face, some were muttering words of disgust and some were sporting scowls of anger and frustration that they could not react violently towards me as there was a person of authority in the room.

"Thanks man, yeah I definitely do not swing that way," Lukas laughed and looked over his shoulder at me. His eyes narrowed before he turned back towards Caleb.

Mrs. Woods had stayed oddly quiet throughout the incident, her eyes darting around the classroom at anyone but me. Finally she let out a resigned sigh and came up beside me. "Maybe you might feel more comfortable skipping the rest of this lesson and doing some studying for your SATs in the library." Her hand came to rest gingerly on my shoulder. "Best not to disturb the rest of the class, don't you agree?"

I couldn't believe what I was hearing; rather than reprimand the class for their obvious discriminatory behavior, she was penalizing me and ejecting me from the classroom like some deviant. I sank my chin to my chest and quickly gathered my things, hearing the muttering of people around me. I knew it was a matter of time before word spread around the school about me, and stories tended to become skewed until they were far worse than the actual event. Once packed, I slung my backpack over my shoulder and hurried from the classroom, making my way quickly to the admissions office to request a change out of Art class. I couldn't protect myself from the eventual onslaught from the school, but I could make sure I would never have to go back to that classroom.

Chapter 2.

Tyler

The incident in the Art Class had been four years earlier. Since that point then Lukas had gone on to become the most popular guy in school, joining the football and swim teams. He had also gone on to make sure that the next three years of high school were nothing short of hell for me. This started out as simple snide comments from across the hallways, shoving me into lockers, tripping me up on the way to or from my desk, and escalated to full-blown violent physical attacks in the yard during break or on the way home from school. I could never have imagined on that first day how much of a misstep I had made by allowing my body to react to the guy in front of me.

Back in History I take in Lukas Ford momentarily and find him staring hard directly at me. He has only grown more attractive with each year, his sinewy arms now taking on a muscular tone, stretching out the material of the dark blue long sleeved Henley he is currently wearing.

Hearing his retort in history class comes as no surprise; it is now a daily occurrence that he will find some way to inject his particular brand of vitriol and hatred into my day. My stomach clenches waiting for what onslaught he has planned next. Heat sears in my gut, not towards him, but in frustration with myself. I should hate him, the very sight of him should make me shake with fury, however, I can't stop my traitorous body from reacting the same way it had that first day. I can feel my trousers tightening around my groin whilst sweat begins to bead at my brow. I refuse to follow the sound of the voice to meet Lukas's blatant menacing stare again. I know from experience that if I confront Lukas or in any way stand up for myself, the beatdown I receive later will be so much worse.

Miss Allen saunters between the rows of desks of the classroom towards the back of the room where Lukas and his friends sit chuckling amongst themselves. Walking slowly towards the group, her gaze never dropping, she stops mere inches from them, placing both palms at the top of the desk and leaning down towards Lukas as she sneers at him.

"Mr. Ford, if you spent half of the time studying that you do applying this cheap hair gel and pound store deodorant," she motions to his hair with the flick of her wrist, "and spent that time with your head in a book, you wouldn't be failing out of nearly half of your classes. Us teachers talk Lukas and frankly we are surprised you've managed to make it this far, but I guess anyone can find someone to do their assignments for them if they pay enough." Her mouth twists into a cruel sneer as she leans down further, her mouth inches from his ear, but words are clear as day for the class to hear, "I'm sure mummy will pay whatever she can to throw people off the scent of white trash."

She stands up straight, turns around on her heel and heads back to the front of the class. As she moves the realisation of what she has said seems to dawn on her face. She pauses mid-stride as if any moment she will turn back around and try to retract her words. She looks to me with guilt in her eyes as she seems to understand that she may have just made the situation much worse for me.

Hushed whispers break out amongst the class, students around the classroom looking at Lukas and giggling about the verbal smackdown that he had just been handed by our 67-year-old History teacher. I keep a close look out of the corner of my eye, making sure that there isn't an angry hot 16-year-old jock about to smash me into the ground. I see Caleb, his sidekick, whispering something in his ear, which has Lukas nodding and looking over at me.

My heart begins to race as the look of embarrassment on Lukas's face seems to twist into something cruel, his eyes dancing with a plan that appears to delight him. Nearing the end of the school day, I count down towards what I imagine will be some form of physical confrontation from Lukas and his band of twisted freaks. I can't stop myself from sneaking glances back towards him throughout the remainder of the class. The last time I do something is off. No longer glaring daggers at me from the back of the class, his friends are busy trying to fit two hours' worth of History coursework into the last fifteen minutes of the lesson.

Lukas is staring my way, but his gaze is pointed to the floor. I can only conclude that he is lost in thought; whatever it is that has his attention looks as if it's causing a war inside him. His face twists from angry to sad, then to pained in just a moment. As if he notices that I'm looking at him his eyes dart up to catch my gaze. I try to wipe the concerned look off my face quickly but I must not have managed. Lukas stares at me confused for a moment before something resembling warmth enters his eyes. I give a quick nod, not wanting whatever moment this is to end, no matter how trivial. The corner of his mouth kicks up into an almost smirk before Caleb's hand comes down to nudge him out of whatever spell we had weaved for those precious seconds.

The moment gone and his temper seeming to be getting the better of him, Lukas pushes his desk away from him and stands, slinging his backpack over his shoulder as he walks towards the classroom door. "Where exactly do you think you are going Mr. Ford?" Miss Allen calls after him.

"I don't have to put up with this shit, especially from the likes of you," Lukas spits at the History teacher much to her chagrin. The sudden outburst ten minutes after their earlier confrontation earns him an almost confused, delayed chorus of *ooh*s from the classroom. His eyes travel the classroom till they find mine. Taking a deep breath and shaking his head as if to reason with himself, he refocuses back on me.

"You're dead Dane," he says before sweeping out of the room and slamming the door behind him.

Miss Allen, at a loss for words, stands quickly, rubbing her palms on the front of her navy blue pantsuit. Her face contorts into a scowl; my guess is that she is trying to muster up some sort of response: an explanation for her actions, a rebuttal to the remarks made by Lukas, an apology to me. But all that comes from her mouth is, "Everyone get back to work, take out your textbooks and finish off the questions set for you last lesson."

She returns to her desk and rests her head on one arm supported by her elbow. She flicks through the textbook in front of her, obviously not focusing on the book, but desperately trying to not meet the eyes of any of her students. I look up at the clock, as the seconds and minutes tick by, like a convicted felon facing the electric chair. I catch the smiling face of Caleb across the room who stares at me as a lioness would her prey. Hunger darkens his eyes. I quickly look back down at my book, hoping that somehow if I concentrate on the text hard enough, I could somehow transport myself into the world described in the book below. Although, from the looks of the grainy black and white photos in the print, it didn't appear to be the best of times for those people either. I wonder how many of those people had received a beating for being attracted to the wrong person.

The bell rings out in the hallway making me jump slightly. I know there's no point in putting off the inevitable. I'll take my lumps and then make my way home to lick my wounds in front of some trashy TV shows and eat a tube of Pringles by myself; those people in the adverts are kidding themselves when a group of teens shares a tube of Pringles between them. I regularly work out at home and go for a 10 km jog each night so

I know I can afford the calories; however I know after what's surely going to happen this evening, I'll be more than likely skipping my run tonight.

I stuff my books and belongings into my dark brown leather backpack and make my way out of the class. My locker is located all the way at the far side of the building, so I make my way slowly along the corridor, passing students as I go. People tend to avert their gaze when I pass them, as if they're trying to ensure my nonexistence. Every now and again I catch someone looking at me as if thankful that no matter what is going on in their lives, they don't have to be me and live the shitty life in which I appear to exist.

I know of a shortcut through the yard that will get me to my locker in half the time, but the cold rain has not let up at all in the last hour. So I forge my way through the throng of students pushing past me headed for the exit. The school itself is an old-fashioned school built in the 1920's. Sporting a lot of concrete and plastic cladding which was added in the 70's, it is a virtual eyesore scarring the green land around it. Given that I've experienced a lot of the worst parts of my young life there so far, it's quite weird to me that school is somewhere I feel most at home. I know its structure like the back of my hand.

Reaching my locker, I quickly dig through my pockets in search of my padlock key. Retrieving it I undo the lock and pick up my coat and the other assignments I'd gathered throughout the course of the day. I start to hope that maybe Lukas and Caleb had not been talking about me. Maybe I am so insignificant that once they left the classroom and lost sight of me, they'd forgotten I existed, and maybe this once I'll escape the torment that they normally rain down on me. This hope is short-lived when a strongly-muscled arm slams into the locker next to my head. I quickly spin round and come face to face with Lukas Ford. My gaze submissively drops to my feet, I take in a sharp breath and wait for the blow that is sure to come.

"I suppose you think that was funny in class, right? Making me out to be some kind of fucking idiot or a joke?" Lukas's other arm slams into the locker on the other side of my head effectively caging me in.

I look around to see if there is any help coming, then smile slightly to myself. Even if there had been someone else in the hallway beside me and Lukas, they wouldn't help me. No one will help me at this school, ever.

"What the fuck are you laughing at queer?" Lukas grits through his teeth, his face coming down level with mine. I can't help but take in Lukas's natural cinnamon and honey smell, which I have masochistically come to seek out whenever he passes me in the hall or in class.

"Nothing's funny," I stutter, betting that being as submissive and small as possible might weaken Lukas's resolve to turn me into mincemeat. "I didn't say anything to you in class, or about you even. I just answered a question that was asked."

The fist slams into my stomach out of nowhere, Lukas's smile dripping with pleasure and disdain inches from my own. The wind escapes my lungs in a rush and rushes out through my mouth. I am sure that I'm going to be sick and then pass out. The pain of the blow is muted somewhat by the shock of the punch, even though I have been preparing for it for the last 30 minutes. I double over and start to fall towards the floor when Lukas's forearm drops down to block my fall and push me back to his feet, a strong hand shoving against my chest forcing me back to the locker.

"Maybe, but I bet you enjoyed that bitch making me look like a dickhead in front of the entire class."

My head comes up to meet Lukas's icy stare. I try to fight it with as much inner resolve as I can but I am unable to stop the tears welling in my eyes. The world becomes blurry as I stare out through watery lenses. I gaze past Lukas down the corridor as I see what looks like a teacher stopping momentarily to look at us before shaking his head and moving on. Lukas is right, I'm disgusting, I'm nothing. Why else would people who are supposed to protect and teach us behave that way? My Art teacher, just wanting me to leave her room as I was causing a distraction; my History teacher, who needs to put her reputation and career at risk to defend her pathetic student; and then this nameless teacher, who just can't be bothered to stop and help. I truly am nothing.

Normally I would either wince or cry or try to bargain with him or his friends, but this time is different - I feel nothing. A sudden emptiness fills the hollowness left by the punch to the gut I had received.

Lukas seems to falter in his thoughts slightly, a look of slight panic crossing his face as he searches for the whimpering boy he is normally met with when launching one of his attacks, only to now find a shell of a person in front of him instead. I can't be sure whether it is guilt or something else stirring in Lukas's eyes now, but by this point I don't care anymore. My mind drifts to my bedroom, where I'm laying warm in my bed, an empty pill bottle in my hand as I let the darkness and warmth take me under.

The hand on my chest tightens slightly as if to grip me, but at the last moment drops to Lukas's side. The hand quickly comes back up to lightly grab me by the chin and pull me forward ever so slightly until bare millimeters separate our lips. Hot breath skims across my mouth and face as Lukas looks me square in the eye, stopping my heart for just one last moment of weakness. As if pained to say it, Lukas spits out his parting remark, "We have one year left of school. Stay the fuck out of my way you disgusting pervert. Why you haven't killed yourself yet is beyond me."

Lukas picks up the bag at his feet and stalks out of the building. I finally let out a long breath and sink to the floor, my back pressed against my locker. Tears, finally allowed to flow down my face freely, release me of the last three years of schoolboy attraction to the wrong person. *One more year*, I just need to keep reminding myself. I just have to hold out for one more year.

Chapter 3.

Lukas

Pushing the doors leading out of the school and rushing into the cool late afternoon air I let the door slam behind me, my heart hammering in my chest, bile creeping up the back of throat, tears threatening to assault my eyes as I replay in my head visions of the monster I'd always known I'd become. I stop and lean against an old tree next to the school gate, not wanting to leave just yet. Holding my knuckles in my other hand I notice the redness against the bony protrusions from where my fist had connected with Tyler's stomach. I rub the rising skin, realising that if my fist hurt then I had probably done some real damage to Tyler.

Why the fuck does he have to rile me up so much? Everywhere I look there he is, almost asking for my attention. The problem is when he gets my attention, I am filled with so much panic and rage that it inevitably leads to me beating the shit out of him or humiliating him in front of the rest of the class.

If I were the stereotypical homophobic asshole who kicks the ass of every gay guy who crosses his path, it might be slightly better than the reality of my situation. Do I want to kick Tyler's ass for his very obvious attention? Yes I do. Back in the corridor five minutes ago, did it take all of my willpower to stop myself from pushing him back against the locker, shoving my tongue in his mouth and making him mine completely? Also yes.

Yeah, I am the other stereotype. The self-hating, closeted gay jock who to the outside world is as straight as an arrow. The very last thing my family needs is me coming out now, not after what I put my family through last time and not after we spent so long trying to put ourselves back together. We might not be completely functional, but my little sister has friends and is happy, my mother has found her own social circle and is thriving and I rule this school. So if I have to hide who I am, and if Tyler has to pay the price then so be it, I have to be ok with that.

The truth however is I'm terrified: I'm terrified that I'm going to get lost in this character I've created for myself and that I'm never going to find my way out. I'm scared that every time I lay my hands on Tyler that the real me dies a little bit more, screaming at me from beneath the surface that I'm wrong, that I'm bad, that I'm just like *him*. I shake the thoughts away and head away from the school.

In another life, I imagine myself on that first day I met Tyler. In this life I don't make fun, I don't sneer, I don't scowl. I do none of the things that currently make me *me,* in our interactions. Instead I still notice how adorable he is when he's lost for words, I completely appreciate his very obvious attraction to me. I slip my hand in his and press a quick sweet kiss to his lips so he knows that I like him too. He smiles back at me and everything is ok.

I walk down the winding roads through the suburbs away from the school, passing houses I imagine are filled with happy families welcoming their children home from school, asking how their days have gone, sitting around a table to eat together, existing together for no other reason other than that that's what families are supposed to do. I hear myself sigh wistfully, before shaking myself out of the pity spiral I let myself get dragged down.

A heavy thud hits my back and I spin around to start to defend myself, my senses immediately switching to high alert. I bring up my fists to take a swing at whoever is attacking me.

"Woah calm down Ford!" I hear Caleb chuckling in front of me. I realise I have my eyes closed, wincing against a potential attack and the voice inside scolds me, *Never close your eyes boy! How will you defend yourself you little pansy!*

My eyes dart open. "What the fuck do you think your doing?" I snap.

"Dude take it easy, I was just fucking with you," Caleb snickers.

"Well cut it the fuck out ok?" I turn back around and stalk down the road.

"Ok chill," Caleb says, catching up with me and falling into stride, "I see you taught that fucking fairy a lesson then," he says nonchalantly like he is telling me it's warm outside, more of a statement of an inconsequential fact than a question.

"What makes you say that?" I ask, keeping my face straight as my stomach revolts.

"Oh I don't know, I'm a good guesser?" he laughs.

"Douche," I say rolling my eyes before picking up speed.

"Could be that I stopped to take a piss before I left and he was in the bathroom, crouching on the floor crying and holding his stomach. I just assumed that you'd caught up with him before you left."

I think my blood pressure starts to spike; a dull thudding starts in my ears and pressure builds behind my eyes. I have a violent urge to shove Caleb away from me and run back to the school to try and make what I did right. I know that I won't though.

Caleb seems thoughtful and quietness creeps in between us for a few minutes.

"What?" I ask finally when it seems like a tension is developing. Caleb looks at me out of the corner of his eye. Seeming quite nervous maybe. It's odd, even though I think I am quite intimidating, when it comes to Caleb, we have always had each other's backs. Why would he be nervous around me now?

"I don't know. I saw him when I first went into the bathroom and was going to say something to maybe get a rise out of him. Seeing him there though, all sad, alone and pathetic. I felt sorry for him, you know?"

I didn't think I could get any angrier than I am at this very moment.

"I don't want this to be an issue when we get back to school on Monday, I'm just letting you know I helped him out. Not in a fag kinda way," he clarifies, "but I helped him get up and to his car."

I stop in my tracks; I'm fighting every natural urge I have to throw Caleb into the nearest wall and scream at him that he never should have had to help Tyler to the car as I should never have hurt him in the first place, and that one of the reasons I hurt him at all was to make fucking Caleb accept me. My teeth are grinding hard inside my mouth until I start to worry that I might crack one open. I take a deep breath and start to walk on.

"It's all good," I mutter, "But I have to get going now, shit to do at home and you know how my mother gets." I shrug.

"So we ain't hanging out this weekend?"

I shake my head and he lets his drop.

"Well that sucks."

I laugh and clap him on the shoulder. "Take it easy man." I maybe do it a little harder than I normally would, and seeing him rub his shoulder gives me a small zing of satisfaction as I make my way home.

* * * *

I make it home maybe twenty minutes later. My mum still isn't there as her car is not in the driveway. That at least gives me some time to grab a sandwich and a few drinks and make myself scarce upstairs. The driveway up to the house is recently repaved, my mother always trying to ensure that every neighbour knows our house is the nicest on the block. Selling the midsized we had in the South years earlier had left us in the position of being able to buy quite a large house in the North. The three-story Victorian house's facade is covered from ground to roof in thick green ivy. Windows painted brilliant white in stark contrast to the deep green, the deep red front door with a heavy brass knocker at the centre of the house completes its imposing look.

I look to the flower beds on the side of the pathway, remembering my mother used to place a small grey glitter stone with a hidden key inside as I would consistently lose my house keys. My father used to say that people would notice because the stone would shine in the nighttime, but my mother always said that the small specks like stars would remind her of me, shining through the darkness to light up her life. I sigh wistfully at the memory before shaking it off and moving back towards the door.

Pushing open the front door I'm met with the low melodic sound of some 90's grunge band which means my sister Jessica is home. Trudging through the house I make my way into the kitchen, slipping out of my jacket and leaving it alongside my backpack on the table. I open the fridge, rummaging around trying to find anything I can snag and sneak upstairs with. I consider checking to see if Jessica is hungry, quickly ruling out that option; not only does she hate my guts, but she is also a thirteen-year-old girl with the hormones to match.

Settling on quick microwave pizza I take the box out of the freezer and pop it in the microwave. Setting the timer to the recommended five minutes I take a seat at the table. The music through drifting the house shows no signs of stopping any time soon. I rest my head on folded arms on the table in front of me. The heavy lead in my stomach has not managed to shift. This isn't the first time I've had to deal with the aftereffects of hurting Tyler.

I let my mind begin to wander back to when we were both just fourteen a couple of years earlier. Like that's any excuse for the things me and my friends have done to him. The stormy weather outside meant that football in Phys Ed class was cancelled, which sucked, but on the bright side it meant we got to use the school's Olympic-sized swimming pool for the afternoon. So, it wasn't all bad.

"What do you say, butterfly stroke, the last one to reach the other side and back has to pick up the tab for the movies tonight?" Caleb gave me a playful shove from behind. Although I knew Caleb was an absolute douche, he had been instrumental in me fitting in so well with the more popular groups of this school. Before I had arrived, Caleb had been the one that the other boys had turned to for inspiration on how to be a complete dick to everyone else; once I had shown up that honour had befallen me.

"Why do you do this to yourself, you know I'm gonna beat your ass," I laughed.

"You wish, dickhead!" Caleb said with a fake shocked expression on his face. He moved to the edge of the pool, waiting for me to join him. I moved to stand next to him, not failing to notice how the red speedos he wore fit snugly over his ass. I wasn't into Caleb in that way, but I wasn't blind either. "Count of three?"

I smiled at him and nodded. "One, two…" was all I got out before my eyes flitted across to the other side of the pool. The god-damn fag was coming out of the changing rooms. Fucking Tyler. He annoyed the ever-loving shit out of me in every possible way.

My eyes raked over him trying to find every possible negative thing there was about him to justify my anger towards him. He had obviously just come from the showers, his wet hair pushed back away from his face, a few loose strands falling across his forehead. Droplets of water dripped down the bridge of his nose, down onto his chest and flat stomach. There was no large muscle mass there to speak of, just some light definition beginning to appear. My eyes travelled further down, where an impressive bulge pushed out against his light green speedos.

Realising I had been looking at his crotch I pulled my gaze away, my forehead creasing in confusion. Why the hell was I noticing him at all, and worst of all why was my dick starting to take notice?

"Earth to dickhead!" I heard Caleb call from the pool. Not wanting my obvious arousal to be super obvious I dived into the pool.

I breached the surface of the pool, shaking the water out of my hair and away from my face. I caught Tyler giving me a strange confused look as I took in what was going on around me.

"I think gay boy is checking out your package there bud," Caleb said from behind me.

I whipped my head round quickly to face Caleb, horrified that he might have seen me checking out Tyler. "Don't be fucking gross." I scrunched up my nose in disgust.

"Seriously, he can't take his eyes off your ass." Caleb's look became dark, as if daring me to match his intensity.

"He needs his ass kicking up and down this school, fucking pervert."

Caleb nodded in agreement.

I started to formulate a plan in my head there and then. Half of myself was proud that I was protecting my social standing and hopefully making my life easier at school and with my family in general. The other half of myself was fighting the feeling of self-loathing that always accompanied me wherever I went.

The pool started to empty out as the other students made their way to their next classes; knowing Tyler was normally one of the last ones out of the changing room, I hung back. He didn't like to change in front of the other guys in our class so would spend a lot of time pretending to go over things in his bag. Caleb had already had to leave halfway through the Phys Ed class, so it would just be me and Tyler.

I made my way to the shower block. The noise of running water was audible in one of the far stalls. Steam was escaping from the glass doors and partitions separating the different cubicles. I pushed down my shorts and grabbed my towel from the hook next to the door. I showered quickly and turned off the knob, wrapping the towel around my waist and moving back to the changing room. As I opened the heavy door separating the shower block from the changing room I stopped in my tracks. Across the room, facing away from me, naked, one foot up on the bench in front of him, whilst he was bent over drying his feet was Tyler, his ass on full display for me. My dick went from soft to rock solid in one second flat, my towel barely able to hide my arousal. I watched as he caressed the back of his legs with the towel, his smooth skin stretching on for miles. I allowed myself this moment to peruse him from his feet, up his calves that were tense with sinew and muscle. Taking in his thickening thighs, which I noticed had started to get a light smattering of hair, the fluff like an arrow pointing up to two perfect round globes.

A sudden realisation hit me that anyone could walk in and there would be no explaining this away. It would be me checking him out. How the fuck did I let him do this to me time and time again?

Anger coursed through my veins, a bitter hatred causing acid to burn in my throat gripping me. I stormed across the room shoving Tyler hard from behind. His head smashed into the metal lockers in front of him. He cried out in pain and then crumpled to the floor. I moved around him to get a better angle to really lay into him. Tyler lay in what was almost the fetal position, his arms up over his head to protect himself. A quiet sobbing escaped his throat, his back moving with every cry.

I wanted to die in that moment. I wanted to lay my body over his and beg for forgiveness. That wasn't what I did though; I knelt in front of him and sneered. "Look at me that way again faggot, and a cut forehead will be the least of your problems," I said noticing the small wound on his skin. He nodded without moving his arms. Not able to stand seeing what I had done any longer I stood, turned on my heels, quickly dressed and left. Now I had gone and done the same thing again, fought against my own desire to finally have what I wanted, just for a moment's peace. Instead hurting him and myself in the process.

The microwave dings. I grab the pizza and transfer it to a plate, and gathering up some drinks and a candy bar, I move to head upstairs.

"Oh you're home," I hear a small voice saying from behind me.

I turn round to see my mother coming in through the back door into the kitchen. "Yeah not long got home from school, was just going to do some homework in my room."

She nods and purses her lips, seemingly unsure of what to say. "Didn't expect you to be home is all." The hint of disappointment bleeds into my ears. She is disappointed I'm home. I should have just stayed out, maybe spent the night at Caleb's. His parents might think I'm a bad influence but they always made an effort to make me feel welcome.

"I can go out if that makes things better," I snap, placing the pizza and other items back on the counter.

"Don't be like that Lukas," she says, sighing and dropping her keys on the kitchen table, using the wood for balance as she reaches down to undo the straps of her high-heeled shoes.

"Don't be like what? Upset that I'm not welcome in my own fucking house?"

She rubs her forehead with her fingertips like she always does when she is just done with a conversation. Sauntering over to the fridge she takes out some ingredients and places them on the kitchen countertop. Retrieving a knife and a kitchen waste box she starts to peel and chop vegetables, disposing of the skins in the grey food box. I stare at her, wondering if she is even going to respond to my quip about not being welcome in my own home, however, as the seconds tick by it becomes abundantly clear that that is not going to happen.

"Why do you hate me so much?" I whisper, hoping that she will hear me.

She puts down the knife on the chopping board and rests both of her perfectly manicured hands on the countertop. "I don't hate you Lukas, you know that," she says pointedly, "People don't uproot their entire lives and move halfway across the country for people they hate."

"Then why don't you want me here?" I say, biting the inside of my cheek, praying that I keep my emotions in check.

She sighs, picking up the knife she gets back to work. I think she is going to ignore me when she says, "It's just hard you know. I look at you and I remember what you did."

"What *I* did?" I gasp.

"You know what I mean!" She rolls her eyes. "We are all where we are, because of you," she states simply.

Leaving the pizza and other items, I turn and walk out of the kitchen into the early evening air, not exactly sure where I am going, but knowing for sure anywhere is better than here.

Chapter 4.

Tyler

It's been nine months! Nine glorious months since my last run-in with Lukas or any of his band of monsters. Not much has changed - people still avoid me, fearing they may catch whatever social disease I must have, but they don't bother me anymore either. It's like my wish of finally becoming completely invisible has come true. Two more months, two more blessed months and I'll be able to see the back of this school forever.

I no longer hold any fantastical notions that things will turn around and the people who've avoided me for all this time will suddenly welcome me into their friend groups, or that there will be parties or lunches on the quad. I've resigned myself to the fact that I'll be one of those people who does their level best to forget school altogether. To take the knowledge I had absorbed and run. Standing in the central point of the school, buildings all around me, I stare up to the sky, letting the sun beat down on my face.

I revel in the warmth I feel until a large body barrels into me, knocking me to my knees.

"Watch where the fuck you're going!" a gruff voice sounds from behind me. Hands on the rough gravel of the yard I take in a deep breath, recognising that voice anywhere. I push to my feet, grabbing the bag which had crashed to the floor along with its owner.

"Sorry" I murmur without looking at him. I go to move away, hoping that he will once again forget I exist.

"Wait!" Slightly jarred, I stop my retreat and slowly turn around to face him. Expecting to see the curved cruel smile on his face I am shocked to see a look of concern creasing his brow. "Are you ok?" he whispers.

I don't know how to respond. It's a simple question, with what should be a simple answer. This is *not* a simple situation. Any wrong answer could earn me a black eye or split lip. I start to back away from him slowly until I'm out of arm's reach, making small hopefully imperceptible movements.

"I'm ok, sorry," I mutter again. Surely two apologies is enough right?

"I ran into you. Why are you apologising?" His voice sounds irritated.

My heart begins to race, I'd been sure that this bullshit had passed. "Possibly because you told me to watch the fuck where I was going?" I snap.

Do I have a death wish or something? Where the fuck did that come from? I avert my gaze back to my shoes as if the answers to the world's problems were etched on the toes. Thankfully I hear a quick snort of amusement.

"Fair enough," he retorts. "I haven't really seen you around much," he says, chewing his bottom lip. Now it's his turn to avoid my gaze. What the fuck is going on here? When does Lukas Ford give a shit if he hasn't seen me around much? I mean maybe the punch bag at the gym is not accessible and he needs to get his cardio in, I'm not sure. I shrug and try again to move away.

"Hey wait up," he tries again to stop me but I move quickly out of his grip.

Fear ties knots in my stomach, pains lancing through my chest as my muscles bunch in anticipation of attack. Normally Lukas favours a quick punch to my stomach before letting loose with fists and feet. My hands automatically come up to defend my head as I wince and accept the fact I'm about to get a beating.

"Take it easy," he whispers, "I'm just talking to you."

Un-scrunching my eyes, I peer out at him though the gap in my raised arms. "Right, sure ok," I mumble. His face has paled and he looks like he might throw up, beads of sweat on his brow. " Are you ok?" I ask as mildly as I can. Maybe if I play along for a few minutes he will lose interest and let me go on my way.

"I'm an asshole." His words are solemn and grave.

"I don't..." I start but he cuts me off.

"It wasn't a question." A sad smile is playing on his mouth. "I'm an asshole."

I honestly don't know what to say. A part of me wholeheartedly agrees with him, wants to scream *duh* and show him the scar on my forehead from the time he had shoved me so hard into a locker that I needed a stitch to close the wound, or the bumpy skin on my knee from when he pushed me down during PE, when I had skinned my knees so badly they had to send me to the nurses office. The rest of me though sickeningly wants to throw my arms around him and wipe that sad forced crooked smile from his face, smooth away the lines creasing his forehead.

"I'm sure you're not all bad." I try for a smile, but I guess it comes out more of a wince since I see the furrows deepening. He looks up to meet my stare, something like hope sparking there as if maybe I really do think he isn't a complete asshole. Also to be fair to Lukas he hasn't terrorized the rest of the senior class and they all really seem to like him. I don't think saying the fact that my face is the only face he has mangled is an appropriate point however. "Listen, I have to get to class," I say, indicating towards the science building with a thumb over the shoulder.

"Oh ok sure." He kicks at invisible stones on the ground. I have no idea what is happening, which only serves to keep my anxiety just below the surface, just waiting to break free. "Do you have to go to class? I mean would they miss you if you weren't there?"

I smile and hold back a laugh, "What?" His features still as he dead-eyes me. "I'm sorry but that sounds an awful lot what a kidnapper says before he nabs his victim."

Lukas looks like he is replaying his words back over in his head and then a large smile breaks out on his face. His features suddenly harden into something between a smoulder and a scowl. "Is that what you think I'm going to do, kidnap you and smuggle you away to my lair?"

Ok if I don't know any better, and I DO, I would swear that this is Lukas trying to flirt with me. This is something that would never happen in a million years. My mouth dries and I struggle to swallow. Taking in a deep breath I shake my head, the laugh that escapes me seeming manic and forced. "No of course not, that's not what I meant!"

Lukas grins and lays a hand on my shoulder. "I'm just fucking with you Tyler."

My name on his lips and his hand on my shoulder heats my body all over. His fingertips are like bolts of lightning sending shocks down my chest and arms, leaving goosebumps in their wake. I should move away, I should run before he realises the effect that he is having on me. Nothing but pain can come from the reaction I have to him, I should have learned that on the very first day I met him.

"Fancy going to chill out by the tennis courts?"

Surely I've misheard. There is no way that Lukas Ford has just asked me to go hang out with him by the tennis courts. The benches there are where the "Cool" kids congregate during free periods and lunch. I've spent the majority of my lunches either eating alone in a bathroom cubicle or in a classroom if I've successfully managed to convince a teacher to let me stay after class to catch up on revision or homework. I've never dared sit on the tennis court benches, even if they were empty. Feeling a whoosh of air past my face I look up to see Lukas smiling and waving his hand in front of my face.

"Think I lost you there for a minute," he smirks. "So...?"

"So what?" I ask, lost for words and rational thought.

"The benches?" he asks, still with that damn adorable smile plastered on his face.

Obviously I'm going to say no. This is the guy who'd pushed me in the pool fully dressed when I went in to pass a message to the PE teacher, he is the guy who'd split open my lip when I dared to be in the bathroom at the same time as him and his goons, this is the guy who'd basically told me I should kill myself because I was worth nothing. Of course I am going to say no.

"Yeah sure." *Aw hell!*

Lukas gestures towards the courts with an outstretched arm. I give him a shy smile and walk across the yard towards the varnished wooden benches. Tossing my bag on the slatted table I take a seat; not bothered to swing my legs under the table, I sit facing away, my back pressing against the chunky wood. Lukas comes to sit next to me, his feet pushing under the table and stretching like a cat reclining, arms and feet pushing outwards, fingertips reaching towards the sun. He lets out a loud yawn, startling me for a moment.

"Tired?" I ask warily.

"A bit I guess." He seems to ponder his next thought for a moment before continuing, "I thought after we finished sitting our last exams last week that the anxiety would just disappear, it just seems to have gotten worse though." He shrugs.

"Yeah I guess now is the big wait to see how we did, before we could always study to improve our chances, take extra classes and all that stuff, but now there is nothing we can do." Somewhere in the distance a car revs its engine; I look towards the gap between the buildings, but see no-one.

"How do you think you did?" His question is something I've been asking myself hourly for the last week.

"I don't know. Ok I think, but then I could just be hoping for the best." I run my fingers against my thighs, letting them travel towards my knees before pulling them up towards my hips. I notice Lukas's eyes following the tracks of my fingertips, his eyelids lowering as he breathes deeply. "Are you ok?"

His eyes shoot up to meet mine, a smile wide on his face like the Cheshire Cat's, fake and unnatural. "Yeah I'm good, just thinking about stuff you know." This is all so surreal. Things like this don't happen, you don't just have a casual friendly chat with your abuser. I need to get out of here before shit inevitably turns sour.

"Listen I should probably get to class you know." I go to move but his hand comes down to rest on the hand I have placed firmly on the bench next to me.

"Please don't go." His voice sounds small, childlike almost.

"Why?" The question is out of my mouth before I can stop it.

"Because... because I... I just want to talk to you." Concern etches his face, like he is worried at any minute I'll just start running. If that's what he's thinking then he isn't far wrong.

"I wish..." he starts before becoming silent.

"You wish what?" Ok if I'm diving down the rabbit hole, then I'm going to throw in a few twists and turns on the way down to hell. "What do you wish?" I repeat when he doesn't answer.

"I wish things were different. I wish I could be different. I wish that first day in Art class would have been different." A mixture of panic and anger rises up and burns in my chest.

"YOU wish things could be different? YOU!" I demand, "Are you fucking joking me right now?"

His mouth gapes open in shock. This would be the very first time I've been openly aggressive with him, maybe not physically but verbally and that is more than anything I've done before.

"What the fuck do you want from me Lukas huh? You spend years making me feel worthless, bruised, bloody, broken and what, you want to absolve yourself of guilt before you go off into the big wide world? Well don't fucking bother ok." I'm quickly running out of air, I'll need to make my point soon if I'm to have any hope of not passing out. "I will be out of here soon and I am going to do my very best to pretend none of you fuckers ever existed ok?"

Lukas's face falls, the pain on his face evident. I pick up my bag and once again go to move. Just like the last time he halts my movement. "Just fucking wait ok!" he bellows. I still, that voice has featured in so many of my nightmares that it roots me to the ground. A hand comes to rest on my shoulder, turning me round to face him and I see intensity burning in his eyes. Holding me with his stare, I feel like his gaze pins me to the ground. "I'm sorry ok," he whispers, his gaze falling and focusing on my lips. My tongue darts out to lick my lower lips and a small audible gasp escapes his throat. My breathing deepens and I don't exactly understand what I'm doing.

I reach up and rest my hand on the one he has gripping my shoulder. My eyes narrow as if trying to solve the riddle that is Lukas, afraid I will make one misstep and this spell will be broken. Throwing away the last shreds of my sanity I move my face towards his, and his eyes never leave my mouth. A foot becomes inches, which becomes centimetres. Next there is only a breath between our lips, I close the distance and lightly press my lips against his. Lukas sighs against my mouth as if breathing in relief.

I get only a second of happiness before a bell shatters the silence, doors open from all buildings surrounding us. I get a moment to panic, scared that we might have been seen when a force smashes against my face. Stars explode around my head and my vision blurs. I fall from the bench, landing with a soft thud on the grass below. I look up confused, expecting to see a group of guys waiting for their turn when I just find Lukas shaking his hand out, cradling his knuckles. I spot a smear of red against the bone and I almost ask if he is ok. Dread curls in my gut as I reach up and press fingertips to my cheekbones. Feeling wetness, I pull them away to find what I expected to find. My blood.

I stare back up at Lukas, the hurt obviously evident on my face. He looks stricken as if he isn't sure himself what just happened. This lasts a second before his eyes narrow and he looms over me. "Never fucking kiss me again faggot or I'll kill you."

Shame consumes me and I mumble a broken apology. Apparently at some point I've started to cry, my brain not really keeping up with the whirlwind of emotions I've been experiencing. Have I completely read the situation wrong? Have I just attacked someone with my mouth who just wanted to talk to me? Maybe he is right, I *am* disgusting.

I nod to Lukas and push myself to my feet, pulling down the sleeve to my shirt and pressing it to my cheek. I turn towards the gap between the buildings that head to the school gates and I run.

Chapter 5.

Tyler

THREE YEARS LATER

What a difference a few years makes.

High school seems like such a lifetime ago, even though it's barely been two and a half years. After what had happened outside the tennis courts, things had pretty much gone downhill. Lukas had not laid a finger on me after our showdown at the lockers, but his friends had definitely had more than enough fun in his place. Strangely enough Caleb had been mysteriously absent from all of my beat downs, seeming to only shoot me concerned glances afterwards. I wanted to say that helped a little but I'd be lying.

To say that high school wasn't ever present in my mind would be me not being completely honest with myself; however, those days were long behind me. I had graduated high school with very good grades, then I'd attended a college an hour away from my hometown to try and ensure I could start my life over without the stigma of being the perverted gay guy wherever I went, and just be Tyler.

Over the past couple of years, I'd spent an obsessive amount of time at the gym, which had really paid off. No longer was I the slight young boy from high school. I'd packed on a good 25lbs of solid muscle. I knew I looked good now. My T-shirts were intentionally one size too small to get that 'strained over muscle' look. The hem of my shirts barely touched the waistband of my jeans so that when I reached up for anything at all, a slim strip of tanned skin showed above it which had earned me more than one appreciative look over the past few years. I had also grown out of my boyband hair phase and now sported a military back-and-sides buzz cut with a mop of dark blonde curls on top of my head which I kept secured back with an elastic band.

College had been like emerging into a whole new world. Being drawn to the other outcasts of society I had made friends with a group of people that you may not find in your everyday travels to a mall or McDonald's. No, these were the people you found sitting on a bench inside an art gallery, staring at a painting pretending that they could see the depth in the artwork, when it was really just a blue circle on a white canvas. Yeah for the first year we were a big group of pretentious assholes. My mother would roll her eyes when I arrived home, jeans sagging halfway down my ass, shades over my eyes whatever the weather and for one very disturbing week, a beret.

Luckily for me before I ended up choosing the beatnik lifestyle, someone forced their way into my life.

Max.

Standing in line one afternoon before class at a Starbucks I had been leaning over the counter to make sure the barista heard my drink order exactly how I liked it:

"Sugar-free caramel latte, oat milk, extra hot, half caf, with foam and cinnamon sprinkles please."

"You know you have the order of a tiny blonde Valley girl right?" a voice chuckled behind me.

Turning around I was faced with the teeniest girl with the biggest smile. Long dark blonde ombre style hair framed her round cherub face, a wide set mouth below high cheekbones and the most piercing blue eyes I'd ever seen. Taking in the potential angel in front of me I noticed she was dressed like a throwback to the 60's hippy era with a beige frayed gypsy skirt and peasant blouse, a small white rose set into the side of her hair. A tiny waist somehow held a huge pair of tits up without snapping her in half. I imagined she was most men's idea of a wet dream and she was wasting her time talking to probably the only gay guy in the shop.

"Is that right?" I asked, raising an eyebrow at her.

"You know it's all coffee right? I mean do you have a dairy allergy? Are you on a diet, is your name Beth?"

"It's Tyler actually."

"Well I'm Max," she said before pushing ahead of me and leaning over the counter towards the barista, "Cancel his order love and can you get us two venti americanos please with milk." The barista looked from me to the strange vision in front of him. I sighed and nodded at him to go ahead and start prepping the drinks.

"Erm...?"

"I'm sorry but friends tell friends when they are being a dork, and drinking that would be the height of dork-ishness."

"We're friends?" I laughed, squinting at her.

"Well duh."

"You don't even know me." I said placing a hand on my hip and gesturing off to the side with the other hand.

"Well you're Tyler and from the way you're standing like a teapot I'd say you were a big homo as well. See I do know you," she smiled, winking at me and moving towards the end of the counter to pick up the drinks.

We've been inseparable from that day, Max's direct nature counteracting my own shy pretentiousness. When my mother had finally met Max she had thrown her arms around her and thanked her for saving her son from himself, which I thought was a bit much. I'd been becoming a bit of a snobbish twat, not joining a cult.

We've made our own little circle of friends, while always orbiting each other like a planet and its moon. People would assume we were an item, and most of the time we didn't bother to correct them. It wasn't the worst thing in the world for people to assume that I'm this supermodel's boyfriend. Max is truly stunning. All of this is lost on me though – I only have eyes for other men.

After college, Max has applied to the same university as me and we're both majoring in English Literature and Journalism. We share the dream of one day becoming investigative journalists working in London or New York. For now however, we've settled for the city of Manchester, where we share a three-bedroom apartment off campus on the picturesque Salford Quays. We had both devised a plan to convince our parents to help fund the apartment off campus, by tabling an argument that if we stay in halls, we'll never get as much studying done and therefore be wasting the higher cost that our parents are paying for tuition. It had been agreed that her parents and my mother would fund 80% of the costs of the apartment, but we would both need to get part-time jobs outside of university hours to cover the remaining 20%, as well as living costs. We figure that this worked out in our favor.

Max has secured a job as a bartender at an American-style biker bar Desert Rose. She only really has to work there two evenings a week as the tips she racks up more than cover her half of the rent whilst leaving her with a generous wad of spending money. Max's parents are rich, like RICH rich, so I figure that she has a little nest egg saved up somewhere when her funds run a little low.

I have a part-time job at a coffee bar called Sergios on Canal Street, a predominantly gay district in Manchester. I spend my days watching couples as they come in and sip on their drinks while eyeing each other. My heart aches for someone to look at me like some of the guys who come through here look at their boyfriends. Max sometimes stops by between classes and helps out behind the bar; the manager Tess never really minds as I'm fairly sure that Tess would give her right nipple for just one night with Max.

After my morning shift Max calls to remind me that I have an afternoon lecture. Max hates to sit in a big lecture theatre alone and always ensures my attendance is 100% so as to never be in the awkward position of sitting next to a stranger and making small talk. I've reminded her more than once that that's more or less how she met me.

I arrive at the university campus, masses of students moving around like lemmings, herding each other into tightly packed buildings. Making my way to the centre of the maze of buildings I enter the lecture halls.

I sit in the front row of the lecture theatre waiting for the last of the stragglers to find a seat in the rapidly filling up room. A few people say hello to me when they come in. A few try to take the seat next to me, but I always save it for her.

"Hey Homo!" I quickly snap my head towards the door to see Max walking confidently towards me, a huge smile on her face as she makes her way over. "Thanks for saving my seat."

I move my bag from where it sits protectively on her space and put it on the floor between my legs.

"Well I assume since you sit in the same seat every lecture that the chair now has a healthy dose of whatever STI you're currently dealing with, so I'm just protecting the rest of the class, whore."

"Well since you already have been colonised by and developed an immunity to all the nasty dick diseases, I think it's safe for you to sit next to me." She leans over and places a light kiss on my cheek.

We've developed this type of banter and maintained it right the way through college and into university. If she had come in and asked me how I was, or sat without saying nothing jokingly hurtful, then I would have assumed something was seriously wrong. Some people are quite shocked when they hear the level of insults that we lob at each other, but only true friends can get away with calling you the types of names that only an enemy might dare to call you.

"You're coming with me to a party tonight by the way, Dawn from the bar is having a housewarming party and has invited me to go. I've said no to the last three pointless parties she has thrown, and if I say no again, she will probably think I'm not ok with her obvious lesbianism. I say obvious as I saw her in the back with her hand down the front of this lady's trousers like she was digging for the lost treasure of Atlantis…. cause you know…it was wet." I make a gagging face and then wince at Max.

Dawn is the manager of the Desert Rose. She's one of the coolest people I know, sharp-tongued and beautiful. I once watched from the other side of the bar as a group of men hurled homophobic abuse at her, slinging all kinds of vile nasty words. I then watched the corner of her mouth curve into a twisted smile. She had leaned across the bar and whispered something that I wasn't able to hear to one of the men. I had seen his face pale before coughing out something about needing to get home and leaving the bar, taking his boys with him. Dawn is all kinds of terrifying.

"And why is this my problem?" I ask, tilting my head slightly towards her.

"As my bitch, it is your duty to accompany me to parties for which I have no date. And as I am currently dateless, you shall be my date. Don't worry I won't even expect you to put out afterwards." Max gives me a wide grin and then puts on her best puppy dog eyes and pout. "Please?"

"Fuck you Max, but yeah ok I'll be there. When you say housewarming, you mean like a house party and not like a formal dinner party cause I might have to ditch you there if it's a dinner."

"Nah it's a standard party, it's not far from our place so we can walk there later, now shut the fuck up ho I'm trying to listen." I chuckle to myself and turn back towards the lecturer.

Chapter 6.

Tyler

There is always that somber awkwardness of showing up at a party as a plus one, during which you have to appear gracious to be hosted but also have to hide the fact that you would rather be anywhere but here. Dawn opens the door to greet us and immediately shoves a tequila shot into each of our hands.

"I'm sorry but this is the price of entry, down in one please bitches."

"Can I not just pay a cover charge?" I plead.

"Stop being a vagina and just drink the damn thing Princess."

I look down at the amber liquid in my hands. I'd always made a point of staying away from tequila since one night on a beach in Maspalomas, when Max and I had decided to down a cheap bottle of *definitely not 100% Agave* tequila, the type of tequila that was designed for the sole purpose of burning away memories and previous transgressions. We had awoken the next day only to find that the tequila had stolen all the moisture from our mouths. After crawling to the bathroom and deciding that I would have to stand up to drink out of the faucet rather than shove my face in the toilet for relief, I'd thrown up. After that horrendous hangover I had promised myself that under no circumstance would tequila ever pass my lips again. However, as it turns out my promises to myself stand for absolute shit.

"Up the bum, no harm done." I clink my shot glass against Max's and down the shot in one, quickly grabbing a slice of lime from the small plate in Dawn's hand. I hear Max chuckle before the sound of a sharp gag, followed by a deep shudder. The memories of the Spanish bathroom are clear in my mind. We pass our empty shot glasses back to Dawn, a smile like the cat who got the cream plastered on her face, before following her to the back of the house.

"Thank god someone did the shots," Dawn calls over her shoulder, "literally everyone else has said no."

Staring dumbfounded at the back of Dawn's head I start to make my case that she is a total bitch when Max puts a comforting hand on the small of my back and gives me a gentle pat, pushing me forward towards the sounds of people.

People are milling about in groups all around the house. I'd lost Max somewhere around the dining room after she spotted a *Quote* 'Guy is so hot he's making my pussy quiver' *Unquote*. Making my way into the kitchen I make a space for myself by the island in the center. Everyone seems to be helping themselves to the various drinks on offer.

After the tequila I figure anything would serve as a good way of getting the taste of death out of my mouth. I pick up a big red cup and make a sizable Jack and Diet Coke. Someone offers me ice which I turn down... why on earth would I want to dilute the whiskey with water? Looking around the room, I try my best to act casual but approachable. No matter how far I've come since high school, there is always that quiet voice inside telling me to be small. Hide, make sure no one notices you.

I spot a guy that I'm sure has been in Sergio's a number of times and have maybe more than once exchanged a few flirty words with, smiling at me from behind his glass. I see the nearly imperceptible wink he throws my way whilst still chatting with his friends. The guy is seriously cute. Muscular arms, square jaw, crooked smile, dark eyes. Kinda like Jake Gyllenhall but without the weirdness. I smile back at him and give a small wave. Interest flares behind his eyes as I watch him bite his bottom lip, his eyes never leaving mine.

I make my mind up there and then, I'll finish this drink and then I'm taking that guy to the nearest empty room.

I have no sooner downed my first gulp when a voice whispers next to my ear.

"Enjoying yourself?"

The voice hits my stomach like a blast from the past, a past I would rather have forgotten. I know I have no such luck as my dick starts to swell like the fucking traitor it is... I slowly turn my head to meet the face attached to the voice. I pray to whatever god is listening to please just make it a trick of my mind. Like Dickens wrote in *A Christmas Carol*: *'an undigested bit of beef, a blot of mustard, a crumb of cheese, a fragment of an underdone potato.'* Oh how I wish that were the case.

I stare upwards, my brain struggling to catch up, realising I am face to face with the one person I never expected to, and hoped I would never see again.

Lukas fucking Ford.

My mouth slowly starts to gape open, air passing past my lips as I mutter nonsense sounds, as the cup I'm holding slips from my grip. My eyes shoot down and I wince as the nearly-full red cup hits the floor, spilling its contents all over both our shoes and the ground below.

"Shit!" I cry out, jumping out the way of further drenching.

"Hey no worries at all, I'll clear it up, no need to freak out," Lukas smiles at me. I gape with a mixture of confusion and incredulity; is this fucker really here right now and just acting like we are long lost buds who just ran into each other?

My heart begins to race, a million questions running through my head.

What? Why? What the fuck? How? All very good questions for which I do not have an answer.

Lukas reappears with a couple of dishcloths and a mop. He hands a clean dishcloth to me and begins to mop the thinning puddle collecting at our feet. I stare at him as if waiting for the punchline of some cosmic joke.

"What are you doing here Lukas?" I spit at him with much more venom than I'd realised. Anger and confusion immediately start to boil in my stomach making me feel like I might throw up. This time it has nothing to do with the tequila shot. I'd thought I was over the issues I had dealt with in high school, when in reality it seems as if they've just been hiding in the recesses of my mind waiting for the right time to lash out.

Lukas regards me cautiously, as one might do a dog holding its tail low to the ground, stalking its prey. "I live here. I'm Dawn's housemate. I assumed you knew that since you are here?" He begins to reach across the gap between us to place his hand on my shoulder when he must see the look aimed at him; quickly, he withdraws his hand and puts his arms up in surrender. "Hey it's all good with me if it is with you."

The simmering fire in my stomach ignites into a full raging inferno. "ALL GOOD WITH ME? Are you FUCKING kidding me?!" I put one hand up to my forehead as if testing my own temperature as I'm sure it is off the charts, looking around the room to see if anyone is witnessing the absurd outburst and hoping they would understand how unbelievably surreal and unfair this is. However, every eye I meet just seems slightly concerned and maybe a little put out that I'm ruining what is otherwise quite a chilled get-together.

"Listen man, calm down. I was just saying hello is all," Lukas half-whispers, looking around giving apologetic glances to the guests close by.

We've started to draw a crowd of people who are now drawn to the increasingly red-faced psychopath standing in a puddle in the middle of the kitchen. I see Max making her way through it towards me and immediately I notice the look of concern in her eyes. I feel what I think is Lukas's warm palm coming to rest on my shoulder, which spooks me completely. Shoving the hand away from my shoulder I drop back only to notice the look of hurt crossing Dawn's face as she pulls her hand away to her chest.

"I'm sorry Dawn!" I gasp as I realise I've lashed out without any real warning. Dawn moves to stand next to Lukas, who gives a slight shake of his head to Dawn and nods slightly in return to indicate everything is under control.

"Everything ok here?" I hear Max say as she reaches me and puts one arm around my shoulder. This must be as confusing for Max as it is for everyone else in the room. She's never really seen me act this way, and must realise it's completely out of character for me.

I rest a hand over hers and give it a gentle pat. I've always been known for being cool, calm and collected in any situation, never reacting with anything other than an even level of chill to stressful scenarios, which had pissed Max off in the past during exams in college when everyone else was at 'tearing their hair out' levels of anxiety, whilst I read a book at the doors of the exam hall waiting patiently to be allowed to enter to begin the test. "Yeah I'm fine, seriously everything is ok."

I notice the guy she had wandered off to speak to earlier has come to stand behind her. Obviously curious as to the developing situation, but also, it seems, still wanting to be as close as possible to Max. The guy must be almost seven foot, his long thick blonde hair in waves around his face, small plaits running through it giving him an almost Scandinavian Viking look. His broad shoulders and huge pecs atop a thin tapered waist are features I know Max drools over. I see him come to rest a palm against the small of her back, staking some form of claim to her to ensure that no other Alpha males dare encroach upon his territory. I have to admit it's kind of sweet, if slightly Neanderthal-like.

"Listen I'm sorry Max, you should get back to the party. I'm not feeling so great. I'm going to head out." I feel Lukas's stare burning a hole in the side of my head. I only allow myself a quick glance at him, afraid that if I look for any longer that the reaction I always had to him would rear its ugly head, then I would either cry or go completely catatonic. Staring directly ahead I pretend he doesn't exist.

Max shakes her head as if to deny my request. "Absolutely not, I'll go with you."

I know there's no way I'm going to spend any more time in that house than is necessary, but I don't want to spoil Max's fun either. It's rare she shows an interest in any guy, let alone some random dude at a house party.

"No seriously I just want to go home alone, grab a shower and get some revision done. I promise I'm ok." I look around the room, wanting to look anywhere but at the person I could not stop looking at for the worst years of my life.

"Hey if you're not feeling great there is a spare room upstairs, you can lie down in there," Dawn suggests.

I've always liked Dawn since she started working with Max at the bar a few months earlier and took it over, improving the bar and its clientele, but at that moment I just want her to shut the fuck up.

"I have my laptop up there, you could log into the university's portal and do some revision here?"

I see the hopeful look cross Max's face. I know immediately that there's very little chance she's going to let me leave a party alone without ending her own night to go with me. I can't deny her the well-deserved rest from working and studying that she so desperately needs.

"Sure, that would be great Dawn, don't worry about the laptop though. I just need to lie down. I guess that tequila went to my head." I try to smile warmly at her, my eyes casting the first glance in Lukas's direction since my little outburst. Lukas's face is a mask of worry and guilt. He knows exactly why I am reacting in such an outlandish way but is keeping silent amongst the group.

I allow myself for the first time to take in the specimen that is Lukas Ford, just three years later. I'd spent the last few years hoping and praying that Lukas had been hit by a car and left unable to walk, or had discovered a secret love for cookie dough and had packed on the weight and now had to be craned out of the house like in those shows on TLC. Fate however had decided to ignore the absolute monster that Lukas was and smile on him instead.

He is hotter than ever. *FUCK!*

His light stubble is now thick on his square jaw, the dimples just barely visible though the thick growth on his face. His eyes are still so light they make me want to stare at them for hours. His neck shows veins as he cranes it around to talk to Dawn standing next to him, the veins leading down to a very broad chest, dark hair visible through the open buttons of his shirt. The long-sleeved Henley grips every muscle on his densely packed torso. His dark blue jeans hug his thick thighs, hanging loose on his hips. The sleeves of his Henley are rolled up on his forearms to reveal tattoos swirling up in what seems to be an entire sleeve as far as I can see.

A small sigh leaves my mouth, which Lukas obviously picks up on as his own lips slightly part.

He meets my stare. I quickly look to Dawn and beam a cautious smile in her direction.

"Sure, follow me, I'll get you set up," Dawn grins and pats me on the shoulder. "You poor delicate gay guys. Let mama take care of you… that sounded much creepier than it was meant to. Forget it and just follow me."

Dawn starts to move away from the group when Lukas places a hand on her arm stopping her movement. "Don't worry Dawn, you stay here and keep people entertained, I'll show Tyler the guest room."

This night is not going at all how I had imagined it. I was supposed to come to a party, get drunk, maybe flirt a little and go home and eat cold leftovers with Max in front of reruns of Ab Fab. Never once had I imagined a scenario where I would be following the object of my long-(mostly)-forgotten masturbatory fantasies up to an empty bedroom at a house party. What the absolute fuck?

Chapter 7.

Lukas

This night is definitely taking a very unexpected turn. You never really expect to run into someone from your past. It's not like the movies or reality TV where every corner you turn reveals a familiar face. You can walk around the city where you live for days on end and never spot a single person you know. I sure as shit had not expected to run into someone I knew from high school, nor had I expected to feel the rush of adrenaline that accompanied seeing that person. Tyler, who had only ever inspired feelings of panic, guilt and anger from me when we were in high school.

A look of confusion and wariness passes over Tyler's face which I'm not completely surprised by. He catches me watching him with caution. His face settles into a mask of contempt. Tyler shifts awkwardly on his feet; I get the feeling he is considering bolting from the room and out of the house. A back-and-forth between Tyler, Dawn and his friends breaks out stalling my desire to move him upstairs, and I have an intense need to tell everyone else to shut the fuck up and get him out of there.

Tyler's face tells a tale and at the moment I can see the anxiety etched into his features, the confusion and dread palpable. I've seen and been the cause of that look on his face on many occasions, and I need it to be gone. The guilt needles its way into my bones, my back muscles bunch and tense as I restrain myself from grabbing his wrist and pulling him from the room.

The tall Norse god of a guy standing behind him puts a hand on his shoulder, leans down and whispers something into his ear. A smile breaks out on Tyler's face. He turns and nods politely, patting the guy's hand. The guy leaves his big hand pressed to Tyler's shoulder, looking ahead to face off with me. He seems to understand that I am the cause of Tyler's distress and he does not look happy. At that moment that is the last thing I give a shit about. The only thing I can focus on is not pushing forward and demanding he take his hands off Tyler.

Ok, why the fuck am I allowed to care who is touching Tyler?

Tyler obviously has no fucking problem with having Thor's hands all over him. Fire burns in the back of my throat as I glare at the big guy, my teeth grinding together until my jaw aches. The guy pulls Tyler backward until he is close enough to be nestled next to him, an arm thrown casually over his shoulder. Tyler's friend Max is looking up at the big guy like he has just rescued a bunch of kittens from a burning building.

The simmering rage beneath my skin turns into a living, breathing entity just waiting for a reason to strike out. I need to get a hold of myself and calm the hell down. Beads of sweat form on my temples and I curl my toes trying to calm myself down.

Unable to hold back any further I take a few steps forward and place a hand on Tyler's bicep. His skin heats my palms. The contact sends fire through my hands and up my arms, a warm sensation fills my chest. I feel Tyler's entire body freeze at the contact. My breath hitches in my throat and I look up to see Tyler's eyes darken and become heavy.

The moment passes quickly; I can see the shuttering in Tyler's gaze as he pulls his arm away from my grasp, his face settling into a grimace.

"Get the hell off of me!" he whispers so only I can hear, with a fake polite smile still plastered across his face so as not to draw any more attention to himself than he already has. Tyler pushes forward through the crowd towards the hallway as I hurry up to catch up.

"If you just tell me where the room is, I can find it myself," Tyler stops in the doorway and mutters behind him, realising that I am following close behind.

"It's no trouble really, saves you from getting lost." I push ahead of him and bound towards the stairs. I want nothing more than to get Tyler and me away from the crowd and to somewhere a bit quieter where I can think straight. I marvel at the irony at the thought of thinking straight when my reactions at the moment seem to be anything but.

I move quickly up the stairs, stopping every now and again to make sure that he is following like a dog scared that his owner would suddenly disappear. Sure enough he is, but the look on his face conveys that each step he takes pains him.

"Are you ok dude?"

"I'm fine," Tyler bites out through clenched teeth.

"Do you need a glass of water or anything? You look kinda ill."

"I said I'm fine, didn't I?" he snaps.

Accepting that that's the only response I'm going to get, I continue down the hall on the first floor and make my way to the furthest bedroom. I push the door open into the tiny room, stepping down two small stairs that lead into what people refer to as the box room. It's not large enough to be a full time bedroom, but we'd managed to squeeze a single bed onto a box spring and a really tiny pine desk with a mirror and small TV on it. The room is permeated by a musty smell, the result of many a houseguest being poured into here after a rowdy house party like the one taking place at the moment.

I feel Tyler close behind me. I turn to face him and my eyebrows immediately pull together in a frown. His face is severe with anger and getting redder with each passing second.

"I'm sorry it's so small, but it should be ok enough for you to rest in." I know I have a litany of things I need to say to him. Entire speeches I should make. Apologies to be pleaded, forgiveness to ask for. The words apparently have escaped me, leaving me only platitudes in its place. "Wow it's been like forever man, how have you been?"

Tyler just stares at me, his mouth gaping wide as if in disbelief. I'm fairly sure I didn't ask him if he likes sacrificing kittens on a weekend. However, the expression on his face would be the one I would expect if such a question had been asked.

Tyler takes in a deep breath and paces back and forth in the small six foot by six foot space that's left in the room after the furniture. He stops suddenly and whips his head around to face me. "Are you fucking kidding me right now? I mean you must have lost your fucking mind, what the actual fuck do you think is wrong with me?"

What the hell is wrong with *me*? Of course he's going to be angry. Of course he's going to be pissed off just by me being in the same room. What I come to realise I am doing however is trying to normalize the situation as much as possible. The idea of him leaving right now is unacceptable to me. I need him to stay.

"For three years you made my life hell. I spent every single day of my life for those years hoping to god you wouldn't look my way as I knew when that happened you would say something disgusting or beat the shit out of me. Now you have the nerve to ask how I've been? Is this really happening right now?"

It's almost as if he has this rant all cued up in his head like a well-loved playlist, he barely needs to take a break or pause for thought as the words keep spilling from his mouth.

"How the fuck do you think I've been? I've been good because I didn't have to spend every day worried about getting a fist to the stomach or face. That's how I have been! How about you?" Sarcasm and disdain drip from his lips.

"Listen I was just asking if you were ok! I didn't think it would get that type of reaction." I put my hands up in front of me and start moving towards the door to give Tyler some space, but first I need to get past Tyler, who by this point looks like a coiled snake ready to strike.

The past assaults me with visions of my fist hitting flesh, of blood pouring down his face, of kicking him in the stomach whilst he lay on the floor with his arms protecting his head, of spitting at him as he tries to walk past me in the hallway. I hear the jeers and shouts of people cheering me on as I dehumanize him. I want to die right then.

I see the man he has become, not because of what I did to him for all those years, but in spite of me. I don't deserve his forgiveness and I feel like a cock for even thinking I could get that from him. "I'll leave you alone ok, sorry I..."

Tyler starts to back away slowly as if afraid for the first time this evening that I might lash out at him, scared because he fears retribution for his outburst. I want to scream at him not to be afraid of me. I want to shake him to make him understand that the person that he knows is not really me. That was never really me.

I remember high school through the lenses of an adult with some perspective and not through the eyes of a teenage boy who wanted desperately to fit in. I remember slamming Tyler up against his locker and hearing the back of his head smash off the metal doors. I remember the various times I'd sucker-punched him in the stomach or tripped him up as he was passing in the hallways.

"Hey, I'm just trying to get past you ok, so I can leave you alone like I said." I can already feel myself falling into a shame spiral and just want to get out of there. I almost want him to punch me. To let him take out all his vengeance on me. I would let him, I would take everything he had to give and thank him for it.

Tyler's eyes never leave mine as I slowly approach, trying to pass him in the hallway. It is a tight squeeze getting down the hallway generally. You certainly couldn't extend your arms to their full wingspan, but for two fully-grown, quite stacked men, trying to pass each other was going to be a different type of challenge. Squeezing past Tyler in the hallway face to face, I come to a full stop as our chests touch in passing.

My back pressed to the wall and my chest touching his I try to inhale, and I feel the warmth of Tyler's breath on my face, spicy and sweet from the few mouthfuls of Jack Daniels that he had managed to drink before dumping the rest on the floor. A strange tingling begins in my jaw, the sensation catching beneath my skin, and suddenly it feels like my skin is too tight and I need to move. A twitch in my cheek contracts my lips, making the space behind my ears clench. A heat spreads down my arms to my fingers, making my fingertips tingle. I know I need to do something, anything. I'm just not exactly sure what it is. I see heat in Tyler's eyes, it looks different to the anger that I've already witnessed. Being a couple of inches taller than him I look down and gaze at him and mutter, "Hi..."

Tyler stares directly at my mouth, I feel a slight increase in the rate of his breathing. Tyler's plump lower lip falls open ever so slightly. I feel my heart rate speed up, heat radiating from me as if I were throwing a sudden fever. I can't seem to break the spell he has on me, I don't think I want to. I don't think I ever want to leave this space in the hallway with not a breath between us. I want to live and breathe and just exist right in this moment forever.

Tyler's hand reaches up between us and comes to rest gently on my chest. His fingertips dig lightly into my firm pectoral muscles.

As if in exploration and experimentation he begins to rub slow deliberate circles with his thumb against my chest, only thin fabric stopping skin to skin contact. I've never hated my Henley before, it's my favourite shirt. Fitting me perfectly. I hate it now though; I hate the barrier it makes between myself and Tyler.

Tyler breathes deeply and appears to be about to move forward when he suddenly remembers himself. The memory of the last time he touches me roars into my head, of his breath and touch and then my fist colliding with his jaw. He pulls quickly away into the room and walks briskly to the bed, sitting at the foot of the mattress and resting his head in his hands perched on his knees.

"Leave me alone ok, I just want you to leave me alone," Tyler sighs with his head in his hands, not looking anywhere but at his feet. "You made my life hell for all that time for something which I had no control over, you made me feel worthless. I pulled myself out of the funk that you put me in and built a good life for myself, and somehow again in thirty minutes you have managed to make me feel like a piece of shit. So congratulations, you win, as always. Now can you please leave me the fuck alone!"

I had never really known what it meant when people said they felt their heart was breaking, but suddenly I have a very keen understanding of that particular emotion. Seeing him crumble only a few feet away sparks an overwhelming need to go to him, to put an arm around Tyler's shoulder, to place a gentle kiss on the top of his head or to pull him back against my chest and protect him for a few minutes.

"Is everything ok in here?"

I turn to see the giant Viking dude standing in the hallway, a concerned expression on his face. His eyes narrow as he scans me from head to toe. I want to scream at him to leave us alone, I'd finally gotten him away from everyone downstairs and finally it had been just us. Yes it is tragic and I feel as if I'm being flayed alive by the pain on Tyler's face and the guilt trying to rip its way free from my stomach, but at least I can spend my last moments trying to make things better, even if only a little. But this big jarhead of a guy is making it so much more difficult.

"Yeah I'm good. You can tell Max she doesn't have to worry."

"If you're sure?"

"Yeah I'm sure, I'll be down soon." Tyler gives this guy a really warm smile. I don't want him smiling at this guy, I want him smiling at me. I remember right before I fucked everything up, as usual, he had smiled at me that day by the tennis courts. I remember the way he had looked at me that day in Art class. I need that smile, that warm gentle face more than I need my next breath.

The guy nods before glaring at me again in warning and leaving us alone once more.

I take a step into the room and sit down on the top step. I hear Tyler sigh when he realises that I'm not leaving as well.

"I will leave you alone, but I just want to clear the air between us. I know I was horrible in high school." I see Tyler's about to respond so I hold up a hand as if to pause him in his tracks. "I was a horrible bag of shit I know, I can't take back what I did, I can't make any of this ok for you, but right now I can make sure you are ok in my house. That's the very least I can do. Please let me do that."

Tyler appears to regard me as you might do if your dog suddenly started speaking. Shaking his head slightly he stands from the bed and walks over to where I was sitting, squatting down in front of me. Placing each of his hands on my bent knees, Tyler hardens his stare, his resolve now clear to see on his face.

"You made me hate myself."

I feel tightness in my throat like I am about to throw up.

"I have spent a long time getting over the boy who both excited me and made me want to die. I will never forgive you Lukas. I don't want to see your face, I don't want to hear your voice and I have no interest in making you feel better by letting you know whether I am ok or not."

A sharp pain lances my chest as if someone has pushed a chilled blade into me to the hilt and then twisted it to ensure lasting damage.

"What I want, as I said, is for you to leave me alone and never speak to me again."

With that Tyler gets to his feet and moves around me and down the hallway. I hear the door slam at the bottom of the stairs as Tyler leaves the house and leaves me devastated in his wake.

Chapter 8.

Tyler

I spent most of the following day profusely apologizing to Max, whom I'd found out later from Dawn had gone ballistic with worry upon finding out that I had left the party alone earlier in the night. Max had sent me text messages with some choice words about how if I ever left her at a party without warning, she'd rip off my testicles and use the sack to make herself a purse for her change.

I came out of my room the following morning to find her sitting alone on the sofa watching some garbage daytime TV. After reading her text message I know I have some grovelling to do.

"Max..."

Silence greets me.

"Maaaax," I whine, pouting my bottom lip.

Silence once more.

I move to stand between her and the TV; she attempts to crane her head around me to watch some talk show host antagonise his guests. I huff a sigh and think. All of a sudden it hits me. I know what will make her talk to me again.

I crouch in front of her and pat my knees.

"Who's a pretty girl?" I smile at her and coo in a baby voice.

A twitch appears on her cheek and she attempts to hold back a smile.

"Who is? Who's a pretty girl? Who? Who."

Max bites the inside of her cheek hard enough that I'm sure if she isn't careful she will draw blood. The laughter in her eyes betrays her face.

"Who's my pretty girl?" I squeal.

A wide smile cracks on her face and she throws herself at me.

"I AM!" she laughs, and I wrap my arms around her and manage to squeeze tight enough to tickle under her armpits until she is half laughing, half crying. She manages to break away, stand up and give me a playful kick in the side. I chuckle and push to my feet. Max plonks herself back on the sofa and points at the kitchen.

Understanding immediately what she is asking for, I make my way into the kitchen and whip up a batch of chocolate chip cookies. I had found the key to Max's heart was chocolate very early on. I'd also found that if I had a batch of chocolate chip cookies on the go, she could never stay mad at me for long. I hover in the kitchen for the 10 minutes it takes the cookies to bake. Max is not the type of person to wait for a cookie to cool down before she eats them, not a fan of delayed gratification in the slightest. I pour out a couple of glasses of cold milk and bring the plate of cookies over with me. Setting it on the coffee table in front of the sofa, I plonk down next to her, grabbing the beige wool blanket next to the sofa and throwing it over our legs.

"So tell me about the guy." I nudge her in her side. A wide smile appears on her face as she chews her bottom lip.

"He's just a guy," she smiles shyly.

"Since when have you not told me all the gory details about the guys you pick up?" I stare pointedly at her, "Even when I beg you to stop."

"I don't know," she shrugs.

"Oh my god." I gape at her.

"Oh your god what?" she says, her eyes widening a fraction.

"You like him."

"Of course I like him!" she laughs. "Did you see how hot he was?"

Yes I did see how hot he was, so hot that if I wasn't a hundred percent sure he had banged my best friend last night I would save him for the spank bank.

"No, I mean you really like him." I try my best for a gentle probing smile. I probably just look constipated instead.

"Do you need the toilet?" she asks warily. *Yup I knew it!*

"Come on tell me!" I say pouting once more.

"Sweetie you look like a blowfish, stop doing that with your face," she sighs and turns to face me. "His name is Peter, he's from Norway originally, but his parents moved to Cambridge years ago and I want his babies."

I throw back my head and laugh. Max is never one for falling hard over a guy, preferring instead to keep them at a distance and use them to fulfil whatever needs she has.

"Anyway I don't want to talk about it anymore, I don't want to jinx anything." Seeing that however much of a joke she is trying to make it, she is also very serious, I nod and settle back into the sofa, picking up my milk to dunk in one of the soft warm cookies. Half the thing breaks off and falls to the bottom of the glass. I groan and proceed to sip at the milk.

"Tell me about Lukas," Max says, leaning her head against my shoulder.

I sigh, knowing I would have to have this conversation. I take a deep breath and begin.

I had never spent a lot of time explaining to my friends in college how much of a difficult time I'd had in high school. Not because I was ashamed of my past, but as a plan to forget that time and move on to bigger and better things. I had told Max that I had been bullied when people found out that I was gay. She had put her around my shoulders and told me how she wished she had been in school with me as she would have kicked all those guys in the nuts. Max seemed to have a fascination of inflicting pain on the males of the species through torture of their testicles.

I spend the next few minutes explaining yesterday, about my past with Lukas, and how seeing him there had thrown me through a loop. She started apologising for dragging me to the party in the first place before I shut her up by calling her a whore and telling her that she was a selfish cunt who was trying to make it all about her. She smiled and punched me in the arm.

"For someone who hates gay guys, and you especially, he was acting very odd when you left."

"What do you mean?"

"Well he came downstairs and was asking everybody where you had gone, he looked really upset."

"Probably pissed he didn't have a chance to deck me before I left," I grimace.

"I dont think so." She takes a bite of the soft cookies and shrugs. "You would think that he had just been broken up with the way he was acting." I know that should make me feel a lot better but for some reason, I do not want to be the cause of anyone's suffering. Not even Lukas's.

"He asked for your number," she blurts out, keeping her stare on the TV screen. "But of course I didn't give it to him," Max said nonchalantly.

I know her well enough to know that if she isn't making a drama out of a situation, then that means the situation has drama she is trying to hide.

"Anyway, you're on a double shift at the coffee shop all day tomorrow huh?" Max twirls her hair around her fingertips, playing with the ends like an angelic schoolgirl might.

I narrow my eyes in her direction. "What did you do?" My voice slightly hitches.

Max throws off the blanket and shivers. "It's cold right, you're cold. I'm cold. I'm going to make us a nice hot drink." She walks into the kitchen and fills the kettle.

"Max," I say, turning around on the sofa, leaning over the back and watching her shoulders tense.

"Would you like a coffee? Or a tea? Or a hot chocolate! You love a hot chocolate, especially on cold mornings like this." Max busies herself with her head jammed firmly in the kitchen cupboard as if she were trying to search for Narnia.

"Max?" I raise my voice and ask a little more firmly.

"I think we also have some green tea." Max notices the stern look she is receiving, and her voice trails off ever so slightly. "I know we have some rooibos tea somewhere."

I pluck a cushion off the sofa and throw it at her back. It hits her square in the shoulders and they sag. "Ok well I didn't give him your phone number obviously as you would have completely killed me. However, Dawn did tell him you worked in a coffee shop, I just filled in the blanks."

My eyes narrow even further. "Filled in the blanks how?"

Max busies herself grabbing things from the cupboard that I'm fairly sure she doesn't need. She is not great at the distraction. "Well I just told him where you worked and when your next few shifts might be," she whispers.

"*Max*! I don't want to see him. I know I didn't say as much that night, but I thought it might be pretty obvious from my complete freak out and full-on over the wall escape from the party!"

Max walks across the expanse of the room and grabs me by both biceps. "Wow you really have been working out a lot haven't you?" she admires, distracted from what she had wanted to say, shaking her head ever so slightly she looks at me the way a mother would look at her son, when her son was being an absolute moron. "Listen, high school was a billion years ago. I know he did some absolutely awful things to you, things that cannot be forgotten. Can we just agree though that people do grow up and change, and the person they were then may not be the person they are now. Can you honestly say you're the exact same person you were back in high school?"

The only thing I can think to do is grumble at her and her undeniable logic. I was not the same scared wallflower I had been in school. I used to try to blend into the background in hopes that I was not the person that everyone was looking at, to protect myself inside a sphere of invisibility and nothingness. Now however I have maybe at times gone too far the other way. After long hours working out at the gym I have a body that I can finally be proud of, and yeah I am that guy in the gym mirror taking selfies and posting them on Instagram because after so many years of not wanting to be seen, I finally feel good enough about just being me that I want to stand out. So no, I'm not the same person, so maybe I could give him the benefit of the doubt... couldn't I?

Probably not.

Chapter 9.

Tyler

I wake up the next morning gripped by a sense of unease, as if the world were off its axis. Everything seems both too big and too small at the same time, making me cranky. Max makes sure she keeps out of my way after I snap at her, having found her used tea bag in an empty cup in the sink.

"You know we have a bin for that right here?" I say, pointing at the grey trash can sitting not six feet from the sink.

"I know, I just didn't want it to drip everywhere," she defends herself.

"Nevermind, I'll clear up after you, not like I'm going to do that all day today by myself as the new barista can't start till next week now," I mumble under my breath.

"Sorry I'll get the tea bag, your Highness," she says, giving me a mocking bow. I move out the way of the sink whilst she disposes of the offending bag. Giving me a swift kiss on the cheek she retreats to her room.

Looking at my watch I see time has passed by without me realising it. I shout out a quick apology for acting like an ass and head out the door. Knowing I'm going to have a long day at work I decide to run there. Taking the long route means I will stay close to the canalside almost all the way to work. The run is not what I would call picturesque, taking me mostly along residential or industrial units. However, I find running each day gives me the headspace I need to deal with the detritus of the day and stay centred. It also allows me to indulge in the lemon squares at work without feeling too guilty at the high calorific content.

Half an hour later, I arrive at the coffee shop facing the canal, bending down to take the padlock off the bottom of the shutters. The heavy metal shutters push up revealing Sergio's coffee house. The first time I'd seen the space I'd fallen in love with it, decorated like a traditional old English tea room with subtle influences from Moroccan coffee houses. The cream and white of the walls are draped luxuriously in purple and orange silks which extend up to the ceiling making sweeping arches into the room. Dark brown leather seated booths line the far wall, whilst fifteen round dark oak tables are dotted throughout the floor, surrounded by dark wicker chairs. Each table is adorned with chrome lanterns inlaid with colourful stained glass. Wall sconces with amber shades draped with beads have been added every few meters on the walls. In the centre of all this is the barista's booth, a large square platform made of metal and wood.

I take in the smell of cinnamon and nutmeg that permeates the air in the room, smiling. I go to the office at the back and proceed to get the coffee shop set up for the day.

Time passes slowly, customers coming in and out. I put a mixture of discs into the CD changer underneath the counter and press play. The Buffy the Vampire Slayer soundtrack kicks in. Not caring if it makes me a dork, I sway around the shop clearing plates and cups.

The regular lunch rush has me run off my feet for a while, hoping that Max might make an appearance and lend a hand. She doesn't so I manage the place alone. A sense of weary loneliness creeps up on me as I make myself busy, counting the minutes until I can begin closing up.

I remember Max saying that she has given Lukas the details of where I work, which has me looking up at the door with bated breath and apprehension every sound from the bell over the door. I'm not sure if I am disappointed or relieved each time the person turns out not to be him. I resign myself to the fact that he probably won't show up as there are now only 45 minutes before closing. I start to clear away the mess left by some of the previous customers. I figure if I can get as much done as I could before the shop officially closed, I could make an early dart and maybe get home and watch some more trashy TV with Max.

Recently she has gotten me addicted to a show called The Simple Life. There is something endearing about two socialites moving in with a family in rural Arkansas. Initially we'd marvelled at the fact that the girls were even able to do some of the menial tasks they'd been set, until Max one day squinted at the TV and pointed something out.

"This is like a safari for them then?" she mused.

"What do you mean?"

"Well it's like, novel to them, working in a dairy farm or a drive-in, like they are seeing how other species live, hunt and kill in the wild."

I frowned slightly and then tapped her on the knee.

"How about we just passively watch it and not think of the ethical and moral quandaries which might make it difficult for us to watch and just enjoy it huh?"

She seemed to ponder this for a second before nodding and going back to watching.

I look around the coffee shop and sigh. I start to stack cappuccino cups on top of each other in one hand, whilst wiping at the table with a wet cloth with the other. I've become quite adept at multitasking since working here. The first few times I tried this, a number of cups had paid the ultimate price. I make my way back to the counter, feeling just a little too smug with myself. Just as I am about to reach the central stand I feel the top cappuccino cup slip ever so slightly to the left and tumble to the ground, shattering into smithereens on the floor.

"Shit! Motherfucking piece of garbage! Dick!" I wince and look around to make sure the last few people in the shop haven't heard me cursing out a broken cup. *Must be professional!* I dump the remaining dirty crockery on the counter and head to the back office to collect a dustpan and brush. I crouch down on hands and knees to sweep up the first few shards of splintered porcelain under the brown bistro-style coffee tables. As I reach under the table, my arm outstretched as far as it will go to reach a shard of glass, I spy a dark pair of Doc Martens, pushing their toe caps under the opposite side.

"Do you always just drop every drink that you have in your hands, or is this a new development?"

I can't see the face, just from the knee down all I can make out is some black skinny jeans and the boots, but I would know that voice anywhere.

"Need a hand under there?"

I close my eyes and pray to anyone who will listen to turn back time just a few minutes, just so I retain some level of dignity and don't look like a flustered moron every time I'm confronted with him. I quickly back up until I can stand and face the guy in front of me.

"I'm fine," I mutter, obviously not fine, and go to place the dustpan and brush back on the counter behind me.

"Yeah you keep saying that, so far I have yet to see evidence that supports the statement though." My eyes shoot up, surprised he is taking such a light tone with me. I formulate something snarky to say to him, and that's when I come to a halt when I see that same breathtaking smile that I had always sought out while daydreaming in class, the same smile that seemed to draw everyone to him. On the occasions that Lukas had seen me staring from across the room, a beating later in the day was normally what followed.

Remembering the violence is like a bucket of ice water thrown over me on a windy day. Like being smashed in the side of the head by a football kicked by a professional footballer. I force myself to look away and move back behind the counter, the structure of metal, wood and glass seeming like a good physical barrier between me and him. I begin rearranging mugs and cups, keeping my hands busy as I have the feeling that I will start to want to wring them like a nervous wreck.

"What do you want Lukas?" I keep my voice calm and measured since I'm in my place of work. The last thing I need is someone reporting the guy behind the counter throwing a mug at the head of a customer. The sooner he gets off his chest whatever it is he wants to say, the sooner he can get the hell out of my life. Ironically the thought of him leaving right now gives my stomach the same feeling as driving quickly over a hill, a sickening swoop.

The song changes on the stereo system, Bif Naked's *Lucky,* playing out through the speakers. Squeezing my eyes tightly shut, I'm assaulted by memories of lying face down on my bed whilst this song plays on repeat as I imagine an existence where Lukas comes to me one day at lunch hour and tells me how sorry he is, and begs for my forgiveness. I remember waking from those daydreams to realise the heartbreaking devastation that the man of my literal dreams repeatedly told me on a weekly basis to kill myself.

Lukas shifts and seems shy, almost not sure what to say, looking down and frowning as if uncertain where to place his feet. He looks up at me through his thick dark lashes and simply says, "I wanted to make sure you were ok after the other night. I was worried about you."

Like it's been hit by some kind of incantation that has the sole purpose of making my blood boil and heart race all at the same time, my brain stutters, trying to decide whether I should laugh, cry or scream at him. The time for checking if I was ok passed years ago. If he had only come to me once all those years ago and asked if I was ok, then maybe I wouldn't want to punch him in his fucking perfect face right now. I bite the inside of my cheek to stop myself from saying anything that I'll regret later.

"As I told you, I am fine. You can stop worrying now and there's no need to feel guilty, so you can leave," I bite out.

I turn around to busy myself with anything that keeps me from being a part of this conversation any longer when Lukas leans over the bar and grabs me by the wrist, turning me back around to face him. I stiffen at his touch, his grip firm and hard. Grabbing his fingers, I peel them off me one by one, sneering at him.

"Keep your fucking hands off me." My voice is cold and harsh.

The shame creeps back onto his face and he looks down at his hands like they have offended him.

"I just want to stay for a little while if that's ok and talk to you." He looks like a scared little boy in that moment and my heart cracks slightly.

I still feel the heat from his hand somehow all over my body and feel disgusted with myself that I miss the contact; I hate that he's made me react this way after all these years. But somewhere deep down I'm still that guy who could barely form sounds or words when just looking at Lukas Ford.

I can feel my resolve weakening slightly, and a part of me is kind of happy about that. I know subconsciously I just want him to convince me to stay and talk to him for a while, but the rational part of my brain wins out. What the fuck am I even thinking? This guy is a monster.

"What could we possibly have to talk about?" It's a true enough statement, what *could* we talk about? We can't really reminisce about high school, what will I say? *Hey, remember that time when you punched me in the stomach so hard that I threw up and all your friends laughed, then you laughed, and I cried and you all left me there, that was weird wasn't it?*

A harsh smile plays on my lips as I face him. "I know who you really are Lukas, make no mistake." A deep furrow in his brow appears and he sucks in a shuddering breath. "You might have everyone fooled that you're this good guy, but you forget that I know you, the real you. Not this fake nice guy act you have going at the moment."

Seeing the hurt and anguish on his face should give me a bit of satisfaction, for making him feel even a fraction as bad as he made me feel for years but it doesn't. Not even in the slightest. I have spent a long time moving on from high school, from the sickening feeling in my gut that made me feel dirty and worthless. The whole point of moving on is not to become the person who made me feel those things about myself.

It suddenly hits me that everything I've done since, every achievement I've earned, every hard hour at the gym I've pushed through, every relationship I've failed at as I chased the fun single life is all due to the fact that I'm trying to be someone different than the sad kid from high school. My life should not be about proving something to someone else - I need to live for me.

"Please." The sound barely escapes his lips, his eyes moving up to meet mine. His expression is stricken and pale. I can't be the cause of that, I just can't, it's not in me. 'Virgin State of Mind' plays on the speakers, the lyrics telling a story of the singer relying on others for self-validation before taking control and changing their entire life.

Maybe I can talk to Lukas, maybe it shouldn't be about me trying to forget my past and become someone else. Lukas looks pained as if he's known that he would get this type of reaction, but it shows at least some character that he knew this would happen and had made the effort to come here anyway.

"I just want to try and be friends. I know what I did was horrible to you, but I just want things to be ok between us now. Can we try that maybe? Can we try just to talk?" His eyes seem to plead with me for some kind of compromise.

Maybe I can be the bigger person, maybe if I let him talk to me he can get rid of all his demons and leave me the fuck alone once and for all. I'm actively ignoring the inner voice calling me a fucking liar. Of course I'm still consumed with attraction to him. He is beautiful, the most beautiful man I've ever seen. It's just a shame that the face is attached to a complete asshole.

I take a deep breath and bite the bullet. "Fine we can talk, but I still have a little while until I'm finished, and I have a lot of cleaning up to do so maybe another time?" I move from around the counter and step towards him, extending my hand out as a form of olive branch. The asshole gives me a smirk like he has won the pig at the county fair and grasps my hand in his. My traitorous dick starts to plump at the contact.

"How about I stay and help you clear up, that way it won't be so much for you to do?" His lips purse into a tight smile which I couldn't help but find adorable. In no universe have I forgiven him, I just need to see this through so I get back on with the life I've been living before he smashed his way back into it.

"Fine ok you can stay, but there is a lot to do so don't say I didn't warn you," I tell him, the stern authoritative sound to my voice making me cringe a little. *Chill the fuck out Tyler*, my inner voice mocks me.

"Put me to work sir," Lukas says, holding his hands out, wrists together as if shackled.

A million thoughts fight for dominance in my head right then. Lukas laid out for me on my bed, blindfolded and shackled to the headboard. Just the sight of him in such a submissive pose, contrary to his previously constant alpha demeanor has all my cylinders firing. My palms begin to itch, and that damn twitch makes an appearance in my cheek.

His face flushes as he seems to realise that he is having an effect on me, dropping his arms to his sides quickly. "I mean let me know what you would like me to get started with."

I give a small nod and then gesture for Lukas to come around the counter up onto the barista platform. As he makes his way around I realise that we are going to be in quite close proximity. When there is more than one of us working we tend to have one person on the platform with the other collecting cups and cleaning around. The platform is not all that big, a design choice made to fit in more customer tables. Stepping up onto the platform we are only a metre apart, the proximity making my head feel a little fuzzy. Even at that distance I can feel the heat radiating off his body and that warm smell that seems unique to him.

I stare at his mouth, the plump lip pouting out. I inhale sharply, my mind focusing on what it would feel like to bite his lip and slide my tongue into his mouth. His mouth cocks up a little into a smirk.

"Why don't you grab those mugs from the empty tables?" I say suddenly, needing to be away from him. Everything about him is so potent and sharp. The smirk turns into a full smile. He looks over his shoulder to the tables I'm gesturing towards, the corded muscle of his neck stretching, making me want to push my face in there and give him a good sniff, maybe bite down on his shoulder. I remember the last time I gave into that kind of temptation. I had to hide my face from my mother when I arrived home in case she went ballistic and marched me back to the school. I was not able to hide the swollen lip the next day however. I'd begged her to just forget it; seeing the pain in her face had hurt more than the actual punch itself.

I guess he can see the emotional shutters come down on my face as he bites his lip and looks down. I hand him an apron, and he puts it over his head and ties it around his waist as he moves from the platform. No one should look that good in a stupid apron.

The tension seemed to diffuse slightly. I give him a short list of things to do which he does with gusto, making sure each task is completed meticulously, coming back to me when each job is complete like a dog wanting a snack or pat on the head for a job well done. We work in moderately comfortable silence for the next 20 minutes, clearing away the stock, loading the dishwashers, cleaning tables, counters and units.

As I'm counting the money in the till I watch Lukas as he sees out the last of the customers and closes the door behind them, turning the open sign around to closed and flipping the lock on the door. He hasn't noticed the appreciative glances he had been given by the groups of men and women sat at tables as he pottered around the shop cleaning as he went; he had not spotted my frustrated glare either as two men whispered something to each other whilst staring at his ass as he bent over a table to pick up empty plates.

He turns around to face me, and all of a sudden the coffee shop feels far too small, like someone had pushed in the walls and drawn all the air out the room. It had felt completely different with other people in the room acting as almost a barrier between us. The air of professionalism we had to convey kept us safe from any real conversation or interaction we might have otherwise had to have. Not now though.

The space sparks with energy all around me, heat coursing across my skin; looking up to meet his gaze, I know I am not the only one feeling it. I see his chest rise and fall sharply. His muscles are taut underneath his blue denim shirt, the buttons on the front barely able to contain the power behind them. Excitement skitters through my veins and I can feel my cock begin to swell instantly inside my jeans, to the point where I have to physically reach down and adjust myself as so not to appear too obvious behind the counter.

Lukas follows the trail of my hands as I grip my cock through the crotch of my jeans and move it off to one side. His mouth hangs open slightly and the tip of his tongue comes out to trace his lower lip. His eyes rise to meet mine. *Fuck*! I had failed to realise that this side of the counter has a glass front, so he has had a front row seat to me squeezing my dick.

Lukas starts to move toward me, and I know it's a matter of seconds before he's face to face with me. The tension is unbearable so I quickly move back further behind the counter and place both palms on the wooden countertop, the chill of the wood cooling down my hands which feel like they have been plunged into boiling water while I wasn't looking.

"Thank you for helping me close up, it was a big help," I smile at him nervously across the counter.

He moves to kneel on a stool facing me and places his own hands on the counter parallel to mine, his thumb grazing the tip of my index finger. I look down at the brief skin-to-skin contact and move my hand away slowly.

"It's no problem really." Lukas looks at me, not smiling, clear frustration in his eyes as if the counter between us were an evil villain who must be defeated. "Tyler I..." is all he gets out before I interrupt him, not wanting to hear what comes out of his mouth next.

"I should be heading out, I think Max has some kind of movie night planned for us," I say quickly, trying to break the tension. "She will have my nuts in a vise if I'm late for that."

I frown as I see the disappointment clear on his face, and I'm sure he could probably say the same about me. I've had boyfriends and hookups before, but never have I been so acutely aware of someone else's presence, never have I had to stop myself from jumping over the counter and mauling someone. Lukas has a dangerous effect on me that makes me just want to not think, just feel and act. That had been a dangerous mistake to make with him in the past, a mistake I'm not keen to repeat.

"Oh right ok," he mutters under his breath. His eyes meet mine again, slightly hopeful. "Can we hang out again maybe?"

"Why?" I ask immediately.

"Because I want to hang out with you," he puts simply.

"Why?" I ask again. I'm way too confused to try and make sense of his request so he will have to lay it out really clearly for me.

He bites the corner of his mouth and runs a hand through his thick hair. I imagine that his hair must be really soft and would feel great between my fingers. His gaze locks with mine.

"Because I want to get to know you Tyler. Not at a party or around lots of strangers like today, I just want to hang out with just you. Ok?"

There is absolutely no way I'm going to reject the request of the man in front of me, but I had to at least try and make it sound like I wasn't some desperate whore.

"Sure, I mean I have class and I work here a lot, maybe text me and we can figure something out?"

His smile brightens almost immediately. He lifts his torso over the counter, his biceps and shoulders straining as he supports his whole body weight. He reaches forward with one hand and slides his palm into my pocket, his fingertips grazing my already hard dick. I know he must feel it as a small groan escapes his lips. He grabs my phone which I totally forgot was in there.

I'm slightly miffed he doesn't grab something else. He pulls the phone out and smiles. Flipping open the device he starts typing away at the screen. A loud tone rings loudly in his back pocket; he closes the phone and hands it back to me.

"Just in case you tried to give me a fake number. Oh, and I saved my number in your phone as well." His cocky grin pushes all my buttons, making me aggravated and turned on at the same time. I look down, my jeans are so tight I can see the full outline of my cock as it snakes against my hip. I can feel the tackiness of the precum in my underwear.

"I wouldn't have given you a fake number." I narrow my eyes at him and then thinking more about it, I give him a grin. "Maybe..."

Lukas starts to laugh and moves towards the door of the coffee shop. "Well now we don't have to worry do we?"

I only have to make it a few more minutes without acting like a complete tool. As soon as he leaves, I can melt into a puddle on the floor and deal with my confused-as-fuck feelings.

I reach the door ahead of him, moving the latch and pulling the door slightly open. I feel his hand close around the one I have dangling at my side. He pulls me around sharply so that I'm facing him. His chest is heaving rapidly. He looks down at my parted mouth and breathes in.

"I'm sorry I just have to know," he murmurs, leaning down so that his mouth hovers above mine. His eyes are trying to meet mine, but my eyes dart everywhere around the room like I'm looking for an escape. Do I want to escape though? *No you fucking don't*, the voice whispers in my head. I bring my eyes back to meet his and melt at the heat in his gaze. His mouth is bare millimeters from my own when he whispers, "Is this ok?"

Unconsciously I give a small nod. He closes the distance between us and presses his lips gently to mine. Not moving at first, the smooth texture of his lips slides against my own. Fireworks go off behind my eyes, this gentle kiss destroying every other kiss I'd ever experienced. Nothing had ever felt this right and this dangerous at the same time. I repress a desire to grab the back of his head and mark him, tear open his shirt and bite his chest.

His tongue traces the seam of my lips, and I taste the distinctive mixture of cinnamon and honey I can always smell from him. Everything about the situation, the smell, taste and feel, is intoxicating and I feel like I can't get enough. His hand comes up and rests against my cheek as the other grips my fingertips. I pant against his mouth, just bursting with need. My cock continues pumping precum into my shorts; I can feel the tackiness spreading against my thigh.

Then as quickly as it starts it's over, the kiss short and sweet. He pulls away from me and his tongue comes out to lick his own lips like he is tasting me there.

"I couldn't leave without knowing what that felt like." He looks at me; I must look an absolute mess. I feel as if he has just turned my world upside down with a simple kiss. "Text me later yeah?" he asks warily.

I nod my head, maybe a bit too emphatically to which he simply smiles back at me, "Cool."

His hand reaches up to the door and grips the door handle, and I'm suddenly brought back to the present. "Oh sorry you want to leave," I laugh, which probably makes me sound like a complete geek. I scrunch up my face and pull open the door for him. He moves through the door into the walkway.

"Speak with you later Tyler," he grins, and then turns on his heel and walks towards the small park that will take him back to the main road. I close the door behind him, locking it and turning to press my back against the door. I'm not sure if my face is expressing shock or happiness because I'm feeling both in equal amounts. I press my fingertips gently to my lips as if to make sure that that had actually happened. My lips still tingle from the heat of his kiss.

Chapter 10.

Lukas

So that just happened.

I had not planned to kiss Tyler when I'd walked into the coffee shop. But seeing him move around the room, confidently talking to people, cracking jokes and making customers laugh as he worked to close the shop, had made me want him desperately.

I could see the longing looks that some of the guys had been throwing his way in the shop, making my jaw tense. At one point an older lady had patted me on the arm and chuckled.

"Easy Tiger," she smiled.

"I'm sorry?" I had said, a bit confused.

"Sweetie you were growling at that man over there who is checking out your boyfriend."

I force out a quick laugh, "He isn't my boyfriend." *I'm not that fucking lucky.* "We are barely friends."

"Well you best start doing whatever you need to do to change that then, cause you have been drooling over him since you came in here." She gives me a wink before going back to her coffee and paper.

He was definitely a sight to behold. Broad shoulders and a well-defined chest under a tight T-shirt leading down to a trim waist, and his jeans cupping the curve of his high, tight butt. I always hated the term bubble butt, however that was the only way I could think of describing his spectacular ass. His shaggy blonde hair had been cropped really close on the sides and the hair on top was tweaked to perfection. His fucking eyes though, the colour of a Mediterranean ocean. I just wanted to fuck him there and then.

It was as if I had no choice in the matter. I'd had to know what it was like to kiss him. Caught up in our own little spell, with no idea whether later in the evening he would go back to hating me again and I would never get the chance to put my mouth on his, I took my chance and thank fuck I did. The second I got a taste of him I knew that it would never be enough. His taste still coats my tongue; I want to keep him with me.

I make my way back to the house that I share with Dawn, I am all set to rush straight upstairs, knowing that I likely need to jack off before my balls explode. My cock has been pushing hard against the zipper of my jeans since I had walked into the coffee shop and saw Tyler across the room. Since I've gotten a taste of him it's been demanding some attention and will not be ignored.

As I push the door open Dawn appears out of nowhere, rushing from the lounge. She is on me in a flash, grabbing my hand and pulling me into the room.

"So how did it go, he didn't attack you did he? What's up? You look dazed! Do you have a concussion or something? So out with it, have you been forgiven yet? Come on don't keep me in suspense!" She barely takes a breath as her words hit me like a semi-automatic. She is panting excitedly, it'll be only a few more seconds, I reckon, before she starts to shake the information out of me.

I grin at her and just state in three words, "It was nice." I smile and edge around her into the kitchen to pour myself a glass of water.

"Oh *no*! Do you honestly think I am going to let you out of here after just saying *It was nice!*, think again mister. I want the details!" She rubs her hands together as if she were just about to roll a pair of double 7's at the table.

I chuckle at her almost perverse insistence upon details of some sexual encounter that has not actually happened. "Nothing happened, it was nice like I said." I start putting clean dishes from the sink rack into the cupboard to my right, my back to Dawn. "We talked a little." My hand stills on the handle of the cupboard. "There may have been a small kiss." I close the door and move around the island, head toward the living room and plonk myself on the love seat in the far corner of the room.

"What? You guys kissed! Ok tell me more," she shouts after me, following me into the room and perching on the seat next to me, her hands gripping my thighs and massaging gently as if to physically coax more of the story out of me.

"Actually, hang on," she says, standing abruptly and running out the room, reappearing a few moments later with an open tin of chocolates.

"Oh for fuck sake Dawn, it's not that interesting of a story."

"Oh please, this is juicy stuff, and chocolate always helps." Dawn is always a bit melodramatic.

"I don't know what happened, I went there just to say sorry really. I mean yeah I am very attracted to him, but I never thought that he would forgive me long enough to let me anywhere near him." I look down at my feet, the guilt from a few nights ago suddenly rearing its ugly head.

Dawn's face scrunches up in confusion. I have never really gone over my past before with anyone outside my circle of friends in high school. She rests back on her heels and looks up at me. "Why would he need to forgive you? I guessed you guys had a bit of a past from the way he reacted to you that night, but what happened that you would need his forgiveness?"

I take in a deep breath.

There are things about Dawn that make her a great friend, she is fiercely loyal, caring and she will fight your corner when you are unable or unwilling to fight your own. Dawn has been my most fierce defender and promoter since she found out that I liked men.

Dawn had told me one drunken evening about her own experiences within the gay community. Dawn is the youngest child and has an older brother called Niall. They had grown up on a small farm in a rural area of Northern Ireland. She often told me about their exploits growing up, how they would build dens and terrify the neighbours' chickens and sheep.

One day she had walked in on her brother and one of the farm workers Jack kissing in one of the old barns. She had assured Niall she wouldn't tell a soul, she kept her word. Years had passed, Niall had started university in Dublin taking a business course. He had told her of his dream to run his own design and consultancy firm and needed some business knowledge so he could go out on his own and not have to rely on their parents for financial support.

One summer Niall returned home and told Dawn that he wanted to tell their parents that he was gay, he was dating a guy in Dublin and it looked like things might get serious. The guy didn't want to date a closeted bloke, so Niall wanted to tell his parents that he had met someone. Dawn had told him it sounded like a grand idea and that she would support him a hundred percent.

Things took a dark turn for Dawn that night, she had helped her brother cook dinner for their parents. She had also taken on some extra responsibilities during lambing season. They had sat down for dinner; she remembered the driving rain and howling wind outside, and being happy to be inside their warm happy home away from the raging storm. She had prompted Niall to tell them once dinner was wrapping up. No sooner had the words "Mam, Pa, I'm gay," left his mouth, when his dad took a swing at him and ripped open his cheek. Dawn's mother had cried and told her son to stay away from her.

They had called him all manner of revolting names and told him he had to leave the house there and then and never return. They told him that he was dead to them and they no longer had a son. Dawn had screamed and cried and begged her parents to let her brother stay. Her mum and dad had ordered that she not speak of them again in her house. She tried to leave with Niall that night, but he had convinced her to stay. She was only fourteen and he was not able to support her on a student budget.

She had watched as he walked out into the raging storm, his belongings in bags on his back. Having no way to communicate with him and her parents forbidding any chance she had to talk to him, she lost touch with Niall. On her eighteenth birthday she had packed her bags after being accepted into the university of Manchester. She kissed her parents on the head before telling them now they were dead to her and they had no more children. Her mother had sobbed as she walked down the lane that her brother had walked down years before and never looked back.

Her parents' treatment of Niall was not unlike the way I had treated Tyler. I begin.

"Tyler went to my high school as you know, when I moved north. He was actually one of the first people I was introduced to on my first day." I pluck the box of chocolates out of her hands, pick a hazelnut chocolate and begin fiddling with its wrapper.

"The first day we met, Tyler had a very noticeable physical reaction to me, if you catch my drift. I knew I was different at that point, but I just wanted to be part of the school you know?

Not an outsider." I look at her for forgiveness before I have even told her the rest of the story, my voice almost sounding like it was pleading with her to understand.

"So, what happened?" She looks genuinely concerned.

"The kids in school had decided that Tyler was not popular before I even got there, after I arrived they expected me to fall in line. So I did."

"Fall in line how?" Her face blanches.

"It started off quite innocent, well not innocent, but not physical. I would call him names in class, get other guys to call him names. I would spread rumours about him watching boys in the locker rooms get changed. Really stupid mean shit." My throat feels hoarse before I even get to any of the really bad stuff I did to him.

"One day we were on the playground between classes, Tyler walked behind the toilet block, I don't even know what for because there was nothing around there, just an old field and a bench."

She doesn't open her mouth, just stares at me expectantly.

"Some of the guys I was with said they thought they had seen him earlier that day checking me out, they asked me did I like it when faggots looked at me, that maybe I was a faggot too if I got off on it." My breathing becomes erratic as the shame fills my chest.

"What did you do Lukas?"

"I got scared, I couldn't let people know I was maybe like him, I just couldn't."

I stand up from the seat and walk towards the fireplace, switching on the electric heater. The air had taken on a miserable chill. I return to my seat, noticing a distance between us that was not there before.

"I told them to follow me. He was trying to get back to the playground from wherever he had been but I stopped him. I grabbed him by the arm and took him back behind the building. They surrounded us and were looking to see what I would do. I asked him had he been looking at me, he said no but I could tell by his face he was lying. I called him names, faggot, queer, things like that."

Dawn bites her lip. I see her eyes gathering moisture.

"He wouldn't say anything after that, but they kept on watching me. I punched him in the jaw, kicked his legs out from under him, I kicked and spat at him whilst he was lying on the floor. He just kept looking up at me with those damn blue eyes like he was forgiving me whilst I was hurting him." A tear drops down my cheek and lands on my knee. I wipe it away with the back of my hand.

She stills completely, and I can almost see the cogs turning in her head, questioning everything about our friendship from the day we met. She backs up away from me as if physically pulled back by an unseen force.

"What happened next?" she whispers.

"We left him there, I think he went home because I don't remember seeing him the rest of the day. That's how it was for the next few years. We would torture him if we were bored, if he even looked at us the wrong way."

"I don't understand, you wouldn't do that!" she gasps. "That poor guy!" She stands up and moves back to sit on the large couch.

I physically shrink back in my seat.

Dawn is my closest friend, but I never thought I would need to have this discussion with her. It was a part of my past that I was so ashamed of. I'd told myself that I was just a kid, that I was doing what any guy would do at my age. I knew though that in reality I never really wanted to face my history as a bully, as a closet case who cared too much about what people thought of me.

"After what you went through with your Dad, how could you do that to someone else?" It's as if she has punched me in the gut – she does not mean for her words to affect me on such a brutal level, but they do because she is right.

"Don't you think I know that? I already feel guilty enough, please don't make me feel any worse," I plead with her.

She sighs and shakes her head slightly.

"Listen Lukas I love you ok, I need you to know that," she says, standing suddenly.

"Yeah I know, I love you too."

"I can't be in the same room as you right now, it's like you're two different people. The person I love and trust, and then this monster. I don't know why but I feel betrayed. Like you have lied to me all this time. I think I just need some space right now ok?" She moves towards the living room door to make her escape.

"We are still friends right?" I ask, my voice small. I know if I look at her properly I'll cry, and she doesn't need that from me right now.

"Yes," she shrugs, "but Lukas you *have* to make things right with that boy. He didn't deserve what you did to him. The fact that he didn't break your neck at the party and let you kiss him today without snapping your arm is a fucking miracle. You can't fuck this up. Be sure what you want because if you hurt him again, I'm going to hurt you. Friend or not."

With that she walks out the living room, closing the door behind her.

Chapter 11

Tyler

I sit staring at my computer screen in the darkness of my room. A handful of meaningless words hover over an otherwise nearly blank document. The Journalism class is kicking my ass in a very real way. The lecturer assigned an essay over two months ago which I had completely forgotten about until last week. The due date is of course two weeks away and I have nothing. Max, being in the same boat as me, has decided that she needs complete focus and has spent the last two days at her parents' house trying to make sure she has the time and space to complete it.

I stare again at the title, *Journalism and its Role in Politics and Warfare between World War One and the Vietnam War.* I'm completely sure that any essay on this topic will be completely fascinating, if only I have the slightest idea on how to begin. Letting myself get distracted, I open the MSN messenger program on my desktop and sign in. I see Max online and open a chat screen straight away.

TY-Dane: How could you leave me all alone! I'm going to fail this essay, then fail university, then I'm going to have to give hand jobs outside Manchester Airport to businessmen to pay my rent.

HippyChic: That escalated rather quickly! You didn't even consider government benefits or shop work, you just went straight to the hand jobs.

TY-Dane: Well you work with what you're good at.

HippyChic: How far have you got?

TY-Dane: The title. I mean the title says it all right. If I just write the title and then in big bold letters write *"Ta-Da"* will I get a mark?

HippyChic: I hear you get a mark for getting your name right, but I'm not sure how true that is, maybe I just made that up. I do that sometimes.

A notification appears on my screen notifying me of a friend request from someone called KasFocus. Not recognising the name I ignore it for now.

TY-Dane: Hang on, got a random chat request. Must be someone from the course.

HippyChic: Erm...

TY-Dane: Erm what?

What the fuck has she done now?

HippyChic: Well Lukas stopped in at the bar a couple of nights ago and maybe mentioned that you guys swapped numbers but he has not heard from you. I mentioned we have a big essay due, but that maybe you would like to hear from him online. I said that you are basically a slave to MSN Messenger when you are trapped in an essay loop. Anyway, I have to go now. BYEEEEEE!

With that, I see her go offline. I remind myself to axe murder her later.

It has been nearly a week since Lukas stopped by the coffee shop. Whilst it was one of the best kisses of my life, I need some space from him to figure out where my head is at. One kiss cannot erase the history between us. I know I need the space because the second he left, all I wanted to do was to run out into the street, drag him back into the shop and fuck him there and then. So I'm taking my time. I hover over his username for a second, deciding whether or not to accept the request or not.

In for a penny, in for a pound. I click accept and the chat window opens almost immediately.

KasFocus: Hey it's Lukas, I got your contact details from Max. I hope that's ok. I realise I probably seem a bit like a stalker now.

KasFocus: Hello?

Ok so maybe he was a bit adorable. Like a cute vulnerable puppy. I was so fucked.

TY-Dane: Hi Lukas.

KasFocus: How have you been? I haven't heard from you. I texted you but I didn't hear back.

He's right, I had received a text message from him the next day. I haven't responded as I've been so freaked out at my reaction to him that I don't really trust myself to have a measured response to him again.

TY-Dane: Yeah sorry about that, things just got really busy. Also you shouldn't be texting me, those things cost like 50 pence per text. We are students buddy, gotta save those pennies for beer and junk food.

I send this across with a smiley face emoji hoping it will break some of the tension with us and maybe let us get back to just casual chatting.

KasFocus: Oh ok then.

KasFocus: But now I have you here.

KasFocus: When can I see you again?

Excitements skitters up my spine, a shudder spreading out through the rest of my body. I consider just sending him my address and telling him to come over now. I still want him. I always have.

TY-Dane: I kind of have a big essay that's due soon so I don't really have much time to be going out.

TY-Dane: I'm not saying I don't want to see you Lukas. It was nice seeing you.

I feel like I have to get that out there, I haven't been able to stop thinking about his lips on mine. His hands on me, pulling me, tight and hard. I have jacked off so many times since we saw each other last imagining all the things we could have done together in the shop.

KasFocus: It was really nice seeing you too. I really want to see you again though.

I can't stop the smile as it spreads across my face. I am unreasonably happy that it's him asking to see me. Other than the fact that he is ninety nine percent the evil villain from every high school movie. Lukas Fucking Ford is telling me that he wants to see me again after kissing my fucking face off. The teenager in me is trying to live out his pubescent fantasies as they finally come to life. *LET US HAVE THIS,* he screams inside my mind.

TY-Dane: Well you were VERY helpful to me closing up the shop the other day!

KasFocus: Yes I was! Very helpful! So much so I think I deserve a reward.

TY-Dane: I think you got your reward that night buddy.

KasFocus: You are right I totally did.

He replies with a winky face emoji.

KasFocus: I feel you are about to ask me a favour.

TY-Dane: You must be related to Mystic Meg from the lottery. So you must know what I'm going to ask you then.

KasFocus: How about you just ask me so I can say yes if it means I get to see you again?

I bite my lip to stop the smile that is sure to split my face in two.

TY-Dane: My room is looking pretty shabby. I want to paint it. Max says the smell of paint fumes makes her gag, so I was thinking...

KasFocus: Absolutely.

He sends the message back almost immediately without reading the next message.

TY-Dane: You haven't heard what I want yet.

KasFocus: Yes I'll come over and paint your room, no problem.

TY-Dane: Well I was more thinking that you could come and help me paint my room.

KasFocus: When? Now?

TY-Dane: Easy tiger, I have to finish this essay which will take the whole of the next two days, then I have work on Monday so I was thinking maybe on Tuesday after class. Max will be with her parents until Wednesday so we will have the evening to get the painting done before she gets back. I don't fancy cleaning her vomit off my carpet.

KasFocus: Shame.

TY-Dane: What's a shame?

KasFocus: That I don't get to see you for almost four days. Of course I'll help you though. I'll even bring over some pizza to sweeten the deal.

TY-Dane: You realise I'm supposed to supply the food when you're putting in the muscle.

KasFocus: Where will I be putting in the muscle? ;)

I blush furiously and hammer out on the keyboard.

TY-Dane: You know what I mean!

KasFocus: I'm sorry, but I meant what I said. It really is a shame.

I consider this for a moment before I agree with him. I really do want to see him. I just know with the way I am feeling right now, if I invite him over I will just drag him to my bed and then hate myself the next morning when it gets all weird and he leaves. I can do the next best thing though. I click the small camera button on my icon on the right of the screen and my webcam whirrs to life. He accepts the request and does the same to his. I grab the microphone off the shelf and plug that in too. He must do the same as I hear grainy sounds coming from my speaker. His camera connects and Lukas's smiling face comes into view.

The way he looks at me has my heart racing like it's running the Grand National. "Hi there," he greets me.

"Alright mate?" I chirp out as breezily as I can, not exactly sure how I'm supposed to act.

His shoulders sag a little and his eyes dim. Is he disappointed with me somehow? "Yeah so, are you sure you don't want me to bring anything over?"

"Nah just yourself will be fine."

This is really awkward, like, I'm no stranger to webcam chats. I might also be no stranger to breaking tense moments with guys over webcam by whipping my dick out - that tends to break the ice. That usually works when you know you're never going to actually meet the random online guy, and it is a handy tool to jack off to when inspiration fails to strike. I don't think that's appropriate in this situation though.

"So tell me something about yourself." His hopeful smile is back. Wrong question though buddy.

"What do you want to know? High school was awful thanks to you, college and university I've spent getting over high school, here I am." I smile, then realise the screen must be practically dripping with sarcasm from my words. A little too much venom in my voice, I admonish myself.

"Tyler..." He starts.

"Ignore me, I'm an asshole." I gesture his response away with a flourish.

"You're not being an asshole." Seeing the smirk on my face he continues, "Ok you're being a bit of an asshole, but you have the right to be. You have the rights, the deeds, the pink slip, and all the authorisations to be as much of an asshole as you need to be. You earned it."

I don't like the darkness he exudes as he says it.

I have to learn to get over this, high school was a million years ago, although it feels just like yesterday. I can't keep punishing him though. Kids have bullied and beat up other kids since the concept of school started, I imagine, and they can't have been held to account forever. I either had to move on, learn to accept the past or pull the cord and get out.

"Listen, I can't say what happened to me is all water under the bridge, but I can't keep doing this to myself either." I realise what I'm saying is the absolute truth as it comes out of my mouth. "It takes a lot of time and energy to keep this grudge, and to make you suffer only leads to me suffering in turn. I'm making the decision to give myself a break, an easy way out."

"I'm not exactly sure what you just said." He looks puzzled.

"What I'm saying is, I'm going to move on and we can try to be friends," I begin. "I can't say there aren't going to be times when I just say 'fuck that guy', because I probably will. But you deserve a second chance. I'm going to give that to you."

Hope radiates from him as he listens eagerly to me.

"Can you deal with that?"

"Absofuckinglutely!" His response is immediate. "Take all the time in the world, just let me try to make things right ok? It means a lot that you're letting me try."

"Well the fact that you're hot as fuck and easy to look at doesn't hurt." I try for a serious expression but he barks out in sudden laughter.

"If you think I'm the hot one here buddy then you obviously are not as smart as I assumed." He winks at me and by god it makes me feel like a giggly schoolgirl.

"Well assuming makes an ass out of you and I've got a nice hole," I say thoughtfully.

Laughter lines crease his face as he struggles to compose himself. "I dont think thats the saying."

"Saying, Schmaying," I brush it off.

"Are you sure you're an English Lit major?" he says, and I swear there are tears in his eyes from trying to hold in the laughter.

"Yup, which just proves how right I am, I'm smart and I will have the degree to prove it."

"I'm looking forward to seeing you," he says, and again these moments of stark honesty have me reeling slightly. I'd be lying if I say that I don't get butterflies in my stomach when I speak to Lukas, but I can't be THAT for him. Enough water hasn't passed under the bridge and maybe it never would.

"Yeah don't wear your Sunday best, cause you're going to be getting messy."

He chuckles and nods.

We talk for the next half an hour about unimportant shit before I tell him that I have to get back to writing the English paper. I don't miss the sad look on his face when I wave to sign off. I wish I could just erase all the memories of before the kiss. Maybe I'm not the bigger man.

How do you be friends with someone who not only made you his personal punching bag, but whose lips and taste you just can't forget? I guess I'll find out.

Oh who the fuck am I kidding, I want him. We are both grown-ups. It's time to take what I want.

Chapter 12.

Tyler

After finally trudging through the misery of writer's block and hammering out what might pass as a legible essay, I submit my work and take a deep breath. There is a kind of timeless quality within the walls of the university campus; you can almost sense the ghosts of the thousands of people who have wandered its halls in the many years it has been open.

"You're cutting it close Mr Dane. I assume since you took all this extra time that this will be a work of art?" My English Lit professor looks over the top of her glasses at me and scowls slightly. This chick seriously needs to get laid.

"Well what I *can* say is that it has been thoroughly spellchecked, so there's that," I smile hopefully.

"Oh yay," she deadpans, then waves me away with a dismissive hand.

Not wanting to be there for the inevitable signs of disappointment when she actually reads my paper I scurry from the room. I don't allow myself too long to worry about my sure-as-hell borderline pass, possible-fail paper. Today is the day that Lukas is supposed to come over to hang out. I've checked my flip phone excessively all day assuming that any moment I was going to receive the inevitable flake-out text. None came.

Making a pit stop at the hardware store on the way home, I pick up all the supplies I will need to paint the room. In truth I'd planned to do this in a few months, but it had seemed like a good excuse to see Lukas, not have any awkward conversations and get my room painted in the process. However, I am the king of procrastination so being ahead of schedule is a big deal for me. My phone starts to ring in my pocket. An unknown number flashes on the screen. I flip open the phone and press it to my ear, braced for disappointment.

"Hello," I murmur, sadness already tinging my voice.

"Hey bitch! So did you submit your assignment?" Max's voice chirps on the end of the line.

"Where are you calling from? I thought you were staying at your parents' house, that's not their number you're calling from." She makes a noncommittal cough and I frown. Girl's hiding something. "Max?"

"Oh it's nothing, I decided to come back early, my parents were pissing me off." My heart sinks. A wave of guilt engulfs me. I'm not going to blow off my best friend because of some guy, some guy with whom I share a horrible history.

"Oh right ok I didn't know you would be back." I try to school my voice to not sound so bummed.

"I'm not back, I'm staying with a friend for a few nights." My ears immediately prick with interest. Max is such a homebody. She wouldn't just be crashing at a friend's house for no reason.

"Max?" I question.

"Oh ok!" she grunts; she always breaks quickly, "I'm staying at Peter's house."

I wrack my brain for a moment before it snags on a memory. "The Viking?" I gasp.

She giggles and makes a confirmatory noise. "He is so hot," she sighs. I laugh and she spends the next few minutes detailing how he had called her every night and they'd spent some time getting to know each other. He had then asked her if she would like to spend a few days together.

"Aww your poor vagina," I coo. She makes a mock-scandalized sound. "So I'm guessing since you're still there that he is good in the sack."

"I don't know," she muses, "Is it good sex if you can feel it in your throat when they are fucking you?"

I snort out a laugh, loud enough that a few people passing me on the street give me annoyed glances. "I just think it means that you should invest in a fuckload of lube."

"Amen sister," she giggles. "I mean I can come home if you're super lonely and bored." It's the voice she uses when she really doesn't want to do something, but thinks she will be a bad friend if she doesn't at least make a cursory offer.

"No it's cool, you keep getting plundered by Ragnar."

She lets out her own muffled laugh.

"Plus I've got a friend coming over soon to keep me company anyway."

"Quelle surprise, what friend?" The suspicious tone to her voice lets me know she already has a pretty good fucking idea.

"Lukas, he is coming round to help me do some jobs," I shrug off.

"Hand or blow?" she asks seriously.

"Fuck off," I laugh, "Painting."

"You with his jizz?" she asks. This is why I love her so much.

"My room, with paint." I respond quickly, trying to hide the mirth in my voice. I look at my watch and my heart starts to speed up. "Listen I have to go, he is coming round soon and I'm not home yet and I need to make it look as if we haven't been burgled by pirates."

"Ok but you have to fill me in later," she insists.

"I think Peter is filling you in enough, no?" I laugh before disconnecting the call.

I hurry back to our apartment on the Quays, hurrying past the commuters and joggers along the canalside. Making it back in record time I try my best to tidy around the house so I don't look like a complete savage before jumping in the shower.

It's been over a week since Lukas showed up at the coffee shop. A whole week since I felt his lips on mine. Both of us had had quite a busy week, on top of the existing shit I had to do, one of the girls had phoned in sick, so I had offered to pick up her shifts for some extra cash.

The idea of him, in my room, maybe shirtless, and watching his smooth muscles ripple under his skin as he stretches upwards to paint the tops of the walls has me erotically charged. I grab the soap from the small caddy attached to the wall and start lathering my body until I wrap a fist around my thickening cock. I notice in the mirror a pink blush is creeping up my neck; I tell myself it's just due to the hot water. I stroke along the length of my dick, feeling the skin pull back away from the head. I look down to see the engorged head of my dick pulsing out of the top of my fist, a bead of precum washed away immediately by the shower. A zing goes up my spine as I feel my balls pull up tight against my body and the feeling I'm about to cum overwhelms me. I tug on my balls to stop myself from going over the edge.

Laughing at how ridiculous I probably look, almost cumming after a few pulls of my dick over a boy from high school, I grab a towel and wrap it around my waist. I brush my teeth and am about to go find a hairdryer when a buzzer sounds from downstairs.

Hurrying to the front door I press the intercom button. "Hello?"

"Hey, I'm downstairs, can you buzz me in please?" the voice on the line says, exciting me way more than it should.

"Sure sorry, I'll let you in now." I press the intercom button to let him into the building and instantly start to panic. I go to make a dash for the room until I realise I have left the shower running, having failed to turn it off when I stepped out. Making a quick two-second stop to the bathroom I switch off the shower, then try to head towards my room.

I hear the front door click open and his voice calls down the hallway. "Hello, I just let myself in, the door was open." I freeze in the hallway as Lukas walks through holding a couple of pizza boxes. He looks up and stops moving, his mouth open slightly as I hear a small strangled sound escape from his mouth.

I take a step toward him. "Are you ok?" I ask, concerned.

"What?" His eyes are darting about the room.

"I said are you ok?"

"Yeah I'm fine, why wouldn't I be fine, I'm totally fine and I have pizza."

Something is disturbing him. I thought I had cleaned around enough, but maybe it still looks like this is a squat or something. "Lukas?"

"You're naked ok!" he spits out quickly. I look down and realisation suddenly dawns on me, he's checking me out. I look at the old antique mirror hanging in the hallway, that Max insisted we bring home from a car boot sale we had frequented one Sunday morning. I have to admit I don't look half bad. My wet hair hangs loosely around my face dripping droplets of water that track down my neck and onto my chest. The gleam of a thin film of liquid makes my chest muscles appear more pronounced. The remnant of my previous boner is still slightly visible beneath the towel making an obscene bulge.

"I'm sorry," I chuckle, enjoying his flustered reaction a little too much, maybe. "I'll get dressed, go through to the living room and make yourself comfortable." I gesture through to the room behind me. I walk into my bedroom, dodging the paint cans, brushes and drop cloths I left there earlier. After taking more time than I normally would, I glance at myself in the mirror appreciatively. I'm not looking too shabby today at all. I've settled on a black gym tank vest top and dark grey jogging trousers. I probably should have worn something a bit more appropriate for painting, but I don't look nearly as hot in a loose white T-shirt and bulky jeans.

I pop my head quickly out of my room to see him browsing a bookshelf in the living room, picking things up and inspecting them before putting them down again. He's opted for the more traditional and practical dark fitted black T-shirt and ripped denim jeans. There's a rip quite high on the back of one of the legs, so I can just make out the precise curvature of his brief-clad ass. I think he might be trying to kill me. I'm unsure exactly how I am going to make it through the day without having some kind of sexual meltdown.

I follow him into the living room and perch against the sofa. He turns to see me and smiles, his eyes roaming down my body and back to up to my face.

"Wow. I mean hi," he says, still seeming almost on edge. "So painting huh." It's the kind of lame-ass statement that someone might say when they are at a loss for words. The fact that I have this effect on him fills me with nothing but absolute joy.

"Yeah thank you for helping today, I thought it might go a lot quicker if it's the two of us." That's a lie; I suspect this might be quite a lot slower with the amount of times I imagine I'll stop what I am doing just to steal glances at him.

"No problem man, as I said anything I can do to help. So shall we get started?" He gestures towards my bedroom and my brain unhelpfully supplies me a million different scenarios of what getting started could mean. I nod and move back towards my room. He follows closely, so close that I can feel his heat against my back. We both stop and stare at the bed as he enters; it's almost like it's waiting there for us with a *let's get this show on the road* kinda vibe.

"Nice room." His voice sounds hoarse and he clears it with a quick cough.

"Water?" I grab a bottle from the little mini-fridge and offer it to him. He reaches for the water and his fingertips brush against mine. I tell myself the shiver that runs through my body is due to the coolness of the water bottle against my skin and nothing else. He unscrews the cap and puts the bottle to his mouth, his bottom lip cradling the rim as water pours into his mouth. His Adam's apple bobs in his throat as he swallows and I don't think I've ever been this turned on in my life by drinking. I gulp harshly and shake my head, my own throat becoming dry. He offers me his water which I accept quickly, wanting my mouth to be on anything that his has just touched. I take a quick swig and hand it back.

Lukas stoops down and searches through the items from the hardware store. He rips open the bag of plastic sheeting and spreads it across the floor, securing the sides to the edges of the room with tape. He then goes about covering all my furniture with more sheeting as I just watch him move around the room.

"What?" he says suddenly, catching me as I gaze at him from across the room.

"Nothing, you just look like you know what you're doing. I would have covered the floor, kinda. I wouldn't have gone to the trouble of covering furniture though."

"That explains the speckles of old paint I can see on your furniture then," he says pointing at my pinewood dresser. Sure enough there on the front and top are small speckles of old dried paint.

"Exactly, so it's good you're here." I give him a wink and he smiles back at me.

"I'm going to start cutting in around the doorways," he tells me, opening up a tin of paint and pouring some out into a black plastic roller tray, depositing the handle and wool sleeve on the floor beside the bed. I plug in my 3-disc CD player and put on a playlist I think might be conducive to our work. I see Lukas's shoulders shaking as if silently laughing as he starts to apply a thin coat of paint around the wooden doorframe.

"What are you laughing at?" I smile at him. "Do you not like my music?"

He turns around and shrugs at me. "I don't know, I guess it's just funny watching such a well-built guy sway his hips to Girls Aloud's 'Sound of the Underground'." He bites his lip to presumably stop himself from full-on laughing at me.

"Hey leave off Girls Aloud! There is absolutely nothing wrong with liking terrible music."

He holds up his hands in surrender and turns back to continue cutting in. I move towards the door to crouch beside him and start to paint around the outlets, mainly just so I can stand closer to him.

Realising I'm actually kneeling at crotch height I suddenly feel really exposed. His breathing rate seems to pick up, I notice that he keeps swallowing heavily. We work together side by side for the next half an hour. Every now and again one of us would catch the other one staring, and then quickly look away and go back to what we were doing. And that's how it goes for the next hour after that, polite conversation about school, friends and TV. The disappointment starts to weigh heavily on me and I can feel myself becoming grouchy and irritable. After the kiss at our last meeting, I had been sure there was something there. No, I'm *certain* there was something there. Even now I know he wants something more, so what is stopping him?

"You ok?" he asks me suddenly.

I look up at him and frown, I don't think I've said anything out loud. "Yeah I'm ok," I say, smiling. I can tell it probably looks like one of those forced fake smiles.

He nods and gets back to work.

I reach across to dip the brush into the paint tray, and my hand connects briefly with his. That same jolt of electricity crackles along my skin, making the hairs on the back of my neck come alive and my gut begin to clench. Just as quickly as the touch begins, he pulls back his hand like it's been burnt. He frowns and then resumes painting like nothing happened.

The little restraint and control I've maintained since he arrived at my fucking apartment crumbles in an instant, beaten down by the fury of my frustration. "What the hell is going on here?!" I yell at him. "Why are you so afraid to touch me? I honestly thought you liked me! Is this all about some stupid guilt you have about what happened between us because I am a fucking grown-up who can deal with my own problems, seriously if you're just here to clear your..."

That's all I manage to get out before he whirls round and slams me against the wall with such force that it knocks the air out of my lungs. His mouth crashes down on mine, claiming me in a brutal show of force. His tongue forces entry into my mouth which I grant immediately, because why wouldn't I? This is Lukas Fucking Ford in my bedroom taking what he wants. I can't think of anything else I want in the world right now other than more of him on me.

His hands roam down my chest, slipping under the hem of my vest and reaching up to press into my muscle, his fingers pulling slightly on my nipple as he passes over it. I gasp into his mouth and ground my hips against his trying to gain some friction against my rapidly swelling cock. I can already feel the wetness of the paint on my back, but I couldn't give less of a shit as all I want is more of whatever he is giving me.

I reach around and grab at his ass, my fingers sliding into the torn section and rubbing along the bare flesh of the crease of his legs and butt. He pulls back his head slightly and I moan in frustration and chase his lips. I push my fingers further into the tear, making the gap wider as I force my hand in and grab one cheek completely. I massage the tight globe in my hands, my finger slipping past to make a brief swipe at his tender flesh.

"Yes, fuck!" he moans against my mouth, forcing his tongue back into my mouth and sliding it against mine. My finger seeks out his hole and I lightly tap against it. I shift my leg between his thighs, pushing up against him. Lukas grinds down against me insistently.

Breaking away, he pulls me off the wall, and leads me over to the foot of my bed, then pushes me down onto my back. I watch him as he stands between my open legs and pulls his T-shirt over his head, revealing a hairy but neat, well-muscled, tanned body. My mouth salivates at the sight of it, I can't help but want to run my tongue along the groove of his abs. I promise myself I will do that later, but I want to see where this is going.

He leans over me pressing a hard kiss against my mouth. I reach up to grab his neck to pull him to me but he utters an *uh uh uh,* wagging his damn finger at me. He kisses down my jaw, licking and biting as he goes. I think I might actually combust any minute now. He pulls my vest up over my head and continues to kiss his way down my cheek and over my chest, swirling his tongue around my nippes. I arch up over the bed trying to get more contact, but he places a hand on my chest and pushes me back down. I moan in frustration and he smiles at me once more.

Lukas sinks to his knees and starts to work off my sweat pants. He lets out a gasp in surprise as my hard dick strains hard, jutting outward against my briefs. He looks up from under heavy lids, his pupils blown dark and a sly grin creeping onto his face. He pushes his nose under my throbbing dick, nuzzling the space between my balls and my asshole. I press my hand to the back of his head and force him deeper, demanding more friction. Reaching up he pulls the fabric of my briefs aside and runs his tongue along the underside of my balls, taking one into his mouth one at a time and sucking gently on them.

I feel like I'm about to come out of my skin, my forearm going across my eyes, I feel a sheen of sweat across the surface of my brow and neck. I'm all for foreplay when the time was right, but right now I just want to bury myself deep inside him or have him fuck me, as long as we are closer together than we are now.

He pulls my briefs down my legs and throws them behind him; I wince briefly as I see them land in an open can of paint. He runs the flat of his tongue along the underside of my dick, pulling back the foreskin, sucking and licking swirling circles around the engorged head. Never losing eye contact with me, he slowly slides his mouth down the entire length of my shaft, making small sucking motions with each inch he takes down.

"Fuck Tyler you taste so good, fuck you're big," Lukas breathes around my dick, never letting it fall from his mouth. He runs a hand down the shaft and grips it at the base, squeezing it to an almost painful degree. He stares at me intently, his expression becoming serious, "This is mine! Do you hear me? Say it!" It's as if I can't get enough air into my lungs, panting heavily until I think I might pass out.

"Yes, yours. Fuck don't stop sucking me." I grip his hair and pull his head back down onto my dick. I know I should be a little more gentle but Lukas is a big guy, he can take it a bit rough. My head falls back against the mattress as he works me over and takes me apart with just his mouth and hands, I feel my balls start to pull up tight and I know I may have a few moments left before I reach the point of no return. I put my hand on Lukas's shoulder and try to push him back. "I can't... I'm gonna, no! I... I need to..." I start to babble, unable to finish my warning. He pushes a hand firmly against my chest and guides me back down onto the bed. He pulls off my dick, making a popping sound as it drops from his mouth.

"Lie still, I need to taste you." He sucks my hard length back into his mouth and then down into his throat. He grabs my hands and places them on the back of his head. Understanding what he's asking but not asking for, I start to fuck his mouth slowly, raising my hips off the bed, my thrusts meeting his downward push. Again feeling that telltale tingle in my groin I pick up the pace. His tongue slides down the length of my shaft and pushes firmly against the hard veins, making me shudder violently.

Just when I think that I cannot not take any more sensation, his other hand works under my thigh and moves upwards until his digits find my hole. Pushing ever so slightly, his slick finger slides inside, causing a deep pressure under my balls. The sharp burn makes my hole clench around him, but I welcome it. My hands grip tightly into his hair as I force myself deeper into his throat.

"Oh my god, I'm gonna cum. I can't stop, I'm gonna...!" I shout loudly as the first volley hits the back of his throat. He moans around my dick, sucking my cock deeper into him, swallowing every drop I'm giving him. My balls draw up tight as wave after wave of my orgasm rolls over me. For a panic-filled moment it feels like I'm never going to stop spurting, which has me worried for Lukas as he is still swallowing me down.

Eventually I hear him sigh as he slowly pulls off my spent dick, which slaps against my belly as it falls from his mouth. He looks up at me with a satisfied smile. My drive roaring back to life, I hook my hands under his armpits and drag him up my body on top of me until our lips crash into each other.

Now it's my turn to be the aggressor as I devour his mouth, tasting my warm saltiness on his tongue. "You're so fucking hot!" I mumble against his smiling mouth. "I can't believe you're here with me."

He pulls back, giving me a curious look. "Why?" he asks like it's the strangest statement he has ever heard.

"I don't know man, you are you and I'm me you know," I shrug and shake my head slightly. He presses a gentle kiss against the side of my mouth and runs his tongue along the seam of my lips, peppering my face with feather-light kisses until his mouth is lightly touching the tip of my ear.

"Have you seen you recently?" he whispers. I don't know why that pisses me off. Maybe it's because I look so different from the person I was back then physically; what's pissing me off more, is that I am realising he's right. I look back on that person that I was as a different person to who I am now, when it's still just me. Does he mean that he's attracted to me because I'm like Tyler 2.0 now? *No!*

I press my forehead against his and sigh before pushing him off me slowly. "I guess I better get on with this painting, not going to do itself right?" I smile, but I'm sure he can tell it never really reaches my eyes.

"Hey what just happened?" he calls after me as I move across to the other side of the room and pick up my paint brush. I start to focus intently on the wall, keeping my back firmly to him, belatedly realising how ludicrous it is that I'm painting naked, even if he did just suck my dick.

"Nothing, just lots of work to do here." I hear the bed springs creak as he leaves the bed. I assume he is about to start painting until I feel him press against the full length of my back, his hand sliding from my shoulder down my arm until it grips the hand holding the brush. He gently removes the brush from my fingers and places it back in the paint tray.

"Hey, I'm serious, what just happened? Did I do something that you didn't like? Did you not want..." he begins to say, and I can see the panic building behind his eyes. I can't have him thinking he's taken advantage of me.

"God no!" I quickly correct him, "That was totally what I wanted, like you wouldn't believe. I'm just having some trouble separating the past from now is all."

He rests his forehead against the back of my neck and exhales. Goosebumps dance along my skin where his breath meets my neck. I shiver and move backwards until I am pressed firmly against him. I feel the smile on his mouth as he kisses gently along my shoulders. His hand snakes around my waist moving me back towards the bed. The edge of the mattress hits the backs of his legs, forcing him to sit, he turns me round and sits me in his lap. He moves his hands up my back, his fingers roaming through my hair, pulling my head down and pressing his lips along my jaw until they settle on my mouth. Not really moving, just resting his lips against mine. He stops for a moment, pulling back until he is just looking at me and smiling. I would kill to know what he's thinking at this very moment.

"I'm just so fucking happy that you're letting me be here with you right now." I guess I don't need to kill anyone. " I don't want to say anything that screws this up if you know what I mean."

I nod and smile, reassured that it's probably just me overreacting to the situation. I can't stop kissing him; in my head a voice screams at me that this is all moving very fast, but I seem powerless to stop. The kisses turn from languid and sweet to fiery and all-consuming in an instant. I push him backwards until he is laying flat out on the bed, I pin his arms above him and snake my other hand down his abdomen and down over his crotch, palming his hard dick through his jeans.

"We didn't take care of you now did we?" I say innocently as I could, but I'm so flushed and sated from the previous orgasm that I probably look positively debauched.

He lifts his head from the bed to kiss me and whispers, "Do you have any protection? I need you to fuck me, like now."

I stand from the bed and hurry around to the bedside table, pulling out a couple of foil packets and the bottle of lube I had restocked recently. Not that I'd assumed that anything was going to happen with Lukas, but a boy can hope. I straddle his legs as he lays back on the mattress, placing light kisses along his chest and down towards his navel, my tongue drawing lazy circles around his belly button as I unfasten his jeans.

I push down the denim and the underwear beneath it till they are halfway down his thighs. His shaft bounces up thick and heavy, I catch it in my palm and stop its sway. It feels hot and hefty in my hand as I rub my thumb along the slit, collecting some of his precum on the pad and bringing it up to my mouth. I run my tongue around my thumb, sucking the whole thing into my mouth and watch his eyes widen and his hips thrust forward.

"You are killing me, please, I need you... please," he whimpers sweetly, unlocking something primal deep within me.

I pull back and hook my hands under his calves, lifting his legs in the air, whilst pulling his jeans and underwear off and tossing them aside. His tight hole is exposed to me for the first time; my mouth fills with saliva and a wave of need hits me.

I can't hold off any longer; I dip my head down and run my tongue along his crease until the tip pushes into his waiting entrance. His hand flies to his mouth, biting down onto the heel of his palm as if trying to hold in a scream. I lick and suck at his hole, his solid throbbing shaft leaking precum onto his stomach.

"Please, I can't take it any longer, I need you inside me." It almost sounds as if he is on the verge of breaking down, his voice filled with lust and longing.

I reach down for the foil packet at my feet. Tearing it open I roll the condom down my cock and drizzle some lube on the tip, spreading it along the entire length. I collect some more lube on the tips of my fingers and slide them into his hole, the skin reacting to my touch and tightening around the digits. His muscles grip them like a vise; I'm not going to last long at this rate. He starts to move to lay on his stomach when I place my hands on his hips, keeping him in place.

"I want to see you," I say simply. He smiles and nods slightly.

I again hook his knees and push his legs back. I line up my throbbing cock with his hole and gently tease his entrance. Pushing forward slowly I feel the head of my cock push against the tight ring of muscle and feel the familiar pop as it passes through.

Lukas's eyes roll backwards into his head as his hands reach forwards to grip my ass, pulling me deeper into him. Inch by inch I move further into his heat. I feel like I could cum right there and then, but I am enjoying this feeling too much to finish this so soon. I take a deep breath when I feel my balls settle against his skin, fully seated inside him. I lean forward, elbows supporting me on either side of his head.

He pulls me against him and presses an open-mouthed kiss against my neck. I tense and wait for permission to move. He's tight; he obviously hasn't bottomed very often, and I want to let him get at least slightly used to the pressure inside him before I move, because I know once I start, nothing could stop me from owning him. I kiss his mouth hard, gasping as my cock swells.

"Go, fuck me Tyler, I need you to fuck me hard!" That's all I need to hear - I take off like a steam train leaving a tunnel. I piston in and out of him, each time the head of my cock rubbing against the tight ball of nerves of his prostate, making him shudder and groan. I feel the tingling sensation begin as my body rockets towards orgasm. His dick, wet with precum, rubs against our stomachs, dialing up my need to see him let go.

"I'm not going to last much longer," I bite through clenched teeth. He moans at my words and without any further warning I feel his dick swell between us as warm jets of liquid coat our joined abdomens. He's cum without either of us having touched him. The feel of him sliding against me has my own release barreling up my spine, and I thrust into him deep one last time and scream as I pump out stream after stream of cum. My balls pull up almost painfully tight as I empty inside him. Sweat clings to both of our bodies as I collapse my full weight onto him. His arms reach around my back and pull me as close to him as possible, his lips ghosting over the side of my neck and face.

Unable to speak myself I sigh as I hear him whisper against my cheek, "Thank you."

We lay there for what could have been minutes or hours, I don't know. But the cooling of the liquid on our stomachs forces us to move. I slide out of him, holding the end of the condom as I pull out and dispose of it. I return to the bedroom with a warm towel to help him clean up. The sight of him laying on my bed, the remnants of cum clinging to his stomach and the fine hairs of his happy trail leading down to his heavy cock as it rests against his thigh are basically like every porno I had ever jacked off to. The sight of him has my cock filling rapidly again.

I pull him off from the bed and lead him to the shower, reaching in and turning on the taps. We lazily kiss as the water warms. I pull him against me as I move backwards into the cubicle. I take my time running the sponge over every inch of his body, worshipping it as I crouch down on my knees to wash his legs and tight firm ass. Every time I look up at him, he is staring at me like I am something to cherish. It has my heart racing each time.

I'd thought this would be cathartic, a way to fuck the bad feelings out of my system, but it's rapidly turning into something I don't know if I'm ready for. After we finish in the shower I dry him off with a towel and lead him by the hand back to my bed. Pulling back the sheets, we both slide under the cooling covers. I pull him back to me, pressing him against my chest. Hands laying over his side, he locks our fingers together and pulls them up to his mouth, kissing each one of my knuckles and then settling our joined hands over his chest.

"Do you mind if I stay with you tonight?" he asks very gently, like he's afraid to hear the answer. I should say no. I should say *hell* no. I should make excuses, that I have work the next day. That we both need time to think. That this is going really fast. That even though we have known each other for years, we have only really liked each other for a few days.

But I hear myself saying, "Absolutely." I close my eyes, press my face into the back of his neck and let sleep take me.

Chapter 13.

Lukas

I wake to feel a warm hard body pressed hard against my back, arms and legs intertwined like vines around a tree. I can't remember a morning when I've felt so calm and peaceful. I pull his arms tighter around me, hoping to get a few moments more of this connection before he inevitably wakes up and starts to freak the fuck out.

Last night had been amazing; I've had plenty of sex before, but I've never felt that connection so quickly with anyone. Every time I've had sex, I've wanted it to be hard, rough and quick, and then I usually can't wait to get the fuck out of there. But this is different. The sex hasn't made me want to bolt. It's made me want to get closer to him, and no matter how much I try, it's as if I can't get close enough. Each time his arms tighten around me in the night, I can only keep repeating one phrase in my head that I never thought I would think about anyone: *I need more.*

I feel his lips skim across the surface of my neck. "Morning, what time is it?" he mumbles sleepily. A sense of hope rises as he doesn't immediately dropkick me off the bed. I reach across to the bedside table and check my phone, then bolt upright, shocking him in the process.

"Jesus it's like 10 am." He grumbles and covers his face with the pillow I had been spooning.

"Well, I've already missed my first lecture. I'm just going to send Max an unreasonably expensive text and ask her to sign me in and grab some notes for me, hopefully no one will notice if I'm not there." He grabs his phone from the bedroom floor where I guess it had fallen during the night and shoots off a quick text before lying back down.

I turn around to face him, press a hand lightly against his chest and lean down to kiss him. The kiss starts off smooth as I don't want to come off as a bit of a bunny boiler, but it becomes quite urgent after only a few seconds. I smile against his mouth and whisper, "Not possible, they will notice you're not there. Well, I know I would."

He hooks his arms around my neck and presses his forehead against mine, eyes still closed. "That's so cheesy, I feel really embarrassed for you right now," he says sweetly.

"You're fucking killing me dude," I chuckle and pull back from him, keeping my hand on his chest, not wanting to lose contact for a moment if I could help it. "Last night was absolutely amazing, I mean like it blew my mind. I had planned to take things slow, but I can't seem to keep my hands off you." I motion with my head down to my hand, which has begun kneading into the skin of his pecs. "Like this for example."

His hand comes up to cover my own. "If you're looking for any complaints, you're not going to find any here."

The atmosphere is getting pretty intense and I am feeling words bubble up in my throat that I know I should not say. I stand quickly and move across the room to find my clothes. I leisurely get dressed, stealing moments here and there to glance over at him as he dresses himself, taking more than a moment to stare as he bends down to pull up his briefs. I get the thought that I might attack him here and now and never let him leave the bed. My hole twinges and I can almost still feel him there from the night before. I imagine what it would be like to return the favour and my breathing hitches.

"I'd better head out," I say finally, regretting it instantly. Part of me just wants us to stay in this moment all day. Life still needs to happen however. He nods glumly and motions for us to leave the bedroom. I collect my bag and move towards the front door. As he pulls the door open and moves aside for me to pass, I push him against the wall and once more steal a deep heated kiss.

"When can I see you again?" I breathe against his mouth. His pupils seemed large and dark as desire reignites in his eyes.

"Now, later, whenever you want," he says in a rush, flustered. I really love that I have that effect on him.

"Can I take you out to dinner later, or maybe I can come back over and cook you dinner here?" He's about to nod when he suddenly winces.

"I normally spend Wednesday evenings with Max watching bad movies. I don't really want to bail on her. I think she will probably be bringing the Viking over for a sleepover tonight." I again push him back against the wall, my restraint once again failing me as I need to taste him again.

"Wait, the guy from the house party?" I ask wide-eyed.

"Yeah, Max's new beau." He rolls his eyes.

"Oh thank fuck!" I exhale heavily.

"What?" His lips quirk up at the side like he already knows what I've been thinking.

"I thought that he was interested in you and I'd have to compete with a bloody Norse god." I wipe my brow with the back of my hand.

He laughs, pushing at my hip playfully.

"That's fine, why don't I come over and cook all of you dinner. Would that be ok?"

He nods emphatically. "Yes definitely, I might have to fight to keep you though, Max will probably want to jump your bones. Have herself a hot guy sandwich."

I press my cheek against his and breathe heavily against his ear. "Yours is the only bone I want anything to do with," I whisper as I reach down and palm his erection through his chinos. He grips my bicep and moans into my ear. I pull back quickly and move through the doorway. "Text me later and let me know when to come over."

His face flushes and he again nods happily as I walk down the hallway and out into the crisp morning air.

Chapter 14.

Lukas

"But you can't cook," Dawn's voice calls from the living room as I rummage through the kitchen for a casserole pan that I was sure I'd seen here like six months ago. Maybe it was nine months.

"It's a stew, what's the worst that can happen?" I shout back as I create the kitchen equipment equivalent of the stomp soundtrack, baking trays and oven pans toppling out of the top cupboard and spilling over the tiled floor. I sag my head and sigh. Dawn appears a moment later to seek out the source of the apocalyptic noises.

She gives me an evil smile. "Erm let me see, *E. coli*, Campylobacter, Salmonella, the shits?" she counts off on her fingertips. "Also it might also just suck."

I throw my arms up in the air in surrender. "So what do you suggest I do? I already offered!"

"I suggest that you don't offer to cater a dinner party when you have the local pizza place and Chinese takeaway on speed dial." I glare at her. "But there is always the option of just telling the truth and bringing some ready-made, non-lethal food with you?"

I make a pouty face and nod. So that's what I did, swinging by Mrs Wong's Noodle bar picking up several containers of different types of fried rice and noodle dishes, a couple of servings of Chow Mein and a fuck ton of spring rolls.

Arriving at Tyler's apartment ten minutes before I'm supposed to be there, I figure it might be a bit keen to show up this early. Maybe I should just play it cool by waiting outside. Or should I go up early so that he knows I'm serious about getting to know him properly? But then again, his friends are there so maybe if I do they will say I'm overeager and kind of a stalker.

As I ruminate I have my finger poised over the buzzer, and I jump back when it squawks to life and a voice booms over the line.

"Are you trying to see if you can make it buzz using just the power of your mind?" Tyler's voice sweetly croons.

"Worked, didn't it?"

"Shit you're right," he bursts into laughter, "come up then Uri Gellar." The door buzzes and I pull open the heavy door. Making my way up the stairs, excitement bubbles under my skin in anticipation of getting to see Tyler again. Between graduating high school and bumping into him again, literally, at the party, I'd very rarely allowed myself to think of him. The guilt had weighed too heavy on me, so taking the coward's way out I had banished him from my memory. However, since he came back into my life, he's managed to work his way under my skin, the pull of him becoming all-consuming.

Strangely, I smell his cologne before I see him at the top of the stairs, the Davidoff Cool Water fragrance tingling in my nose. "Hey," he says, leaning cockily against the wall, blocking my way past.

I continue walking up the stairs until I'm standing on the top step, nose to nose with him. "Hi," I murmur.

"Glad you could make it." His eyes drop to my mouth.

"Couldn't keep me away," I say before pressing my lips against his, he gasps before sinking his hand into my hair and pulling me off the stairs toward him. The bags of takeout food bang against my leg, warmth radiating through the plastic. He groans into my mouth, his tongue sliding across my bottom lip. I catch it with my own tongue, sliding them along each other.

I push him against the wall and slide my thigh between his, pushing up against his dick which I discover to be hard as steel. He ruts against me, causing my balls to tingle and the hair on my arms to stand on end.

"Where's the fucking chef!" I hear Max's voice call from inside the apartment. I wince, remembering they are expecting me to cook. Tyler looks down at my hands and laughs, pressing his forehead against mine.

"From what I can see and smell, it's safe to say that the chef is still in whatever Chinese takeaway kitchen Lukas has been to." Tyler holds on to my free hand and pulls me behind him into the flat.

"Are they going to be disappointed I'm not cooking?" I sigh, I'm such a fucking loser. I could have at least made something simple like a stir fry or spaghetti. Why the hell did I let Dawn talk me out of cooking? Now his friends are going to think I'm lazy and don't give a shit.

"I think as long as you have some spring rolls in there, Max is going to forgive you pretty quickly." He winks at me and my heart sings. How the fuck does he do this to me?

"I got forty." He gives me an incredulous look. "I wasn't sure how much that big guy eats!"

Tyler laughs and pulls me into the living room.

Max peers at me over the top of a pair of red-rimmed glasses; presumably she uses them for reading as I've not seen them on her before. "Hi," she says sweetly, "glad you could make it." I do not fail to notice the slight edge to her tone as I move into the living room.

Behind Max sits a wall of solid muscle with long messy blonde braids. I give him a slight nod which he returns, standing up from behind Max. I can't help but feel slightly intimidated due to his size and height. He thrusts a giant paw at me. "I'm Peter," he states simply, and there is an air of enthusiasm about him which I suddenly find endearing, like he is a big puppy that just wants to play.

We make our introductions with some polite small talk that feels rather stunted. Tyler suggests we move to the dining table to eat. Feeling completely out of place and almost set adrift, I move to make sure I'm sitting next to him, shifting my chair a bit closer so I can slide the palm of my hand against his thigh and give it a small squeeze. He turns around, his eyes lifting in a smile. I shake away the deep and meaningful words that want to escape my mouth.

There is something primal that pulls me to him, a distant voice in my mind that screams for the connection that it craves. It's not as if we have just met, we had known each other for years. Max catches me staring at Tyler intently and makes a small coughing noise. I look up and meet her eyes guiltily, then start to open the boxes of food spread out on the table.

"I think we need to clear the air Lukas, don't you agree?" Max sits across the table from us with a smug smile on her face. "Ouch!" The table shakes and Max reaches down to rub at her leg.

"I think we need to shut the hell up and eat this food before it gets cold." Tyler bites through his teeth at her.

A look of indignation on her face, Max continues, "No, I do think we need to talk about this."

Tyler sighs and hangs his head slightly, looking at me from the corner of his eye and mouthing the word *sorry* before wincing. I give his thigh one more hard squeeze before taking a deep breath and looking at Max, who at the moment presides over the table like judge, jury and executioner.

"So Lukas, high school huh. You were an absolute cunt." My mouth gapes open. I'd expected some grilling about this, but Max isn't pulling any punches. She looks at me expectantly and gestures for me to speak.

Realising I'm just staring at her with my mouth open, I come back to life and splutter out, "Yeah, you're right I was."

"So what are you doing here?" she continues. "Normally we don't get all chummy with people who were dicks to us in high school. So…?"

"Max!" Tyler grimaces.

"No it's fine," I say, placing my hand on his arm and smiling to reassure him. "She's your friend. It would be weird if she wasn't looking out for you." Tyler gives me a sweet smile and nods. I turn back to her. "You're right. I was horrible to him, there is absolutely no excuse for what I did."

Max considers this. "Maybe you should leave then?" she asks pointedly.

"Babe." Peter puts a huge hand on Max's shoulder. She turns to him with an accusatory glare. Rather than look upset or annoyed by her obvious anger towards his intrusion, his face shows surprise which quickly morphs into admiration. He smiles gently at her and gives her a pat before looking at me with an apologetic expression. Kinda like, *you're on your own buddy*.

"Do you have any idea what that did to him?" The fire in her eyes burns into me and I can only be thankful that Tyler has someone like this in his corner. I only wish I'd had someone like that for me when I needed it most. "Beating him up every day just because of who he is - do you have any idea what that kind of violence and trauma does to someone?"

The question pierces me like a knife and I wince. I look down, unable to meet her glare anymore.

"Max that's enough!" Tyler yells from next to me. I immediately put my hand on his arm to calm him down. I don't want my fucked-up nature to come between him and his best friend. That isn't what I'm here for.

"Yes I do," I say quietly.

"What?" Max turns her attention from Tyler and looks at me, clearly confused.

"You asked if I knew what that type of violence does to someone. I'm saying yes I do. Cause it happened to me."

Chapter 15.

Tyler

My head snaps to the side as I see Lukas appear to shrink in his seat. For a moment, I can't seem to process what he has said. I can't remember anyone ever giving Lukas any flack in High School about anything to do with sexuality.

"What do you mean you know?" I ask, turning to face him, "not Caleb or any of the guys at school?"

"No," he smiles grimly, "my Dad. It's one of the reasons he is currently serving a life sentence in prison." I reach across and grab his arm, unable to stop the shock from spreading across my face. Of all the things I was expecting him to say, that was not one of them.

I know that Lukas had moved north with his mum and sister, and that his dad was no longer in the picture, but not that he's ever experienced anything like what he is implying. I turn to Max who has gratefully shut her mouth, but is sitting back in her chair waiting expectantly.

"You don't have to do this here," I say to him, realising that baring their soul to strangers is not everyone's idea of a great time.

He smiles sadly at me and shakes his head. "I want to." He places a hand over the one I still have gripping his arm. "You're important to me, you should know. But it's no excuse for what I did."

"Lukas."

"No I'm serious Tyler," he says sternly, "no matter what you hear now, you can't excuse me for what I did."

"Lukas," I try again.

"Promise me." He looks at me pleadingly.

"Ok." I know I might not be able to keep that promise. I bring his hand up and kiss his knuckles before settling his hand in both of mine.

Lukas takes in a deep breath and starts.

"Ok, well I loved my dad. What am I saying, I mean I do love my dad, no matter what he did I still love him." He looks down as if trying to find the words but they are not coming easy.

"Anyway, my dad was a difficult man. He had very strong views on a lot of things, immigrants, the unemployed, woman and most importantly I guess to this, gay people. Gay men specifically. He had a very hard time accepting the fact that gay people were just people. He would call them all types of names."

"I know the type." Max says sympathetically, her gaze softening as she listens.

"Well he made no qualms about the fact that he hated gay men. He used to say they were dirty, paedophiles, disgusting. If there was a horrible name, you can be sure he used it." His face falls, I can almost see the pain etched there. "Which was just wonderful for me when I realised that I was gay."

Lukas gets up, picking up an empty glass and pointing towards the sink. Max nods. Pouring himself a glass of water he returns to the table, taking a big gulp.

"I had done my best to not feel it, plastering my bedroom walls with girls from magazines, talking crudely about them, dating girls from high school, My dad would look at me proudly each time I brought a different girl home. He told me that it was like looking at a mini version of himself. I hated that thought, I didn't want to end up like that. But I played the part of the straight jock son that he wanted. I just wanted my dad to love me, you know?"

I shift my chair closer to his until our thighs are pressed together. I rest my hand on the small of his back, hoping the connection will help in some way.

"Then I met James." He smiles wistfully. "We knew each other in passing in school, but he approached me at a party one weekend. I tried to get him to leave me alone but he was insistent and said that he knew I was hiding and that he wanted to get to know me. So I let him. We were completely inseparable that summer."

A spark of jealousy flares though me, I shake it away quickly. Lukas must see the frustration in my eyes. He taps my knee reassuringly.

"There was one night that I somehow convinced my mother to let him stay over at our house. I told her that we had some homework to get done before school started up again. She said it was ok but not to tell my father as he said that young men didn't have friends sleeping over, that it was a girl thing to do." Lukas bites his lip. "I remember we were laying on the bed, just talking about nonsense. I was telling him about a girl at school I was going to ask out when he just sat up and pulled me up with him. He asked me if he could try something and made me promise not to freak out." Lukas looks down. I see the tears pricking his eyes.

"You don't have to continue, it's fine."

He shakes his head. "He pulled me against him and he kissed me. It was like he opened all the doors and all the windows and suddenly I could see. It was the best thing that had ever happened to me." He looks at me and winks. "Up until that point, at least."

Oh fuck I was falling for him hard.

"We kissed for what seemed like forever, it was everything." A single tear falls down his face, he reaches up and wipes it away. "My bedroom door slams open and my dad comes tearing into the room. He pulls me off the bed and screams in my face that I'm disgusting and a faggot, the next thing I know I'm on the floor, blood pouring from my face as he punches me over and over. My lip busts open, he broke my nose, turns out he fractured both my eye sockets and my cheek and through kicking me in the stomach he broke four of my ribs and my arm."

The words are pouring out of him too quickly, and my head spins at the list of atrocities coming from his mouth. I can't fathom that he is talking about something that's happened to himself, basically as a child. I feel bile creep up my throat, burning at the back of my mouth. I instinctively reach a hand up to encircle my neck like it might stop the rising acid. My eyes fill and the world looks topsy turvy, like I'm seeing it through a kaleidoscope.

"I remember looking up from the floor and seeing my dad scream at James to get out. He was poking his chest and shoving at him. James should have left then. He was trying to get to me, he was crying like he was scared for me, when he should have been scared for himself." Tears are flowing freely down Lukas's face now; I look over to Max to find her face buried in Peter's chest, his hand stroking her head as she grips his shirt. His face is etched with deep frown lines as he continues to listen to Lukas.

"My dad grabbed him round the back of the neck and dragged him down the stairs. My mum was standing on the top of the stairs screaming bloody murder. She looked at me and I could tell that she was broken. She didn't know what to do. Somehow, I got off the floor. There was blood everywhere, I thought I might pass out from the pain but from somewhere I found the strength to run down the stairs. I was holding my arm against my chest which just made my ribs feel like they were being cut out with hot knives."

I want to stop him, I want to cover his mouth and stop all the words from coming out, like it might stop them from ever having happened in the first place.

"I got to the front door and James was still trying to get inside, to get to me. He was standing on the stairs outside the front door, screaming that he was sorry and that he didn't mean it. I didn't care if my Dad had killed me at that point. I just wanted him to get away from James so I could tell him to run. With the one good hand I had left," he says instinctively flexing his fingers, "I punched him in the back. He let go of James and I started to tell him to run, but my dad put his hands around my neck and was strangling me, I could feel the bones in my neck starting to break."

I hear Max sobbing quietly into Peter's chest. Peter himself looks like he might throw up. I know the feeling.

"James jumped on my dad's back and tried to pull him off me. My dad called him a faggot again. He let me go and that's when I saw my dad pull his arm back and he punched him so hard. James' head smashed off the door frame before he fell back, he... he... he fell backward and his head crashed into the paving stones outside." I realise I'm squeezing Lukas's fingers so hard that it must border on pain. "They don't know if it was the punch or the fall that killed him, but by the time I got out the door a second later there was blood on the street, his eyes were open and staring at me, but he was already gone."

Lukas's lip trembles and I immediately pull him towards me, burying his face in my neck, hoping he doesn't feel the tears falling from my eyes onto his shirt. When I look up, Max's eyes are as red-rimmed as her glasses and she whispers something to Peter. He nods and they both stand up and move around the table. She rests her hand on Lukas's shoulder, bending down to kiss him briefly on the top of his head before they leave the room. I hear the door click shut to her bedroom.

I hold him there for a long time. Leaving the food untouched, I pull him to his feet, lifting his head to meet mine. I press small kisses to his cheeks where tears have fallen before I kiss him gently on the mouth. He sniffles and pushes his head back against my shoulder. I reach down and link his hand with mine, pulling him gently behind me to my room. Sitting him at the end of the mattress I pull off his boots and jeans, slip his shirt off his shoulders until he sits there quietly in just briefs and a T-shirt. I peel back the covers and make him lie down. Climbing in behind him, I move until I'm pressed against the full length of him. I wrap my arm around his waist and press a small kiss to his neck, rubbing small circles on his stomach until I hear his breathing even out.

I lie there for a long time, comfortable in the fact that I can truly move on now.

He's mine.

Chapter 16.

Lukas

I wake up with a massive sense of disorientation. I'm definitely not in my own bed. An arm tightens around my waist and I'm immediately gripped by panic. I hear a hum from behind me, the sound like honey, it soothes me and I smile. I reach down and grab the arms encircling me, pulling their owner tighter around me. Lips press into the back of my neck, hot air rushes across my skin, making me shudder.

"Morning," the deep voice says sleepily, as Tyler clutches me impossibly tighter to him.

"Morning to you too." Memories rush in from the night before and I groan. "Oh my god your friends are going to think I'm such a loser. Did I actually cry at the dinner table?"

I'm suddenly pulled onto my back and a very naked Tyler straddles my waist, pushing me down. "Hey, I don't want to hear you talking like that." All traces of sleepiness are gone. "What you did last night was so brave and I'm really proud of you." He leans down and kisses both my cheeks before kissing my mouth.

I smile against him. "Ok," I mumble, not really convinced but touched by his sincerity.

Just feeling him against me is like a dream, the miles of skin pressed against my own. I feel his soft cock resting against my thigh. My own dick starts to twitch in acknowledgement of the hot guy currently plastered along the top of me. I reach around and caress the round curves of his ass, giving them a playful tug towards me. I leave one hand where it is and slide another between us to grab his now semi-hard cock, playing with his foreskin, rolling it back away from the head, smoothing my hand down the soft skin before I give his balls a small squeeze.

He hisses out a breath and dead stares me, "You're evil!"

I laugh and surge up to take his mouth in mine. I groan loudly into his mouth, seemingly unable to stop the noises that come from my mouth anymore.

He frowns at me and winces, "I'm sorry my morning breath must be terrible."

I pull him sharply back down to me. "I don't care." I flip us until he lays out spread underneath me, seeming shocked that he is suddenly on the bottom without warning. My head dips down and I run my nose along his jawline, taking in his scent. I lick his neck, sucking his supple skin against my mouth.

"Don't you dare give me a hickey Lukas Ford," he warns.

I laugh. "Nah, I have other things I wanna suck." He looks down quickly to meet my face and I grin up at him. I continue moving down the bed, licking and sucking along his chest. Teasing his nipples between my teeth. Giving them an experimental bite. His back arches off the bed and he cries out. I'll have to store that reaction away for a later date.

I nose down his abdomen, dipping my tongue into his navel. I palm his dick which is like a steel bar, pushing urgently against my chest. Wrapping my hand around his length, I pull back the foreskin. A hiss escapes from his mouth as he tries to push his cock deeper into my fist. I press down against his groin, pushing him back to the mattress.

"Easy baby, let me take care of you." He makes a keening sound which gives my inner porn star the ego boost he needs right now. Running my nose down the length of his shaft I breathe in the dark and heady smell, kissing the tight skin which makes his dick enlarge each time I do it. *Neat trick.*

I look up to meet his eyes, he watches me as I swallow his thick cock inch by inch until he is pressing against the back of my mouth. I breathe out through my nose and swallow more around him until he is nestled in my throat. I feel his cock flex and see his eyes squeeze shut. I pull off his dick until the head comes to rest on my tongue, and then push him all the way back in again. My eyes begin to water as I struggle to breathe, but I love it. Resting my forearm on his stomach I begin bobbing up and down on his dick, the head pushing into my throat every few strokes.

"Baby, fuck me. Fuck. Oh my god. Fuck." A string of curse words follow as his fingers thread into my hair. I pull off his dick, making an obscene wet suckling noise as it falls out of my mouth and slaps against his own stomach.

"Sweetheart I need you to fuck my face ok? Don't stop until I tell you." He nods emphatically and I suck his cock back into my mouth. I smile up at him and nod, and he starts to thrust up into my mouth. I moan around him, squeezing his balls in my palm. His breathing becomes laboured, his mouth open slightly as he looks down at his dick disappearing into my throat. He must see my eyes water, but realise how much I love it. He pounds into me and my throat feels raw and well used. I reach down with my free hand and shuttle my own dick through my fist.

"Fuck Lukas, I'm not going to last." I moan and suck harder as he picks up the pace. Incredibly I feel his cock thicken further as he stutters and thrusts spurt after spurt of hot salty cum into my mouth and throat. I can feel his legs start to tremble as he empties into me. I suckle on him lightly as I feel his prick start to soften. He twitches, sensitive. I let his cock fall from my mouth, giving it one last kiss as I rest my head against his stomach.

"What about you?" he asks sleepily, stroking my hair.

"It's all good." I lift my palm to show I'd actually cum in my hand. He grabs my wrist and brings my hand to his mouth. His tongue darting out, he licks my hand clean. I scurry up the bed and press a hard kiss to his mouth, tasting myself there. He sighs against me and I fall back onto him, sated.

* * * *

Waking again later that morning, we stumble out of bed and make our way into the living room. We find Max and Peter sitting on the sofa watching Hocus Pocus whilst eating some of the Chinese food I'd bought the night before. She holds up a carton of chow mein to me in offering, but I shake my head, smiling.

We settle in and watch the rest of the movie with them, Tyler lying back against my chest. My arm is pulled tight around him, every now and again he cranes his neck upward to steal a kiss. I catch Max looking over at us with hearts in her eyes. I guess that is her signal that she approves of me and isn't going to rip my nut sack off. Not that I'm under any illusion that she won't do exactly that if I ever hurt her best friend again.

We spend the remainder of the day alternating between watching movies, eating junk food and napping. I didn't go home that evening either. Instead, we fall asleep completely sexually satisfied, wrapped around each other like vines.

So that's how it goes for the next few weeks. We see each other most days. There are some days when it's just not possible to make our schedules match, and those days are hard. We make up for them the next chance we get to see each other. We spend the nights exploring each other's bodies, and the mornings lazily kissing until we are forced by our alarm clocks to get up.

I'd been nervous to tell Tyler I prefer to top; bottoming for him our first time had been a rare exception and I'd worried Tyler would be dissatisfied that I'm not as versatile as he seems to be. He just smiled his perfect smile and proved to me he didn't mind one bit, by sinking onto my hard dick and riding me till we both came.

I love that Max is fiercely protective over Tyler. She had followed me into the kitchen that first morning I'd slept over and hugged me tightly. She then made it clear in no uncertain terms that they would need to use dental records to identify my body if I in any way hurt her friend. She'd smiled sweetly at me whilst saying it, but I have no doubt that somewhere under the smoking hot façade is the quiet beating heart of a maniacal psychopath. Better to have one of them on your side than against you I guess.

Her new boyfriend, the Viking Thor look-alike from my house party, has now become a permanent fixture in her life. Peter isn't actually a Viking, but he's a nice guy who lives down my neck of the woods in a small town whose name always makes me giggle, Six Mile Bottom.

Dawn joined the group on a number of occasions, but always uses the excuse that she works in a bar so drinking at one kinda feels like she's on the clock. When Dawn can't make a night out, Max secretly likes that she is on a night out with three well-muscled guys: she likes the glares of envy she receives from other women and men. For me though, it's the times when it's just me and Tyler I enjoy the most.

One lazy Sunday morning Tyler says that we need to get out in the real world and away from one of our bedrooms as he's fairly sure his dick will fall off from overuse or that we'll need to start mainlining vitamin D supplements to counteract the extreme lack of daylight we've been experiencing.

"You bored of my body already?" I pout at him.

He smiles and straddles my waist as I sit at the edge of his bed. "No definitely not, but I'm not ready to upgrade you for a better model yet so I have to watch the wear and tear." I smack his ass lightly causing him to jump a little. then squeeze his cheeks and pull him against me. He groans and jumps off me. "See, we'll just end up fucking!"

"Ok ok, what do you want to do today baby?" I say, striding over to him and wrapping my hands around the back of his neck.

He considers this for a moment before pressing forward to kiss my cheek, then whispers in my ear. "Let's go for a walk."

After showering, which takes half an hour longer than it should as I protest against separate showers, using the excuse that I'm saving money and the environment, only to end up sucking his dick until he coats my tongue. Satisfied I got my way a little, we dress quickly and leave the house.

A short drive later we pull up along the outskirts of Sefton Park, a large greenland in the centre of the city. The park has become a tourist attraction within the city, with its wide pathways, the large greenhouse filled with huge tropical plants which regularly serves as a venue for jazz concerts and tea dances, meadows and fields spanning the entire space framing the green spaces, and <u>two natural watercourses</u> flowing into the seven acre man-made lake.

As we stroll around the lake, Tyler's hand finds its way into my own, linking our fingers loosely as we take in the sights. A now familiar tightness in my chest takes hold, which only grows in intensity each time I sneak a peek at him when I think he isn't looking. If I were a hypochondriac, I would say that I'm having a mild heart attack, but I know better. It's a feeling that I'm too scared to name, so I stay silent.

Being a university city and it also being term time, the park is moderately busy. Couples, friends, families and small groups, too caught up in the day-to-day of their own lives to notice us as we stop every now and again to steal kisses from each other. We sit on a small hill overlooking the lake, the giant glass atrium in the distance behind us.

I let my eyes glance across the expanse, finally settling on a young family. A small boy throws seeds from a paper brown bag into the lake, causing a flock of ducks and pigeons to swarm all around him. A gay couple watch on from a short distance, one of them with his arm around the lower back of the other, pulling him closer to his side and pressing a gentle kiss to his temple. The recipient of the kiss seems to shudder slightly before moving closer to his partner and resting his head on the other man's shoulder.

My heart catches in my throat as a silent longing detonates in my chest, my fingers gripping Tyler's like we're on a white-knuckle ride.

He reacts to the sudden pressure by turning to me. "Hey are you ok?"

I relax my grip and stare at him, a deer caught in the headlights. Shaking my head out of the unspoken fantasy I smile at him, the back of my hand quickly dashing to my eye. "Yeah, I'm fine, I think I just caught something in my eye is all."

He looks at me, face filled with concern. My eyes stray back to the family scene. I realise in this moment that I want to have that myself someday. I want a guy next to me as we watch our child explore the world around them.

No, not any guy, I want the guy next to me in that picture too. I see Tyler follow my gaze as I watch the couple stare lovingly at their child. "Pretty cute huh?" he whispers into my ear, his warm breath causing an instant reaction down my spine.

"Yeah, I guess so." I shrug and move away from him slightly.

Sweat beads on my forehead, fear and panic grip me. This is all getting very real, very fast, and it's messing with my head. I both love and hate the fact that this guy is becoming integral to my peace and happiness. In such a short time I've reached a point where I don't know what I would do if he ever decided that he didn't want me anymore. If our past becomes too much to overcome. If I'm just too damaged.

"What's wrong, did I do something?" The sound of his voice, quiet and a bit scared, makes me want to throw my arms around him. I can feel the tingling in my muscles ticking under my skin as I hold my arms at my sides.

"No sorry, I was just getting a bit of space is all." His eyes close slightly and he dips his head, he looks a bit resigned as if he has been waiting for me to pull away from him. "I don't mean it like that, I just..." I begin, but he places his hand on mine and squeezes.

"Don't worry I get it, I understand." He doesn't understand anything. He starts to move away from me as if to stand up.

I grip his hand, scared I'm fucking up again. "Listen, it's not like that, this is all moving really fast and I'm just not sure... No this is all coming out wrong!"

Tyler pulls his hand away from me and gets to his feet. He walks down the hill towards the lake, waiting for me at the edge. I follow him as he starts toward the perimeter, back towards the entrance of the park. We make our way back to the car. I feel a lump in my throat forming along with a sense of dread burrowing its way into the pit of my stomach. He unlocks the car and then tosses me the keys he'd been holding for me, then climbs into the passenger seat and waits for me to get in.

I have maybe 10 seconds to fix my fuck-up before he starts to completely pull away from me. Taking a deep breath, I prepare myself to eat a full helping of humble pie. I gather my thoughts, as best I can, and get into the car. I turn in my seat to face him and begin.

"Listen, this is all really new for me, I don't know how to navigate this thing that we are doing. I don't know what's normal." At that word he tenses, I can almost see him begin to shut down so I continue, "I didn't prepare myself for how much I was going to like you and how quickly it would turn into something more."

His back straightens slightly at this. My palms begin to sweat as once again I bite my tongue to stop myself from saying those words that will, this early in a relationship, make any guy bolt for the door, the words I really want to say. "I'm just having some trouble separating who I am now, from the person who treated you the way I did back then. I don't want to hurt you, I don't want to fuck this thing up between us as it's important to me. I'm just scared you will remember the way things were and you are going to run."

My phone starts to ring, sliding my hand inside my pocket I find the button I need to send the call to voicemail and press it.

"Do you think I have some form of fucking amnesia; do you think I don't remember exactly what you, what all of you did to me? I'm not some lovestruck teenager who is just forgetting the shit that I had to put up with just to get some action from a hot guy." I ignore the term *hot guy*; I also stop myself from clapping like a schoolgirl at the term 'lovestruck'. So, I let him continue. "I am with you because I want to be with you, in spite of all that. I believe you have changed, well I hope you have, but if you're going to keep bringing the past up all the time then you can just go fuck yourself, because I've worked too hard and too..." My phone begins to ring again. "Just answer the fucking phone Lukas!"

I fish the phone out of my pocket and see that it's my mother's name on the caller ID. That feeling of dread is back. It's weird because she never really calls me. I put the phone to my ear.

"Hello" I bark into the phone.

"Lukas, Lukas is that you?" My mother's voice sounds small, feeble almost.

"Yeah, it's me, what's up." I cast a glance at Tyler who stares out the windshield at the joggers passing by.

"Lukas I need to talk to you." I huff into the phone, I need to fix whatever it is I've fucked up with Tyler. I can deal with my mother later.

"Mum can I call you back, it's…"

I never get the chance to finish that sentence. She quickly rushes out the words that I can tell it pains her to say. I allow the harsh reality of the conversation to wash over me, I feel my skin go cold. I don't really speak for the duration, apart from saying 'yes', and 'I understand', at the right places. I was no good at dealing with these conversations. I feel Tyler's warm hand resting on the back of my neck. I say my goodbyes and hang up the phone. My heart sinking into my stomach I breathe words I am not prepared to say out loud:

"My father's dead. I have to go home."

Chapter 17.

Tyler

I get out of the car and rush around to the driver's side, opening his door and pulling him out onto the pavement. He still hasn't really blinked or made any movements other than to open and close his mouth mutely. I take the keys from him and walk him around to the passenger side, watching the road to make sure no passing drivers take us out. Getting him secured in his seat and fastening his seatbelt around him, I press a small kiss to the top of his head before closing the door.

I take a deep breath and my hand drifts to my chest. It's hurting me thinking that he is in pain. I can't stand it. It's a terrible time to realise I'm completely and utterly in love with him. There's no denying it though, and the pain I feel for him is so acutely intense that I take a second to remember how to breathe. I make my way to the driver's side and get in the car. I reach across the middle panel and rest my hand on top of his. Automatically he turns his hand over and links our fingers, taking my breath away slightly. I squeeze his fingers and he returns the gesture. I hope this connection is giving him some strength, even if only a little.

Squeezing one last time, I pat his hand and start the car. We drive home in relative silence until I pull up outside his house. I'd made him text Dawn on the drive home, mostly to give him something to do as his silence was becoming endless and dark. Dawn is there to meet us outside as we pull up. She opens his door and pulls him from the car, gathering him up in her arms and bear-hugging the ever-loving shit of him. He stands motionless in her arms waiting for her to be done so he can move into the house.

I know by now he's too out of it to even notice I am there, so I rush up behind him and put my hand on his shoulder.

"Listen, I am just going to run back to my place to pack a bag, I'm going to borrow your car, but I'll be back in about an hour ok?" I squeeze his shoulder lightly and his eyes crease in confusion.

"Why are you packing?"

I look sheepishly down at the floor, uncertainty and caution colouring my face. "I'm coming with you. Home." The words seem to shake him out of whatever black hole of despair he's tumbling down.

"What do you mean, you're coming with me down to Suffolk? You don't have to do that Tyler, we have only been dating for a short while and you have school and your job and…" I put my hand on his chest and push against him slightly.

"I'm coming with you, ok," I say a bit more firmly. A weight seems to lift from him, he throws his arms around my shoulders and sobs into my neck. I wrap my arms around him and place a hand along the back of his head. "It's ok baby, let it go."

A sharp wail escapes from Lukas through clenched teeth as his tears begin to soak the top of my shirt. I slowly move us a few steps into the house, and Dawn moves silently around us and closes the door. I walk with Lukas to his room and get him settled in bed under the covers, lying down behind him for a few minutes, pressing right against him. Eventually his crying turns into low sighs, and then I hear his breathing become more even and realise he has dozed off. I press a kiss gently against the top of his head and slip out the room.

"Look after him ok?" I say to Dawn whom I find sitting in the kitchen drinking coffee.

"Sure thing honey," she smiles at me sadly.

"I'll be back soon, just going to get a few things from my place." She nods and sees me out. I make it home in record time and fill Max in on the situation. She helps me get ready and chases me back out of the apartment, promising that she'll sort everything out with my job and school. I'm back in Lukas's bed before he wakes up. I slide my arm over him and pull him back against me, placing a kiss to the back of his neck. He stirs from his sleep and turns to face me, kissing me on the lips and then pressing his forehead to mine as the memory returns to him that he is now without a father.

"I'm sorry I didn't mean to fall asleep." I pull him forwards and press his head to my chest in response. "Thank you so much for coming with me. I really need you there," he speaks quietly. "If you need to go and pack your bag I'm ok here."

I motion behind him to my bag on the floor. He turns around and whips his head back quickly. "Wow you are good!" I smile at him and pull him back against my chest.

"Whatever you need, I'm here ok?" I whisper, I feel him smile against me and nod.

We get out of bed a little while later, giving him time to spend with Dawn. She becomes a complete mother hen, making sure that he has eaten enough, that he has showered and will be getting the correct number of hours of sleep. She shoos us off to bed early in the evening telling us we have a long drive ahead of us tomorrow. I don't argue; any extra time I get to spend alone with Lukas is a bonus in my books.

We wake early the next day, and Dawn has gone through the trouble of preparing us breakfast as well as travel mugs of coffee for the road. Lukas, whilst still obviously dealing with his inner turmoil, looks better than he had yesterday.

"Call me ok," Dawn says while squeezing the ever-loving shit out of Lukas.

"Yes mother," he chuckles.

"You look after him." She points at me over the car. I nod and slip into the driver seat. I tell Lukas to put some music on for the drive. He had been insistent on driving but I'd convinced him that his mother might call to make sure we were on the way. I'm surprised she has not checked in on him at all after her initial call to Lukas yesterday. One would think a mother would want to check on her son after dropping a bombshell on him like that. Lukas eventually had agreed and settled in for the drive.

It takes us around four hours to drive back to Newmarket in Suffolk. His family were originally from here before moving up north. Driving down a long straight road, high bushes on either side blocking the view of the famous Newmarket racecourses beyond I break the silence.

"Why did your mother move back here?" I turn to look at him briefly, noticing his gaze immediately shifts downwards. "If that's a tricky subject, pretend I didn't ask," I say as cheerfully as I can.

"No, it's fine." He takes one long breath and lets it out. "After what happened with James, my mother called for help. An ambulance came and took James away. Another one came for me. I saw the police question my dad who very honestly told them what he had done. When they tried to put the cuffs on him he pulled away, lunging at me and saying I was dead to him and that I had destroyed his family."

I reach across and stroke his thigh.

"I was in hospital for a week whilst they set my leg and gave me facial reconstructive surgery. In all that time my mother visited me once. That was only really to sign the consent forms to operate on me. When I was discharged home she told me that she had to take care of my sister and didn't want to upset her any further by bringing her to a hospital."

How could a mother do that to her son? I couldn't even begin to fathom my mother treating me in that way. My heart breaks for him.

"I just wanted her to love me, so I said I understood and that she did the right thing. During my dad's trial she convinced me to tell the police and the judge that I'd thrown the first punch. I did, but it didn't matter because they gave him life for what he had done to James. When we came home she cornered me one night in the kitchen to tell me that we couldn't stay there no longer, that she was a laughing stock and that she couldn't walk the high street without people talking about her son and what he had done."

"That can't be true!" I gasp, already hating every resident of this fuckwit town.

"No, they were probably saying *there is the wife of that child killer,* but she couldn't see him for who he was. So she placed the blame on me. When we were packing up our house to move north she sat me down and said that I had put my dad in jail. She said I'd made her lose her husband, made my sister fatherless, that I'd gotten my friend killed. She said that I needed to put my deviant thoughts to the back of my mind and protect my family." He puts his hand over mine. "I think I believed her, I think from that point I just associated my desires with destruction and evil. I think when I saw you that first day and I felt that instant draw to you, it made me worry that it was happening again. I couldn't let it." The tears flow freely down his face as he squeezes my hand.

"Lukas..."

"I'm so fucking sorry baby, I'm so fucking sorry," he repeats over and over. I indicate and pull over to the side of the road. Unbuckling my seat belt, I turn to him.

"I need you to stop that right now ok?" I tell him sternly. "It's just you and me, no one else. No matter what happens today, you have me. I need you to believe that."

He calms eventually. Wiping tears from his face with my thumb, I lean across and kiss his cheeks. Settling back in my seat I start up the car and head towards his family home.

*   *   *   *

There are a few raised eyebrows amongst Lukas's family when they see he has brought a man home, a man with whom he is clearly in a relationship. His mother is extremely welcoming in a southern polite kind of way but remains noticeably distant to Lukas. Lukas's sister sat with us outside in the garden and explained that his father had gotten himself into a yard brawl in prison and had been stabbed by one of the other inmates. It troubles me that Lukas doesn't seem at all surprised.

The funeral goes relatively well, with Mrs. Ford remaining stoic and sombre, wiping a single solitary tear away from her cheek during the procession. Lukas reaches across to offer his mother a show of support, only to have his hand brushed away without a glance at him. Back at his family home, I make sure to steal a few moments with him and pull him to the window seat.

"Can I get you anything?" I move to sit next to Lukas as he perches on the large box window seat in the lounge of his childhood home. He's still wearing the black suit that he'd picked out to wear for the funeral. I lightly place my hand on his knee and squeeze gently.

He rests his hand on top of mine before smiling sweetly at me and placing his head on my shoulder. "No I'm good, thank you for today - it really meant a lot to me that you were here."

I squeeze his knee lightly once more and kiss the top of his head. "Anytime baby."

"I think we should head back home late tomorrow if that's ok with you?" Lukas asks, squeezing my hand.

I'm not sure that's the best idea considering all that his family must be dealing with now. "Sure, if that's what you want. Do you not think it would be best for you to stick around here for a few days though?" I hope the slight suggestion won't be taken in a negative way.

"They don't want me here any more than I want to be here." He dips his gaze to the floor. "They'll be able to move on properly once I'm gone."

The sadness in his voice makes my heart ache. Clearly his mother isn't the only one who secretly blames Lukas for his father's death; Lukas does as well, if only subconsciously. I move closer to him, my body squeezed up against his side. I throw my arm over his shoulder and pull him in towards me. "You're an amazing man Lukas. Can you tell me a bit about your dad?"

Lukas pushes himself to his feet and turns to face me, stretching out his hand as he mutters, "Sure, I suppose I could. But not here, let's go to my old room."

I take Lukas's hand and he leads me through the house, giving people small nods as he passes. We settle ourselves in his childhood bedroom. He leans against an old desk piled full of boxes of old clothes and books. He looks over the contents of the boxes and smiles sadly. "They aren't wasting any time in making sure there isn't a trace of me left here."

"You can bring some things to my place if you want," I offer meekly, hoping he won't feel too pressured by my very obvious *moving this relationship on* tactic.

He smiles at me and nods. "I don't know where to start really," he said, breaking the awkward silence. "My dad was never the paternal type of person. We never played football, he never came to any of my parent/teacher evenings, he never told me he was proud of me. What he was however was fiercely protective over his family and the image they portrayed to those around us." Lukas looks past me, staring at the wallpaper as if seeing his memories play out on the crisp blue surface. "My dad was one of the most active members of the jockey club near the perimeter of the town and a pillar of the local community. Anything that potentially could affect that was dealt with swiftly."

"How do you mean?" I ask, going cold.

"If I failed a test, or messed up a game of rugby or football, if my grades dropped, if I appeared weak in any way, he would give me what he liked to call *Straighteners*."

"What the hell is one of those?"

"He would take me into the garden, tell me that if I was going to be a man then he would have to teach me. He would then proceed to beat me for hours. I mean really brutally. He would tell me I could fight back, that I was allowed to hit him. He was just so big. I couldn't stop him."

"Lukas," I wince.

"You'd think after all the stuff he put me through and what he did to James, that I would be the last person in the world to dole out that kind of violence." I huff in a breath, knowing he is talking about us again.

I move across to him and put my hand over his, squeezing gently. Seeing him so vulnerable makes me want to wrap myself around him and try to make everything ok for him for once. I place a small kiss at his temple and breathe over his ear; I feel him shudder next to me. "You have nothing to apologise for anymore, do you hear me? We've said enough about the past, let's just leave it where it belongs and move forward from here, alright?"

He smiles and slowly nods, turning his head and looking up into my eyes. I dip my head and press my lips against his. He sighs against my mouth and I feel his turn up in a smile. "I don't know how I got so lucky with you, I don't deserve you."

I pull back from him slightly, my face showing nothing but seriousness and resolve. "Lukas, you have me, all of me."

Like a bomb has detonated nearby, Lukas throws himself at me, pushing me down into the mattress, his body covering mine, every inch of him pressing into me. His hands seem to be everywhere at once, tearing off my jacket and pushing up my shirt, reaching up and pressing his palm over my chest, his thumb grazing my nipple. His mouth presses urgently against mine, demanding entrance. I open up to him and immediately his tongue slips inside my mouth, exploring and tasting every part of it.

I run my hand through his hair and grip the back of his head, pulling him closer to me. Teeth clacking and lips smashing together, we eat at each other's mouths with a raw unbridled fury.

He moves back and makes quick work of removing all my clothes, each item of my three-piece suit seemingly offending him for keeping him from my body. Once naked I lie back on his pillow and look up at him standing astride me. Now moving slowly, he peels each layer of his clothes away from his body, uncovering each part of his physique at a leisurely pace so I can take my time to savour everything. Standing naked before me he gives his length a few slow heavy strokes. He looks down at me, his eyes glassy.

Dropping to his knees on either side of my waist, he leans down over me, kissing me tenderly. It's such a change of pace from everything we've been doing up to that point that it steals my breath away. My hands drop to his waist and hold him to me. Resting his forearms on either side of my head, he regards me with a hint of apprehension in his tender gaze. "You can't ever leave me. You're mine now. You know that right?"

I feel a sharp tug within my chest that seems to burrow into my soul. I nod at him and smile.

"You have to say it," he said with more insistence.

"I'm yours," I tell him whilst tightening my grip around his waist. He mashes his mouth back against mine. Reaching down between us he slides a hand down beneath my crotch and taps his index finger against my hole. I gasp into his mouth and a triumphant smile appears on his face. I reach down to the floor where he had flung my trousers and retrieve a condom and packet of lube from my wallet. Tearing open the lube I pass it to him along with the condom. He regards the condom with a frown.

"Listen, I have something to show you." He moves off the bed and grabs an envelope from his bag. "I went to the sexual health clinic and got tested for everything. I'm negative. You?" I take the letter to check his results and nod.

"Me too, I got my six-monthly check two weeks ago and I'm negative as well." He grins at me and reassumes his place straddling my waist.

"I want to be inside you with nothing between us, would that be ok?" It is more than ok, it's suddenly all I want. Any restraint I have suddenly dissolves as I pour some lube into my hand and rub it down his length, almost frantically fisting down his cock. He chuckles and pours some lube against my hole, pushing his digit slowly inside me, prepping me.

I don't want him taking too long, so I grab his forearm. "I'm good, please just get inside me. I need it." I probably sound like a whore, but I don't care – I just need him.

He hooks my legs over his arms and positions his dick against my entrance. I can feel heat radiating off him down below, driving me insane. I push back against him hoping to get some friction and maybe get him in me as soon as possible. He puts his hands against my waist, stilling me. "Easy baby, there's no rush."

I groan and turn my head into the pillow, not wanting to seem overly desperate. In fact, I am very desperate, almost painfully so. Moving slowly, he inches forward, the head of his cock sliding past the first ring of muscle, the familiar feeling of fullness which just about borders on pain. I grit my teeth and push through the sting until it turns into the pleasure. Inch by agonizing inch he makes me come apart at the seams, my hands clawing for something to hold onto, sweat beading at my skin. Finally, he's fully seated himself inside me, no condom between us, I feel all of him, his heat and desire pulsing within me.

The heat of his stare bores into me and I turn my head to meet his gaze. It's almost too intense, but I can't break the hold he has on me, his hips rocking in slow motion against me and pulling back only to piston into me again, somehow feeling fuller each time. His eyes lock with mine; I feel something pass between us. Energy crackles across the surface of my skin, passing into him. I feel my orgasm barreling up my spine and my balls begin to tighten up. As I bite my bottom lip to stop myself from screaming out words that I knew I shouldn't say right now, his palm comes to rest on my chest as he moves in and out of me, moving slowly up to my neck and eventually cupping my jaw.

"I love you," he says simply.

My orgasm explodes, causing thousands of tiny stars to explode over my head. White hot flames penetrate my skin, every nerve ending singing under its surface. With one final thrust I feel his own release spilling inside me, coating my insides as he trembles above me. I wrap my arms around his neck and pull him down to me, his soul-crushing kiss cleaving away the last pieces of my heart that weren't already his before.

"I love you too," I whisper against his mouth. I feel him sigh against me, he presses his forehead against mine, staring intently into my eyes.

"I can't be without you anymore, you are all I think about, every minute of every day. You got under my skin Tyler and I don't want you to ever leave." I feel my heart fill to capacity. How the hell has this happened - going from hating every fibre of someone's being, to them becoming the one person you could imagine a future with?

We lie there for a while, him still inside me but slowly deflating. We clean up and decide to take a walk around town then drive around to see some of the sights. We drive back up north the very next day, and I'm overjoyed to see that a kind of lightness has overtaken Lukas. He seems freer, his laugh and smiles without restraint or worry. Every now and again he pulls my hand across the console and brushes a kiss across my knuckles. I never stood a chance saying no to him. As much as he is mine, I am his.

Chapter 18.

Lukas

I open my eyes to find myself alone in his bed. I reach across to his side of the bed. Feeling the warmth of the sheets, I look across the room to see him moving about picking things off the floor and I smile.

It's strange how integral someone can become to your life in such a short amount of time, that your body seems to yearn for them when they are not around. It's as if when they aren't there, things just don't feel all that normal anymore. That's how it's become between Tyler and myself.

The trip to Newmarket certainly changed things between us. We haven't felt the need to put a label on whatever is happening between us; there's no need to. He's mine and I'm his, that's the only truth I know. We've both become regular guests in each other's homes, and our respective housemates have come to not expect to see us alone. We've somehow organically become an *"Us"* and that's just fine.

I'd never really had any interest in pursuing a serious relationship with any of the people I'd dated. They were more a means to pass the time than someone to form an actual connection with. This time is definitely different. I have been acutely aware of a small but powerful voice in the back of my head, that screams at me that if I had just had a backbone years ago, we could have been doing this for years by now. I cannot let those thoughts fester for too long though. I'd mentioned them to Tyler and he suggested that maybe it just hadn't been our time until now. Something about that perspective is soothing, as if it means we were destined to happen.

I stretch out my body along the length of his bed, like a cat before it falls asleep. I watch as he potters around his room, stopping every now and again to pick up clothes from the floor to put into the laundry hamper. The fact he is doing it in just a pair of skimpy black cotton briefs is a huge bonus. The thin material clings to his groin and buttocks, stretching taut, barely covering the lower half of his ass. My mouth parts, a small gasp bubbling up as he reaches forwards to grab a stray pair of socks under his dresser and the material pulls away from his crevice, giving me a glimpse of his hole.

I'm off the bed in record time, taking strides across the expanse of the room, dropping to my knees, gripping the taut round globes of his ass. I pull them apart, catching the cotton material with my thumb and pulling it to one side then driving my tongue into his hole.

Tyler gasps, lurching forward, his hands going up to press against the wall in front of him, instinctively pushing back against my tongue. He reaches back and pulls my head to him, trying to get my tongue deeper. "Fuck Lukas, are you trying to kill me?" he breathes heavily.

"What a great way to die though." I smile against him, my face buried between his ass cheeks. I rub my tongue across his opening and kiss and suck until I can hear him begging me for more. "What do you want, baby?"

"Hnngh!"

I laugh and pull away from him. "I don't think that's a word you know," I say slapping his butt gently.

"I need you to shut your mouth and fuck me now," he gasps.

I stand up, unbuttoning my trousers as I go and pulling out my already hard dick. "I need to go get the lube, be right back."

He twists around and grabs my arm to stop me from leaving. He sinks to his knees and engulfs my dick in his mouth. Sucking and slurping along the length, making it shiny with saliva. He massages my balls whilst holding on to the base of my shaft with the other. He looks up at me, his pupils dilated and dark.

"No time for that, just fuck me." He stands, turning around and putting his hands against the wall, sticking his arse out towards me. I spit into my hand, rubbing some moisture against his already wet hole and sliding a single digit inside him. He is so tight that my cock jumps in anticipation. "Take your finger out of there and fuck me now Lukas!" Tyler's voice drips with desperation.

Lining up with his hole I push forward sharply, my dick popping past the initial ring of muscle until I feel him grip my dick with his ass. "You're so fucking tight sweetheart, you have to relax. I don't want to hurt you." He moans and slams the wall with his fist.

"I know you love me, I want it to hurt a little. Please fuck me." His voice sounds harsh with need. I grab his hips and force my dick the rest of the way home until I feel my Levis against his ass. "I need to come," he shouts, his hand reaching down to grab his dick. He begins to jack himself off quickly, the intensity in his movements making me start to thrust into him like a horse out of the gate. I try to match his speed but he is tugging on his dick so fast.

"Do you want me to cum inside you?" I ask through harsh breaths.

"Yeah please, I need it. Give me it," he cries out, "Oh fuck I'm gonna cum."

My balls pull tight against me, I'm right there with him. "Fuck, me too!" I thrust into him once, twice, three times more. My cock swells as I empty into him, sweat dripping from my head onto his back. I hear him call my name as he starts to pulse jets of cum from his thick throbbing shaft.

I sag against him, completely exhausted. I hear him chuckle. "What?" I ask against the skin of his back, not moving from my hunched position.

"Good job it's laundry day." he chuckles.

Curious, I look around him to see he has cum in his basket of laundry. I laugh and slowly pull out of him. He winces as I pop out. I reach down and rub his used hole with my fingertips. Feeling myself there leaking out of him, I smile.

"Wait," he says, opening one of the drawers of his dresser. He pulls out a small metal object. "I have an idea." He reaches behind him and gathers a small amount of cum onto his fingers, smearing it on what I now know to be a small metal butt plug. "Now you'll know you're still inside me when we are out tonight," he says winking, reaching back and sliding the plug into him. What should technically be quite gross fills me with a sudden heat and desire to drag him back to bed and fuck him for the rest of the night.

His words suddenly hit me. "We're going out?"

He frowns at me. "Remember, you said you would meet me after work for a drink?" He looks at me expectantly and I pout, remembering we've made plans that do not involve us falling back into bed as soon as possible.

Tyler had suggested we go out for a few drinks later that evening to a bar close to the café where he worked. It's a well-known gay bar whose primary clientele appears to be eighteen to thirty-something gay guys or rowdy hen parties. The split seems to be about 50/50. Why parties of women on hen nights think that gay guys want them invading the clubs is anyone's guess. The guys in this club *are* looking for any type of connection they can find, albeit a romantic one or just a one night stand, and a hen party won't provide either of those. The gay guys in the club take it in their stride though, telling the girls they are beautiful and "Hey Girl!" or "Hey Queen" it to the best of their abilities to give the girls their fill of a 'true gay experience' for the night.

We enter the bar on a particularly busy Wednesday evening. As soon as we walk in, I can feel the stares on Tyler as he stalks his way through the bar. I feel the hair on the back of my neck rise and my blood slowly starts to boil beneath my skin. I quickly shake off my irritation. I have no claim over Tyler, we had both agreed to not put labels on anything. I wish now I had a fucking label maker cause I'd cover him in the word 'mine'. Tyler can do whatever he wants, and I'll just have to be fine with it. *Liar.* Tyler presses his stomach up against the bar, leaning forward slightly to see what they have in stock in the fridges.

"What can I get you handsome?" The sultry voice comes from the very attractive, well-muscled bartender currently perusing the goods and leaning across the bar, his eyes overtly gliding across the tight jeans stretched across Tyler's ass and the narrow strip of skin exposed as his T-shirt rides up. Is everyone going to hit on my... on my what? My date? My friend? My boyfriend?

This is going to be a very long night.

Tyler politely smiles back. "Do you guys have any Brewdog Punk IPA?"

"We sure do. Is that all I can do for you?" The douche actually winks at him. My fists clench at my sides, and I register slight pain in my palms. I'm certain that any tighter and I would draw blood.

Tyler turns around to face me. "Do you want the same?" I grunt and squint my eyes, nodding slightly. Looking at me slightly confused but wary he turns back to the bartender, "Two please."

The bartender nods and eventually passes the drinks to Tyler. We work our way through the crowd and find a seat on a lower level with a small table between us.

"Are you ok?" Tyler asks with a furrowed brow.

"Yeah I'm fine," I say, my mood improving a bit now I have him all to myself. "So, what do you want to do tonight?" My shift in mood seems to quell any concern that he has, his smile brightening his face.

"I don't know, maybe a movie at my place? Max will be home, but I think she is staying over at Peter's later so we will have the place to ourselves." He wiggles his eyebrows and gives me a cocky smile that basically strokes my dick in all the best ways.

"Why are you so sure that you are going to get lucky?" I tilt my head and take a mouthful of the pale ale.

"Oh I don't know, I guess I just..." is all he gets out before someone's voice booms:

"Tyler!" I snap my head to the side to see a huge guy walking down the few short stairs towards us. Tyler turns his head towards the incoming visitor before turning back towards me quickly mouthing the word *Sorry* to me. "Where the actual fuck have you been hiding?"

The guy is a tank, around 6 foot 5 and built like a brick shithouse with a shock of long jet black hair trailing across his face. He looks like he's just stepped right off a Greek god's pedestal.

"Hey Mike," Tyler says, standing up to greet him, putting a hand out, but having it slapped away and being pulled into a fierce embrace with strong fingers digging into his back and waist. It takes everything in me to not to get up and remove the guy's hands from Tyler and drag him back towards me. A sudden piercing pain lances through my head, I bring my hand up to my forehead massaging the space between my eyes to dull out the pain. As suddenly as it arrives, it goes. I shake my head and then turn my attention to this *Mike*.

"So where have you been?"

Tyler pulls away from the hug but smiles sweetly at the guy. "I've been around, work and studying takes up a lot of my time."

It bothers me that he doesn't just say that he's been spending his time with me. I need to pull my shit together. I'm acting like a needy douche and I need to get a hold of myself.

"I feel like I haven't seen you in a lifetime." The guy reaches across and squeezes Tyler's shoulder. My foot automatically starts to tap against the floor whilst I take another big gulp of my drink. "We should catch up soon, maybe grab a drink or something." Yeah, there's definitely history between them. I can feel my fist squeezing around the glass, my breath starting to come in short sharp huffs. Yeah, that's for sure the unreasonable side of my brain, jealous that anyone has ever touched him before me. Why the fuck couldn't I have found him just about to join the priesthood or something?

"Yeah that sounds cool, I have been super busy but I could grab a drink sometime I guess." There is a level of uncertainty in Tyler's voice as if he's trying to gauge my reaction. I can't seem to take my eyes off where the guy's hand is still lightly resting on Tyler's shoulder, gently massaging it. Before I do something I would later regret I stand up and push back the chair.

"I'm gonna go grab another drink," I say whilst polishing off the can in my hand, "I'll let you guys catch up." I quickly make my way up the stairs and head towards the bar. But alcohol isn't what I need, air is. I make a quick turn and head outside the bar, taking a seat on one of the bistro chairs. I put my head in my hands, willing my heart rate to slow and the sudden fever in my head to cool off.

A cold hand presses to my neck, I lift my head to see Tyler standing there. "Hey is everything ok?"

I stand and move a couple of feet away from him. I know I'm acting like an asshole, but I can't stop myself. "Yeah I'm good, everything ok with your friend in there? Sorry I just wanted to give you guys some privacy."

Tyler smiles and moves a little closer to me. "I didn't need privacy, I needed to see if you were ok."

The insecure little man in my brain does a victory dance that he chose to leave the muscle god in the bar to be with me. "Are you guys... I mean were you... you... like you know... Was he someone you were dating?"

Tyler closes the distance between us and gets into my personal space, pressing his groin against mine causing a sharp breath to escape my lips. His hands travel up my chest, and he settles his palms on my cheeks, forcing me to meet his gaze.

"If you are asking if I dated him and other people before you, then the answer is yes. If you are asking if I'm currently dating him then you're an idiot. You're the only person I want in my bed at the end of the day and the only person I want to wake up to in the morning. So no, I am not dating him. I'm dating you, you moron," Tyler chuckles and his tongue came to swipe across his bottom lip. He pulls my head forward and presses a kiss to my lips, teeth nipping at me lightly. One hand moves back and presses against my abdomen, his fingers finding their way under my T-shirt. He trails light, gentle kisses up the side of my face, his tongue mapping the outer rim of my ear before breathing heavily.

He links fingers between mine and pulls my arm around him and down, beneath his waistband. I feel the ridges of the buttplug still planted deep within him. "Does that answer your question?"

This man is going to kill me. I nod at him before reaching up to take his hand.

"I believe you said something about movie night and getting lucky." I nearly trip over my feet dragging him from the bar.

Chapter 19.

Tyler

Today was supposed to be about me showing him one of my all-time favorite spots in all of Manchester, about sharing a special place that meant a lot to me. So how it's ended up as such a clusterfuck is beyond me.

"So we both have the day off work, we could right now still be in my bed getting up to god-knows-what and you've brought me out to study?" Lukas grumbles, taking the coffee from the Starbucks barista.

I nudge his side and kiss his cheek. "Trust me, you're gonna love it. And we are not going to study! It's just a really beautiful library."

He scrunches up his eyes and nods. "Fine, I'll take your word for it."

I've been coming to the John Ryland Library for a few years now, the Gothic design inside coupled with the magical feel of the great hall with ancient books lining the walls gives me goosebumps whenever I visit. I sometimes spend hours just browsing through the old manuscripts or touring the changing exhibits on local history. It's become my go-to place if I just need to get away and think. Until now I've never taken anyone there with me, wanting it to be something that's just mine. Something is different now, I want to share everything with Lukas, which is why I want to show him this amazing place. Somehow I know, taking him with me will make this place even more mine.

We make our way down historic Deansgate, pausing every now and again to browse shop windows, his hand never leaving mine. We finally reach the side visitors' entrance to the library as the heavens open and a torrential rainstorm comes from nowhere. Pulling me through the automatic doors and past the visitors' desk, Lukas brings us to a stop in front of the bank of elevators.

I feel him rubbing lazy circles with his thumb across my palm. He pulls my hand behind and around him; forcing me to stand directly behind him, he maneuvers my arms around his back so I'm pressed along the length of him. I tighten my grip around his waist and my nose finds its way into his hair. He moans almost silently and pushes back against me. "I fucking love you," he whispers.

I feel my pulse kick up a notch as I reach around, turning his head towards me at an awkward angle, but not caring as I just needed my mouth on him, taking his in a blistering kiss as I gasp against his mouth, "I love you too." I take this moment just to bask, remembering that due to his past, our history and my stubbornness we nearly missed our chance. I'm so fucking glad we didn't. I press one last kiss against his cheek.

The elevator dings, opening on an older couple of ladies who gave us curt nods and a knowing smile as they make their way to the visitors' center. We travel to the top floor, strolling casually through the exhibits. I show him around my favorite parts of the building, traipsing along the great hall, noting the amazing neo-Gothic architecture on each of the archways above, the searing lights from the huge candelabras down the center of the room. "This really is something isn't it," Lukas says, unable to tear his eyes away from the magnificent stained-glass windows at the center of the room. I'm beyond happy that he's taking just as much pleasure from this place as I have in showing him it.

The library has always felt like one of the most romantic places I've ever seen, which to some people might seem slightly odd due to it being a Gothic library with cold stone facades. It's the history though that blows me away.

A philanthropist called Enriqueta had commissioned the library in the eighteen hundreds. She had moved to the North of England from Havana, Cuba with her family years before. She had fallen in love with a local merchant John. At the time however, he was in a committed, loving relationship with his wife Martha. Enriqueta spent a lifetime watching him from afar, even becoming friends with his wife Martha. Sadly Martha had died in her seventies, leaving John a widower. A year later Enriqueta could not take it anymore and declared her love for John. They were married a year later. He showed her his love for charity, expressing his desire to provide the public with a huge library so everyone had an opportunity to learn. Sadly their marriage would not be a very long one. He died never having realised his dream, leaving Enriqueta a wealthy woman. She invested her wealth into building a massive library in the heart of the north of England, holding the naming dedication ceremony on the anniversary of their wedding day. The John Ryland Memorial Library. I stare up at the statue of Enriqueta and smile.

"Come on, I want to show you this really cool candelabra in this crazy-as-shit staircase." I take his hand and lead him from the room, excited as a child dragging his parents around the school on a parent / teacher evening showing off their work. Making our way through the building we come upon a huge black iron candelabra casting amazing shadows over the stone walls.

"Go on stand next to it, it'll make an awesome Instagram picture," I said with an almost sarcastic drawl. We had established earlier in the relationship that he was a bit of a social media fiend.

"Shut the fuck up... but yes I will," he says with a shy grin. I go to push him lightly on the shoulder when a shout from behind startles me and I end up thumping him with a lot more force than I had meant to.

"Ford! Is that you? You dickhead where have you been?" I watch as the color drains from Lukas's face as if someone has opened a tap and I'm watching all the blood run out. The voice itself carries a hauntingly familiar tone, one which settles on the periphery of my brain but refuses to give itself a name. I slowly turned around to put a face to the name when Lukas does that for me.

"Irwin is that you! Jeez Caleb how long has it been?" I move behind Lukas as he talks, my subconscious 16-year-old brain taking over and trying to make me become as small and insignificant as possible. I peer over Lukas's shoulder and see Caleb making huge strides towards us, with a petite beautiful girl around our age in tow. With shoulder length blonde hair in tight curls swept in a loose tie on top of her head and sharp angled black-rimmed glasses, she appears to be what most teenage boys would imagine if the words 'sexy librarian' are mentioned.

"I don't know, about a year and a half." Caleb turns back around to the sexy librarian, "Lukas here was my best friend in high school, but dropped me like a hot piece of shit when he got accepted at University of Manchester on the Psych course we both applied to, but only one of us got in." Caleb jokes, but I couldn't help but agree with his description of 'piece of shit'.

"Lukas this is my girlfriend, Lydia." Lukas reaches across and shakes the girl's hand, his fake-as-shit smile plastered all over his face, the one I had come to hate. "Aren't you going to introduce me to your ma…" I think the word 'mate' was about to come out of Caleb's mouth before it drops open and appears to hang against his chest. "No fucking way… I mean no offence but… anyways hi, what the fuck are you two doing together?"

Caleb sounds rightly shocked out of his initial reaction and maybe unintentionally sneering his words.

"Hi," is all I can muster apparently. I want to say so much more, but 16-year-old me is in full fucking control right now, and I want to crawl up into a ball and disappear. I shrink further behind Lukas. "Tyler here went to school with us," he leans back and explains to Lydia. Went to school with? More like their high school past-time was trying to destroy Tyler.

"Oh cool, so you all hung out?" she smiles. It's an innocent enough question, but Lydia has no idea about the can of worms she's just opened. Caleb looks quickly from me to Lukas, unsure of how to answer, but also I guess unsure of how not to come off as a monster to his girlfriend whom he's obviously trying to impress. Otherwise what the absolute fuck is he doing anywhere near a library? He hadn't exactly been academic in high school and as he pointed out himself, hadn't gotten into the university. Ok, it makes me feel like a jerk to think that way, but I'm being vindictive and protective.

Caleb clears his throat and chuckles nervously. "Not exactly, Tyler was a bit of an outsider in school, me and Lukas hung out with other kids, you know, football, rugby kids and all those types."

Did he just say 'a bit of an outsider'? Understatement of the fucking century. I was absolutely popular, just for all the wrong reasons. If you wanted to take your frustrations out on someone, then you kicked Tyler's ass, if you had just gotten yourself dumped by one of the girls on the swim team, it was Tyler's ass you kicked the crap out of that day. So yeah, I guess you could say I'd been a bit of an outsider.

I do remember in the last few months of high school, Caleb seemed to back off his usual taunts and beatings, somehow seeming plaintive as he watched his friend do the job instead. There had been one time that he had helped me to my car after a particularly rough afternoon. I assumed at the time he was looking out for his friend and thought that if he showed me a scrap of kindness that I would be less included to report an assault. He was right. I'd not said anything.

I finally turn to see how Lukas is reacting to the current turn of events. I notice he is looking everywhere but at me, his features stiff. An icy chill sweeps through my body and settles in my heart.

"What, were you like one of the drama kids or artsy kids then Tyler?" Lydia continues to smile, and if it isn't for her terrible choice of boyfriend I would have thought she was a really sweet person.

"Erm not exactly," I think I say with a certain amount of conviction, though part of me is pretty sure I'm whispering. Lydia gives me an odd look, a mixture of confusion and empathy that for some reason is starting to piss me off. A sudden realisation crosses her face as she looks between the three of us.

"I'm guessing these guys weren't the nicest to you back then?" she grins sadly and makes for a playful punch on Caleb's upper arm, maybe also giving it a bit more force than the gesture intended.

"It's all good now, we're all grown up." Caleb smirks and nudges Lukas's arm in the same kind of way Lydia had his, "From what I remember, our Tyler had a bit of a thing for Lukas here. Well I guess not so little anymore - wow man you beefed up! Managed to win over Lukas in the end huh?"

Lukas's eyes darts up to meet mine and panic floods his face. Then with one sentence he manages to destroy any stability I had started to feel with him. "He wishes, just bumped into each other. Making sure I keep my back to the wall with this one, you know what these gay guys are like around a hot piece of ass like this." Lukas laughs and reaches across to ruffle my hair.

I'm fairly sure I can hear the sound of my heart breaking, the sting behind my eyes building until I'm sure I won't be able to stem the flow of tears. I need for no one to ask me a question at that moment or speak to me as I know my voice will break. Holding back a sob I smile, heave out a sigh and shrug.

I can feel him tense next to me, anguish coming off him in waves. I won't look at him, I can't and more than anything I don't want to look at him. The guy whom I've spent every waking moment with, the guy whose hand I held and whose hair I stroked as he cried against my chest, is now someone I want to go through the rest of my life never laying eyes upon again.

I hear Caleb chuckle nervously, he shoots Lukas a sharp look. He pats Lydia hand; she is holding onto his bicep giving Lukas a murderous glare. She drops her hand as Caleb moves around Lukas and comes to a stop in front me. "Listen Tyler, I know it's the last thing you want to hear from me, but I was a complete dick back in school. My brother came out a few years ago, after I left high school."

I look up to see shame in Caleb's eyes mixed with pain. "He came home and said someone had given him a black eye after they had seen a profile of his online. I wanted to kill the fucker. That was until I realised that had been me not so long ago with you. I told him about you, about what I had done and he didn't speak to me for like a week."

"Shit man really?" Lukas pipes up, Caleb ignores him and continues.

"I can't take back those years, I would if I could but all I can do is say how sorry I am and hope that you won't think I'm a total dick forever." He holds out his hand; it hangs there for a moment. I see his shoulders sag and I dart out my hand to shake his. A smile lights up his face. " I'm really glad to see you're doing well man!"

That is as much as I can handle emotionally for that day, so before anyone could witness me breaking down I gather my composure as much as I can and nod very quickly at Caleb. "Thank you. That means a lot. Anyway it was nice bumping into the *three* of you. I have to get going. Lots of work to catch up on. Later."

Without looking in Lukas's direction I head out the building as quickly as I can. I don't turn around to see if he's chasing after me because a part of me knows that he won't. A part of me knows that whatever embarrassment he's feeling will make him stay for a few minutes to catch up with an old friend.

What the hell has happened? One minute I'm showing him a part of myself that I've never shown anyone and the next I'm finding it difficult to breathe. I leave the library and head back onto the busy road before I can no longer hold back. I let out a harsh sob, my hands coming to cover my mouth. Thank god it's the middle of a workday and the road is relatively empty.

I receive a few concerned glances my way, but people have meetings to get to and targets to meet so no one bothers me. I wipe my eyes with the back of my sleeve and hurry towards the tram station. If someone had asked me how I made it home safely that day I would not have been able to tell them. I find myself standing outside my apartment, unsure how long I've been standing there, my heart racing a thousand miles a minute with the key in my hand poised to go inside when the door opens in front of me.

"Tyler what's wrong?" Max stands before me, immediately reaching out and guiding me into the house. Fuck her for knowing me so well - I look at her face, full of concern for me, and whatever wall I had built in that short time comes crumbling down and only then do my tears truly begin to flow.

Chapter 20.

Lukas

No no no no no no! What the fuck have I done? I know as the words are leaving my mouth that I'm tying a hangman's noose around my own neck. I see the life leave his eyes, I see the spark I had put back into those eyes diminish. With every millisecond that passes I want to die a thousand times more. I cannot stop myself though. I let him leave and I watch the person that matters most to me walk out of my life.

It had been instinctual, like I had no control over what I was doing. Like an age-old defense mechanism kicking back into life. I'd come out after high school and am openly gay to everyone at university, even my god-damn family know I'm gay. Confronted with an old high school friend on whose opinion and acceptance I had craved for my formative years, I turn back into the part of me that I hated the most.

I slam into the same barrier in my head. Who did I want him to see? The closeted gay kid who was so ashamed of himself that he tortured someone like him for years just to stay on top of the social ladder, or the dumb high school jock who was just same old Lukas? My brain had apparently chosen for me.

I stand in front of an old friend, staring vacantly but not processing any of the words he's saying. Finally I feel pressure against my arm and look down to see a small delicate pale hand gripping my bicep. I look down to see Lydia regarding me with concern.

"Are you ok? We kind of lost you there for a minute." I'm not even sure if I respond in any meaningful way to her question or just stare at her slack-jawed. Panic continues to rise within my gut. I feel a full-blown anxiety attack about to break to the surface, my heart begins to pound rapidly and I take in big gulps of air. I feel like my lungs are empty and I'm about to pass out. My head spins and I place my hand over hers in an effort to gain some equilibrium.

"I have to go, I'm really sorry," I try to say between gasps of breath. I move away from them swiftly with only one goal in mind, to find him and lay myself down at his mercy. I look in every room of that damned library, thinking I can see him everywhere I look, but he's just gone. I run to the entrance of the building and into the main road. Barely avoiding being hit by an oncoming bus, I start as a hand reaches out and grabs me from the road.

"Are you ok man?" Caleb looks at me wild-eyed. "You nearly just died, like right there."

My head darts from side to side, praying to anyone who would listen to make Tyler still be there somehow, to understand and to forgive me again, but he isn't, he's just gone. I don't think I could have stopped the tears from sliding down my face then if I tried, which I didn't. I cannot care less who can see me, who might judge me, I'm a piece of shit who deserves whatever is coming to me.

"No, I'm not ok," I tell him simply, "I think I just ruined the best fucking thing that ever happened to me." I run both my hands through my hair and shake my head not sure exactly what to do.

"You have to go find him Lukas, like right now." Caleb eyes me cautiously whilst gripping my shoulder. "*Go.*"

I find myself an hour later standing outside Tyler's door, soaked to the bone as a torrential downpour has decided to further mar the day. I feel a chill settle in my chest which I don't think has anything to do with the worsening weather. Reaching out, I knock gently on the door and wait with bated breath. The door swings open to reveal Max, standing there, her eyes settling on me. I had hoped to see anger, rage or fury. Something I could relate to, as it had been what I was feeling towards myself for the last hour. But all I see is sad disappointment.

She moves back away from the door, giving me entry into the apartment. A horrible foreboding like standing in a relatives room waiting for news that you did not want to receive, but sure was coming. "He's in his room. He's waiting for you," she says simply and shuts the front door, making her way into the living room and closing the door behind her.

I stand outside Tyler's room and knock.

"Come in." His voice sounds so different, smaller somehow. I push the door open. Tyler sits at the edge of his bed, his feet crossed at the ankles whilst he holds onto a small brown bear I had bought him from a stall at a Christmas market we had visited in Manchester over the holidays.

"Hi," I say cautiously. He doesn't look up at me, just takes in a deep breath.

"Hi," he mutters back. I need him to look at me, I need him to see me, I need him to smile at me, I need him in my arms and my nose in his hair breathing in the scent that I had come to rely on for my own wellbeing. The more I look, the further away he seems. I need to do something now to fix this shitshow I have created. To stop this ball of lead in my stomach expanding.

"Listen, about what happened I'm so sorry, I don't know what happened." He turns to look at me, the hurt and betrayal in his eyes telling me that had been the wrong thing to say. He stands up from the edge of the bed and moves slowly towards me, his fingers playing with the small red bow at the bear's neck. He looks almost like he is becoming sicker and sicker with each step he takes towards me. When he's barely a foot from me, he reaches out and grabs my hand, placing the small bear in my palm and closes my fingers around it.

"You know exactly what happened. You were ashamed to be with me, you were ashamed of what people would say if they saw you with the loser from high school. You were ashamed of what it would say about you, to be with me." His voice is a hoarse whisper, his eyes drop to the floor. "What's worse is that you made me feel like you did back then, ashamed and small. I made a promise to myself that I would never be that person again."

He moves backwards away from me, fuck that, I wasn't letting this go without a fight. I reach out to snag his elbow and pull him forcefully towards me. His body crashes against mine, he gasps as my hand wraps around his waist, the other resting against his chin, tilting his head up so I could finally see his eyes.

"Please baby, I'm so sorry. I fucked up." A sob bursts from my throat without warning and I feel dampness at my cheeks. I'm not sure when I had started to cry, but I could feel my anxiety at his ongoing resistance to settle in my arms. The thought that this is ending is tearing me apart. "Please... Please just give me another chance... Please." I dip my head so that my lips slide against his. The kiss is brief before he pulls away from me. His hands presses firmly against my chest.

"I'm sorry too, but no. This," he says, motioning between us, "this is over." Tears streak his own face as he dashes at a stray tear with the back of his hand.

"No it can't be over, I just found you again. You're mine," I beg, my hands flailing uselessly at my sides, the instinct to reach up and wrap in my arms strong, but I can see he doesn't want that.

"I was yours," he says, his voice barely a whisper.

I place my head in my hands, a blinding agony roaring to life, feeling like someone has jammed a hot poker in my skull. I shake my head as if trying to shake the truth from it. I can't lose him. It had only been hours since I'd had him warm in my arms, his smile just for me.

"We can still be friends, but I need to be with someone who wants to be with me, no matter what, who is not ashamed of me and feels lucky that I'm with them. That just isn't you." I don't know how to respond. I want to scream at him that that person *is* me, that I'm not ashamed, that I wake up every morning in his arms counting my blessings that I just got to wake up with him, but after what I had done how can I expect him to believe me?

"We just need some time away from each other. I need that time," he says, motioning towards the door. There's no point in saying anything now, so I nod my head and leave his room and his apartment. How had today gotten so spectacularly fucked up?

Oh right, me, that's how.

Chapter 21.

Tyler

"Listen Mary, it's been forever. You've been holed up in this place for too long now. We need to get you back out there in the real world. You need to meet a new guy already. If nothing, for a bit of harmless fun," Max pleads with me. We've been watching a movie side by side on the couch in pure harmony up until a few minutes ago when she suddenly seems to have a brainwave. "If you don't get back out there and use what god gave to you, it will drop off and your butt will close up."

I giggle and choke on the water I'm sipping. "I'm not a hundred percent sure you know how anatomy works, you know?"

Max shrugs and continues, "I just don't want you going all Miss Haversham; I don't want to end up finding you covered in rats whilst wearing a wedding dress in a few years is all." She rests her hand on my thigh. "So that's why we are going out tonight."

I groan and draw the blankets from the back of the couch over me and around my shoulders.

"Before you say no, can I just tell you that you don't have a choice in the matter. So get your stinky ass in the shower and make yourself presentable. We have men to conquer." I groan again and throw a cushion gently at her head.

"You know just because you said I can't say no, it doesn't mean I can't actually say no, right?" I tell her pointedly.

"Come on Linda it's time." She gives me a pretend-sorrowful look. "It's time to get back on the horse, or the penis." I laugh, but I still feel the sharp stab of longing in my chest after all this time.

Three long, long, looong months had passed since I ended whatever was starting between myself and Lukas. It was not so much that I had ended things, but more like I had ejected Lukas from my life completely. I knew in my gut that it was the right move for me. I had thought that I had shed the old Tyler since leaving high school, that somehow that person had been destroyed and from the ashes this new version had arisen, or another analogy that's not as super gay as a bright flaming phoenix.

In the few hours that had followed the incident with Caleb and Lydia, I had started to feel the way I had every time Lukas had assaulted me or told me that everyone would be better off if I disappeared or killed myself. I started to feel that maybe I wasn't the strong, funny, handsome guy that I had come to recognise when I looked at myself. I allowed those thoughts to take root for just a moment before I pulled myself out of the darkness. Any relationship that ran the risk of me feeling like I was worth less than I truly am, was toxic and not for me. So I had to say goodbye.

Max throws her legs off the couch, pushes herself to her feet and turns to me. "I'm giving you an hour and a half and then I'm dragging you out, in whatever state of readiness, so I suggest you get a move on." She throws the pillow back at me, her face resolute in a way that tells me that I really do not have any choice in the matter. With a resigned sigh I make my way to the bathroom. "If you decide to wear hot pink cut off shorts and a tight white halter top, don't cause that's what I'm wearing."

We find ourselves two hours later in Belle's, a basement pub in the city. It's a local haunt popular with the LGBT community, owned and operated by gay men and women. Belle's is kind of like Cheers, if Cheers were designed with gold, red and green art nouveau cladding on the ceiling and local artwork on the walls, giving the impression of a very poor man's Palace of Versailles. Now whilst it isn't the most fashionable or aesthetically pleasing of locations, the place has a great vibe, which is why people keep coming back.

The security guard stopped us on the way in, making sure that I knew it was a gay bar and that me and my girlfriend would need to be cool with guys kissing.

"Oh I think he will be ok my love," Max says sweetly, "I once walked in on him taking one in the ass and one down the throat, so a little kissing shouldn't bother him too much."

I facepalm and push Max past the open-mouthed security guard.

"Stereotype much?" Max whispers to me.

I laugh and tap her on the shoulder lightly. We push through the crowds of people grinding against each other in what looks like a desperate attempt for half the club to get inside the other half. The acrid smell of smoke from the smoke machine by the DJ booth permeates the air as it moves in waves across the heaving dancefloor. The bass from the music travels through the polished wooden floor, making its way through every cell in my body until I can feel the music in my core.

Max pushes me chest first against the bar, using me as a boost so she can shout our drinks order to the heavily glittered guy working behind the ornate wooden bartop. Dressed in a skintight white vest, denim short shorts and chunky brown boots, he's the picture of Village People, construction worker realness. I glare as four shots of tequila are poured and placed in front of us.

"Are you joking?" I scowl at Max.

"Come on, you won't throw up every time." She bites her lip and crosses her fingers. I narrow my eyes and pick up one of the shots.

"If I do then you're paying the laundry bills." I grab the pot of salt that's been placed between the shot glasses and hold a lime wedge between my fingers against the cold glass. Licking the back of my hand, I sprinkle salt until I can see a thin white bed of salt crystals gleaming off my skin in the disco light. We clink glasses, lick the salt and shoot the amber liquid. The heat travels to my throat and I gag in reflex. I place the lime wedge between my teeth and suck greedily, hoping the citrus will burn away the alcohol currently churning in my stomach.

A deep laugh sounds behind me and I turn to find the source. The first emotion that hits me is guilt as I notice the tall blonde gorgeous specimen standing in front of me. I allow my gaze to take it all in with a potentially creepy slow once-over. Around 6 foot 4, his height means I have to look up slightly, which gives me goosebumps as I immediately imagine that with his muscular frame and looming height, he could quite easily pin me down and have some fun with me. The crooked smile playing on his face can only be described as smoking hot, his angular jaw and pointed nose perfectly placed on his tanned face. His eyes are so light blue that he almost has an otherworldly feel. He fills out his red V neck T-shirt to capacity, to the point where I fear or hope that at any moment he might hulk out of it. His tree trunk thighs are encased in skin tight black jeans. He's completely my type in almost every way, my dick immediately takes notice.

"Something funny?" I raise my eyebrow and bite the inside of my cheek.

"No," he winks at me, "I was just admiring the view."

"But I was faced away from you," I tell him plainly.

He fucking winks at me again as he says, "I know." Picking up his drink, he moves through the crowd until he merges with a group of other guys standing near the edge of the dance floor.

"Can you believe that douchebag?" I ask Max, pointing over my shoulder at the cheeseball currently laughing with the group of very attractive men, like an Abercrombie photoshoot that might happen at any moment.

"Oh you mean the guy who got my nipples hard by just proximity?" she says. "No, I don't know what you mean." She turns back around and picks up another drink.

Six drinks in and we're both quite clearly feeling the effects, swaying to some truly terrible music coming from the DJ booth as we move about the dancefloor. I spot the guy from the bar stealing glances at me, and I would be lying if I said I wasn't stealing some right back. Max insists again and again that I should go over and introduce myself properly. But I can't shake the feelings of guilt and wrongness, like I shouldn't even be here, like I have someone at home waiting for me. That heavy crushing feeling once again settles around my heart.

I miss him, I miss Lukas so much. That much to everyone who knew me was obvious, but mostly I'm angry at him, and yes, I'm also a little angry at myself for falling for him so quickly. I watch Max give me a sullen look which gives me pause. I decide I need to shake myself out of this funk before people start avoiding me due to me suffering from a fatal case of being a boring pain in the ass.

"I'm going to get a refill. Same for you?" I say, holding up her empty bottle of Rum Beer. She nods to me and smiles, immediately going back to dancing. I make my way through the crowd of writhing bodies towards the bar. I lean across the wooden surface, trying to get the bartender's attention. The construction worker saunters towards me with a grin on his face. I can easily imagine that that grin and that body has gotten him a lot of action in his time.

"Hey stud what can I get you?" The smile drips with sexual promise, his tongue grazing across his bottom lip. The pure animalistic energy radiates off him, so intensely that I find myself just staring at him. His grin widens as he lifts himself across the bar, leaning seductively over it. I worry he's about to make a move and I will just crumble with nerves. Before any of that can happen however, a deep growl sounds behind me.

"Here, let me get those for you." The voice is deep, husky and a hair's breadth from my ear. I shudder and let out a light groan. A warm hand finds its way to my waist, moving me slightly to one side to make room for its owner. I turn to see the blonde Abercrombie guy staring daggers at the hot bartender.

Realising what he has just said I shake my head and lower my eyes, giving just a slight smile. "No don't be silly, I'm getting drinks for me and my friend. I can't ask you to buy our drinks."

He grins back at me and I don't realise he still has his hand at my waist until he gives it a slight tug towards himself. He whispers against my ear, "You didn't ask, I offered." He turns towards the bar and gestures to the bartender. "Can you just give me another of whatever he has ordered and take it off that please," he says, passing his credit card across the bar.

The bartender gives almost a pouty look before snatching the card.

"You don't need to say thank you for that either," he says, gesturing to the hot guy currently getting our drinks order.

"Thank you for cock blocking me? Or cock blocking him?" I ask incredulously, eyeing him.

"Sorry, you mean you wanted that guy?" he asks, his brow furrowed.

"I guess I would have liked the option," I retort, hoping I don't sound too put out.

"I guess I will just grab my card and leave you to it then," he says, his face falling slightly.

"Don't be an idiot," I laugh, reaching across to put a hand over his impressively large bicep. His face lifts and his smile creeps back on his face. The bartender comes back and slides our drinks across the bar. He turns back to face me and my breath hitches. He is devastatingly handsome, those eyes a blue that I didn't think existed in nature. He reaches out and offers me his hand, which I take and shake a little too vigorously. "Ben," he puts simply.

Slightly speechless and still in a daze over the color of his eyes I mutter confused, "Who is Ben?"

His laugh rumbles low and gravelly in his throat. "I am," he laughs and pauses a moment. "That's my name," he says when I still haven't said anything but continue holding his hand. He squeezes my digits lightly.

I try to shake myself out of my stupor and let go of his hand. "Ben, nice name." *Lame, Tyler!*

I turn back towards the bar and squeeze my eyes shut, cursing my stupid fucking brain and mouth. I hear Ben clearing his throat to get my attention. I turn around and try my best attempt at a casual smile.

"So is your name a secret? Do I have to guess?" *Doh!*

"Oh god I'm really sorry, I'm Tyler," I say whilst thrusting my hand back in his and shaking it harder than before. He laughs and looks down at our joined hands.

"I think we already did this bit, not that I mind holding your hand at all." He winks at me yet again and my dick starts to take notice, plumping and pushing against the zipper on my jeans. Once again I push back against the feeling that I'm somehow cheating on someone whom I owe absolutely nothing to at all. I take a large gulp from the beer in my hand.

"So were we just going to stand across the room and eye-fuck each other all night?" His boldness stops me in my tracks, and I splutter beer down the front of my green T-shirt, wiping at my chest and giving him the stink eye. His laugh is deep and real.

"Apparently not," I manage to get out after wiping the beer from my chin, "as we are currently here having a drink with each other."

He narrows his eyes at me, his smile crinkling the sides of his mouth. "That's only because I made a move."

I shrug my shoulders and give a shy smile. "Maybe that was my plan all night, to get you to come over to me."

He laughs and nudges me with his hip, leaning with the bar against his back, his elbow resting behind him on the smooth wooden surface, his shirt stretching across his impressive pecs and causing my mouth to start salivating like a pavlovian dog.

I have to stop staring at him like a creeper. "I should probably get back to my friend; I forgot to bring her drink over, she might have died from thirst by now or tried to turn some gay guys straight."

Ben smiles and nods before reaching forward and putting his hands into my pants and pulling out my mobile phone... Why do people suddenly think that's an ok thing to do now? I remember Lukas had done something similar months ago. He keys in his number and hands me back my phone. "I won't intrude on your night, but I want you to call me. I want to take you out if that's ok?"

A small part of me instinctively wants to say no, the feeling like I belong to someone else strong in my consciousness. I breathe deeply and smile. "I would really like you. I mean that... that... I mean... What I mean is that I would really like *that*." Jesus my mouth is trying to kill me. His smile lights up his face as he tries to hold back a laugh.

"I'm definitely glad you would like... *that*." He moves towards me and his hand snakes up my waist and comes to rest on my neck. He moves forwards as if to kiss me, but his mouth diverts at the last second, his breath smoothing across my jaw and settling at my ear. "Don't forget to call, now will you?" he whispers before planting a soft kiss against my ear.

I visibly shudder and then curse myself for being so damned responsive. I blush a deep crimson and shake my head. "I won't, I promise."

He nods as I pick up the other bottle and move back towards Max. I can't help but look over my shoulder every few seconds to check that he's still watching me from across the room like I'm a needy whore.

Ben leaves the bar shortly after with his group of friends, looking over his shoulder and grinning at me on the way out. I spend the rest of the evening forensically dissecting our interaction for any signs that he might be a total dick. We leave the bar ourselves around 2am, Max climbing on my back declaring that she is going to ride me like Seabiscuit.

"You have to see him again, you know that right?" she slurs in my ear. "You can't let good man meat like that go to waste. It's like against the gay law. I think Lily Savage comes and puts you in gay jail if you do shit like that."

"I don't know if I'm ready to date anyone yet," I sigh, the warmth of her breath and the smell of booze wafting over my face.

"Date? Calm down Blanche, you know you could just ride him like I'm riding you right now, but with more penetration." I laugh, reaching behind me to lightly smack her leg.

"Yeah I suppose you're right," I muse.

"Just fucking do it, and when you do I want all the details, gory ones and everything." Her voice trails off like she might be about to fall asleep on my back. I sigh and heave Max up my back. The feeling of drool on my neck confirms she has nodded off. I trudge through the night time air in search of a cab, resolute that I'm definitely going to be moving on.

That is how I come to find myself a week later sitting across from Ben at Mama Gita's, an Italian/Indian fusion restaurant on the outskirts of the city. I'm not exactly sure who the restaurant is trying to cater for but the oddity and uniqueness of the place certainly draws a crowd. We've been texting back and forth for the last few days after the meeting in the bar, after I'd worked up the courage (i.e. been bullied by Max) to finally message him.

It's been nice, flirty and easy. Which is definitely something that has been missing from my life - easy. I don't fail to notice how every now and again his foot will *accidentally* brush up against mine. "So you seem really nervous, I hope I don't make you nervous cause that's not what I'm going for," he suddenly says from across the table, his chin resting on his joined fists.

"Well I'm bound to be a bit nervous; I mean look at you," I admit shyly, "everyone in here has checked you out at least once". Ben is very much a next-level heartthrob, like he belongs on the front of some bodice ripper taking a damsel roughly.

"I don't think we should go down this path," he says suddenly, making my heart sink, "cause then I will say have you seen you, and then you will say something nice back and then we will be all in a tizz. How about we both just accept we are both not difficult to look at and thank our lucky stars we found each other?" I appreciate and enjoy how direct and uncomplicated he was, Ben's so easy to talk to.

Is easy and uncomplicated the stuff dreams relationships are made of though? With Lukas I'd felt like I was on fire, and initially I'd assumed that sleeping with him would douse the flames, but each time it only made the fire hotter. My body would reach for him when he was near, like magnets drawn to each other. Ben provokes a different kind of response, his directness and manliness stoking the embers of interest in my groin. I feel I can breathe with him, like he doesn't overwhelm my senses so much that my head swims with thoughts of him. I am attracted to him though, you would have to be blind and stupid not to be.

"You alright, I feel like I lost you there." Reaching across the table he rests his hand over mine, which appears to have been making a tight fist on the table. He squeezes slightly and regards me cautiously. I definitely owe him an explanation as to my weirdness.

"Listen before this goes any further I have to tell you I am just getting out of a... let's say difficult relationship. I'm just getting back out there, but obviously I am coming across a bit weird, so if you wanna make a run for it now, I wouldn't blame you cause I'm kind of a mess and I don't know if I'm going to be good company to be around, and I have weird friends who like to threaten the guys I date, so if you just want to save yourself now I would totally..." is all I get out before Ben reaches across the table and grabs me by my collar, hauling me practically over the table and crushing my mouth to his. I let out a soft groan into his mouth, the other diners in the restaurant fading into the background and blinking out of existence. His tongue seeks entry into my mouth which I gladly give, sliding against mine, sending stars shooting across my field of vision.

He tastes of peppermint which is entirely pleasant. The kiss stops as suddenly as it begins and he moves back into his seat. "So now we've got that out of the way maybe we can move this along?"

My brain stutters and I can't seem to form a rational thought, my lips still tingling from the sensation of his against mine. "Sorry I was rambling, thanks for shutting me up," I smile.

He tips his head and the crows' feet around his eyes crease with his wide smile. "Any time, glad to be of service."

The conversation and wine flow naturally, and I feel more relaxed than I have in a long time. If my cock isn't so damn interested in the guy sitting across from me, I would have said he would have made an amazing friend.

"So you think you want to do this again?" His brow furrows as if afraid to hear the answer.

"What, you mean eat here again? Yeah sure the food was amazing. With you? Mmmm I don't know about that." His knee nudges me under the table as he narrows his eyes in my direction. "Of course, I want to see you again, are you kidding? But are you saying the date is over?"

I catch a glimpse of his tongue as it runs across his bottom lip, his gaze fixed on my mouth. "Well that's really up to you, isn't it."

I have a giddy feeling, like I'm on the kind of date you go on when you're really young and you have all this self-doubt, but it all seems to be working out. I try my best for a coy smile, but the heat from his stare has me reaching down to rearrange my trousers to make myself a little more comfortable. I raise my hand to call over the waitress. "Cheque please." My heart starts to pound in my chest so hard that I would bet anything that everybody in the restaurant can hear it, like something from the Tell-Tale Heart.

With the intensity of his eyes on me and my dick growing by the second, precum leaking from the tip, I look around instinctively like I have something to hide, but I'm not exactly sure what I have to conceal. *Liar.*

I'm really considering going through with this, of lying with another man. Being naked with another man. Letting him touch me in all the places Lukas had, letting his kisses and his touch wash it all away. At least now I can hold on to the fact that the last person to be with me like that was Lukas. If I go through with this I won't even have that anymore.

"Are you ok?" Ben asks, leaning across the table slightly. "You've gone a little pale, should I just call you a cab? We don't need to rush anything." Is that what I want? Visions of Lukas's face pass across the surface of my mind, the pain etched on his face making me want to fall to my knees and ask for forgiveness. Then I begin to realise I have nothing to ask forgiveness for.

I'm a single guy, on a date with a nice guy who likes me and who doesn't care if everyone around us knows that he likes me. That kiss across the table, the way he claimed my mouth like it belonged to him is something that Lukas should have done all those months ago. So, fuck him right?

"No, I'm fine seriously."

Ben looks down at his shoes as if expecting the brush-off that comes with a statement like that. "Oh, I understand, well don't worry…"

I cut him off at the pass, "AND! I don't want it having any negative impact on us. So yeah I maybe got lost for a second to make absolutely sure that this is what I want, as I don't want to mess you around," I reach across the table and put my hand over his, "and this is what I want, *I want you*."

The heat returns to his eyes with a vengeance, and he raises his hand. "Can we get the cheque over here please!"

Chapter 22.

Lukas

To say I've been an asshole to my friends and family over the past few months would be understating the level of dickish-ness I've shown, but somehow I can't seem to reign it in. I've been snapping at anyone who has shown an interest in my wellbeing or who simply just wanted to help.

The idea of leaving the house at times just seems so incredibly hard that I've spent days at a time locked in my room, leaving only for bathroom purposes or to forage for food. The sunlight hurts my eyes and my head aches just thinking. I've lost some weight due to my lack of exercise, and Dawn's pointed out I look like Casper's crack addict dead cousin. If I could find a way to pin the cause of my social isolation on any other living human I would do it, but I only have myself to blame.

I sit at the edge of my bed, my hands resting on my thighs, staring into the middle distance. My emotions swing in a heartbeat from hating myself to hating him: hating him for leaving me, for not understanding, for not giving me a chance to explain. I love him though, so I know I'm full of shit.

My phone rings on my bedside table, the piercing shrill of my ringtone like a knife inside my brain. The light illuminates the room, causing a momentary flash blindness before my eyes readjust back to the dark room. I've made sure the room is pitch black by my purchase of the blackout curtains currently blocking out all sunlight. I'm going full emo. The number on the screen indicates it's the university again; my attendance has been sporadic recently. I grimace and put the phone to my ear.

"Can I speak to Lukas please?" The voice of my lecturer booms out of the phone, making me pull the handset away from my face and rub my ear against my bicep.

"Hi, yeah it's me." I wait for what I assume will be the ceremonial tearing open of a new asshole she is about to give me.

"Listen Lukas, I think it's probably a good idea that you come into my office during clinic hours, we really need to talk about how, if possible, you might continue on with your studies. You have missed quite a lot Lukas and I've tried my utmost to be understanding, but I'm not sure how you are going to catch up or if I have the kind of time you would need to help you catch up."

My vision starts to blur, the now familiar pounding in my head increasing in intensity until a dull roar echoes in my ears. How dare this motherfucker try to kick me off the course? I'd had perfect grades until all this shit started to happen. So yeah, I've missed a few deadlines and my grades have taken a bit of a hit. "Are you serious, I spoke to you about everything that was going on with me and you said you understood for fuck sake!" My hand tightens its grip on the handset as if to stop myself from launching it across the room, the pounding in my head intensifying and building behind my eyes till it borders on agony.

"Lukas, please do not take that tone with me. I am just trying to help you out here and I don't appreciate being spoken to like that by one of my students!" She finishes the sentence with a huff as if daring me to continue.

I know I should apologise but the pain splitting my head apart drowns out all logical thought, everything I think I should say is thrown out the window as I spit, "Fuck you!" down the phone and end the call. I move backwards onto the bed, my arm covering my eyes to block out the light of the phone screen. Climbing to the top of the bed and throwing the duvet over my head, I squeeze my eyes shut till sleep takes me.

I wake several hours later, the sunlight now extinguished in the darkness of the night. I reach across the bed and look at my phone to see several missed calls and texts from my friends. Throwing the phone down the end of the bed, I groan into my pillow. I need to get myself out of this quagmire that seems to be dragging me down more and more. I fling my legs off the side of the bed and make my way through the house into the kitchen. Dawn sits leaning across the island, stirring what appears to be an empty cup given I hear the clattering of a spoon against porcelain.

"Hey Dawn," I say as cheerily as I can muster but it likely still sounds like a groan. The headache from earlier is almost gone but a slight pressure still makes its presence known. Dawn turns her head slowly to look at me, the expression on her face a mixture of surprise, anger and confusion, as if she couldn't believe I had dared speak to her.

"*Hey Dawn?* Are you fucking kidding me? Don't you dare fucking speak to me Lukas." The venom in her words literally makes me take a step back towards the kitchen door.

"Hey, what the hell have I done? Did you hear me shouting at my lecturer earlier or something? I mean I know the way I spoke with her wasn't cool or anything, but I didn't think you..."

She moves quickly around the stone island separating us in the kitchen and stands just inches from my face. "Are you off your fucking meds or something?!" she yells at me, her breath hot on my face, "I'm talking about what happened earlier when we spoke, or when I got verbally abused in your room."

She could have been yelling at someone else for all the sense this is making to me. I go to put my hands on her arms but seeing her flinch at my approach I stop and hold them up in supplication. "Listen Dawn, I have no idea what you're talking about. I haven't seen you since yesterday."

The crease in her brow furrows a deep river across her forehead, her anger slowly morphing into deep confusion.

"Lukas, I came into your room earlier to see if you wanted any dinner ordering. You bolted up in bed, looked me dead in the eye and began screaming at me. I think some of the words I caught were *Go fuck yourself* and *Bitch* and *Whore*, at which point I decided to leave you the fuck alone. Are you saying you don't remember any of this?"

I feel my face drain of blood and a cold shiver courses through me. I feel faint on my feet and move towards a bar stool to sit down.

She sees the panic on my face and her eyes widen. Surely, she has to have been making this up.

"Listen, I was as shocked as you look right now, you've never spoken to me like that before. I thought you were still asleep at first but you were talking directly to me and you said my name, so I knew you weren't."

My heart begins to race as the drumming in my head begins to re-emerge. This time I feel my stomach doing somersaults as her words settle heavily in my chest, that feeling that creeps up your throat that tells you that you have moments before you throw up hitting me like a ton of bricks. I launch myself from the stool and empty the contents of my stomach into the sink. A tingling sensation begins at the base of my spine, working its way out to my extremities. I know this is not right but I'm powerless to stop it, my legs begin to tremble as I struggle to gain cohesive thought. My vision begins to blur and dim as I stare into the wall behind the sink. The darkness takes me, and the last thing I hear before everything goes black is a friend's voice screaming for help.

*   *   *   *

I wake a short time later to the sound of Dawn's voice speaking as a warm hand presses against my forehead. I hear her reciting our address for some reason and telling them I wasn't responsive. I mean I've been asleep, why would I be responsive, and why is my bed so hard and cold against my back? I want to tell her that I can hear her, but I can't seem to move my body. Panic starts to well in my gut as I fight through what feels like quicksand just to open my eyes.

"Hang on, I think he is starting to wake up!" she yells at someone down the phone, "Lukas, can you open your eyes, please Lukas can you just open your eyes for me…" The sound of her scared voice makes me want to comfort her, which frustrates me further as I still can't quite work up the energy to move. My eyelids flutter open as I take in the sights around me. I appear to be lying on the kitchen floor, the cold tile pressing hard at my back and head. My head continues to pound, but now a new pressure clutches at the base of my skull like a balled fist pressing against my neck.

I open my mouth to ask Dawn what's happening but I make an unintelligible sound and groan in confusion and frustration. I'm scared and although Dawn is kneeling next to my head, stroking my hair gently, all I want at this moment is Tyler's smiling face to make me feel safe. I don't exactly understand how I know he can make me feel that way, but I just do.

I shiver and Dawn gasps. "I'm going to go get you a blanket ok!" A tear runs down her face and I feel a wave of fear. I don't want to be left alone here on the floor. I don't know if I'm dying; I don't know what it feels like to die, but I don't want to be alone when it happens. Is this what my father felt as he died surrounded by unfriendly faces on the grounds at the prison? I grab at her arm and my hand encircles her wrist. She must see the pain in my eyes as she settles back to her knees, pulls the fuzzy purple jumper she is wearing off and places it across my chest. "I'm not going anywhere ok," she soothes in a shaky voice.

An ambulance arrives a short while later, my mobility coming back slowly until they have me lying on a stretcher as I'm wheeled from the house. A small shallow part of me feels the shame wash over me as I see neighbors giving me pitying looks of concern. The paramedics lift me into the back of the van and Dawn follows me in, making it perfectly clear to them that they would not be going anywhere without her. Even in my daze and anxiety, a small smile spreads across my face as I note that my friend is always fiercely protective, no matter the situation. The paramedics seem to put up a small fight only to acquiesce in the face of her bravery.

The A&E is Crazy Town. They wheel me straight through to the Majors department, the triage nurse moving quickly after being told I had been slurring my speech in the back of the ambulance. I hear them talking about the possibility of thrombosis or stroke and needing clot-busting agents. I think they are going for a quiet whisper, but every word they speak serves only to ramp up my anxiety.

After a CT scan they make the decision that I'm not going anywhere tonight, even after my insistence once I get my voice completely back that I'm ok and probably suffering from a severe case of stress and being a total pansy. From the CT rooms I'm sent to stay in a medical assessment unit, a dire place filled with overworked nurses, frightened junior doctors and yawning consultants moving from bay to bay hearing the same patient histories whilst tapping out god knows what on IPads. Through some joyful turn of events I'm placed in a single side room. I look down to the end of the bed to see my friend nervously wringing her hands, getting up every now and again to pacing the small room. A jovial-faced Asian nurse pops her head into the room to inform us the doctor will be around in a minute or two to discuss my scans.

Dawn sits down on the bed next to me, her hand resting gently on my thigh. "Listen, no matter what happens I'm here for you, right? I mean there isn't going to be anything wrong with you, you're just fine, but I'm here anyway ok?" I give her a small lopsided grin and look down at her hand.

"Listen, I think it's pretty shitty that you wait until I'm vulnerable and in a gown with my ass hanging out the back to put the moves on me." I reach down and remove her hand slowly, dropping it like a lead weight on the bed. "I'm just not into you that way." I shrug my shoulders as she gasps, her hand coming up to cover her mouth.

"I'm sorry I didn't mean to..." she begins before she sees the smile spread across my lips. "You absolute dickhead!" she laughs giving me a small punch in the shoulder.

"It would be best if we didn't assault the patients whilst they are under our care," a voice travels from behind the curtain, the material moving along the metal rail to reveal a short lady in her mid-thirties, tight curls swept on top of her head secured by a bright pink clip. Large glasses frame her smiling face. "I'm Kate, or well I guess I'm Ms. Long, or Dr. How about you just call me Kate?" Her thick Birmingham accent has a friendly lilt and the cute twinkle in her eyes is soothing and even appears to relax Dawn, whose hands have stopped compulsively wringing. "I'm a neurosurgeon here and I've come to talk about some of the problems you have been having and discuss the scan results from last night, do you mind if I sit?" She indicates to the small chair by the side of my bed. I nod and smile, noticing a blush creeping up the side of her neck.

"I can leave if you would prefer," Dawn says, moving to stand up. I reach forward and pull her back down next to me and place her hand in mine.

"Stay. Please?" I ask. She nods and turns back round to face Kate.

"So, can you tell me a bit about what's been going on recently. Has anything like this ever happened before?" Kate questions flipping through my notes.

I shake my head. "No, I mean I've not been feeling myself for a couple of months,but, well I have been going through a bad break-up and haven't really wanted to see people."

She inhales a bit and seems to consider this before moving on. "Can you tell me a bit more about that, not feeling yourself, I mean?" she probes, her glasses slipping down her nose, only to be pushed back up by the tip of her pen. I think back to the last few weeks and how out of sorts I've been.

"Well I guess I have been quite moody." Dawns snorts before giving an apologetic look. "Well a lot moody. Been feeling a bit depressed. Stayed in my room a lot as the light has been hurting my eyes a bit, which I put down to staying in my room. Some headaches I guess." Kate begins to write things down in a language I could only assume is English. Doctors seem to have their own language it seems, as I crane my neck to get a look at her notes to find some indecipherable squiggles that might as well have been hieroglyphs.

"Have you had any weakness at all? Arms, legs?"

I think back and there have been some times where I felt like I was so tired I could not get out of my bed and my arms and legs felt heavy. "I think so yeah, I put it down to me sleeping a lot and just feeling really down." Dawn again punches me in the shoulder.

"Again, can you at least wait till I'm out the room before the abuse starts again," Kate scolds her. "I don't want to fill out any more forms than I have to."

"Sorry," Dawn winces.

Kate closes her notepad and sets it on the floor beside her. "Lukas – can I call you Lukas or do you prefer something else?" I wave my hand as if to say it doesn't matter. "We ran some tests as you know yesterday. We took some blood and we did a CT and an MRI scan." She opens a brown manilla envelope that she has with her, fishes out the scans from inside and attaches them to a light display at the far end of the room. I sit up to get a better look, like I know what the hell I'm looking at. "Now we had the neuroradiologist have a look at your scans and your results have just come back."

She squints at the light box and runs her hand across the dark film. "Can you see this small round looking blob at the front of the head?" She points out what appears to be a circular lump on the scan. 'It's called a frontal convexity meningioma."

I take in a deep breath, Dawn's hand tightening around mine. "Well that doesn't sound like a happy thing," I say, trying to force some levity into the rapidly sinking mood in the room.

Kate smiles tersely and turns back towards the scan. "Unfortunately Lukas, it's a type of brain tumor."

The words sink into me slowly, and I can feel the circulation to my hand being slowly cut off as Dawn grips me tighter and tighter.

"Now typically these tumors are quite benign, and we would normally just watch to see if they grow, or in cases where they are affecting motor function or speech, we can perform surgery to remove the tumor. However, we got the results of your MRI back a little while ago and it indicates that your tumor is malignant. It's cancerous."

A heavy breath leaves me, almost like a sign of relief. It's as if I've been waiting for this news and have been on tenterhooks for someone to just say the words. I can feel the remaining fight leave my body. I hear Dawn weeping behind me, but I can't feel anything. I am numb. I can't say it's a pleasant experience, but it's not the complete breakdown I would have been expecting either. I can't decide what would have been worse.

Kate comes over to the bed and sits facing me. I look past her to see the scan still displaying the small enemy on its surface. "Now it is in its very early stages so we hope that we can take the whole thing out surgically, you are young and fit and we will do our best to help you beat this. We do have to run some more tests, but I have spoken to the consultant in charge and we would like to begin treatment as soon as possible." The small flicker of hope in her eyes is something I feel I can cling to, so I nod and blink back the tears threatening to suddenly spill from my eyes.

"I'm all yours Doc. Whatever you think's best." My eyes once again drift back to the scan on the screen. It's time to fight.

Chapter 23.

Tyler

I hand the two hazelnut lattes across the counter to the middle-aged silver fox and watch as he sidles up to his presumably-boyfriend, placing the cups on the table in front of him and dropping a kiss on his nose. I pine for something I can't have as I watch hands sneaking under the tables to lace fingers together, heated glances across the table making all sorts of promises to each other without saying a word.

People seem to get like this when the university year is ending, and the summer season is on the horizon. Maybe it has something to do with the change in weather; the rainy spring season is coming to an end and the sun is finally here. Whatever it is, I'm feeling it too. Things have been going great with Ben. We've been seeing a lot of each other and with him, everything seems so comfortable and safe.

It's a nice sweet feeling when you know you're able to say what's on your mind to your boyfriend and don't have to worry about some dramatic event unfolding around us. Yes, the passion that I'd felt with *He Who Must Not Be Named* was nowhere to be seen, but we don't always have to have that all-consuming, teeth on edge, jaw twitching passion for each other, right? *Right?* I sneak a glance at the door and feel my cock fill with the memory of Lukas's - *Shit I said his name* - firm hands grasping me and his soft lips pressing against mine on that first day... *That damned first day.* I shake my head and smile as I see another customer approaching the counter.

The sound of the a door opening grabs my attention; expecty to see yet another fucking loved-up couple marching through the shop I sigh. My mood picks up slightly as I see Ben breezing through the door, a smile stretching across his face as he sees me. I muster what I hope is a beaming grin for him as he moves around the side of the counter.

"Hey there, sorry I just wanted to see you." His arms come around my waist, pressing a soft kiss against the corner of my mouth. It's no hardship to have this amazingly handsome man press his hard body against you as if your heat is the only thing which can keep him warm. However, I do miss the electric jolt that I used to get whenever Lukas barely even touched me, and I feel like a shit, comparing them all the time. I know that it's not fair on Ben, he's a great guy and deserves so much better than the half-assed attention he's used to getting from me. I kind of resent him for letting me treat him so coldly sometimes.

I reach up and grab him by the back of the neck, pulling his head towards me and crashing my mouth over his, making a decent effort, I think, to make sure he knows he is being claimed. My tongue slides alongside his, our teeth clashing. He moans into my mouth before pulling away and moving back a few feet. "Woah, I think I should surprise visit you at work more often," he smiles at me and my heart breaks a little for him.

"Yeah I think you should totally do that," I grin back at him. "I have a couple of hours left on my shift yet, wanna catch up later?" He seems surprised which confuses me for a second, until I realise that this is potentially one of the very few times I've requested to see him, normally he's done a lot of the planning and I tend to go along with whatever he requests. I know I'm being such a dick towards him. He's all in, one hundred percent and I'm barely giving fifty percent.

"Yeah that sounds nice, what were you thinking?"

I try to think of the most date-appropriate thing, something that'll scream 'couple'. "I don't know, maybe a movie, then we could grab dinner and then maybe go out for a few drinks?"

The smile broadens across his face. He moves back towards me and cups my cheek with his hand. "Sounds perfect. Listen I have to go, but shall I pick you up around 7pm tonight?"

I nod and give him one last quick kiss before he leaves the shop. The intense feeling isn't there; the attraction is, and as the old saying goes, fake it until you make it.

Later that evening after the movie, we decide to walk to the restaurant. His hand slips down between us and laces our fingers together, his hand warming my own. I really love how open he is with me, how able to show his affections without any need for privacy or secrecy. Like he's proud to have me standing next to him. Still however I have this annoying pang of guilt, as if I'm doing something wrong, almost the feeling of cheating.

"So, what did you think?" His voice shakes me from my thoughts, he couldn't be reading my thoughts could he? Then I realise he's obviously talking about the movie. We'd settled on a horror/slasher flick over the other 1000 romantic comedies that seem to be showing in the theatres recently. At present I still can't handle the happy-ever-afters without getting unproductively cynical about the whole thing, to the point where I come across like a bitter divorcee who had lost half my shit.

"Yeah, I thought it was good, just what I needed you know?"

He looks at me cautiously and tilts his head. "What you needed was to see a campsite full of teenagers get butchered by a serial killer with supernatural powers?"

I realise I sound a bit nuts and giggle. "No but you know, it's nice to think there is someone even more stupid than you out there. I mean did you see that bit with the girl, whose friends had all disappeared, was running through the woods, in the middle of nowhere screaming for help? Who exactly was she calling out for? What was she trying to do, if not give her location away to the killer?"

Ben's eyes soften and he puts his hands on my shoulder in mock solidarity and gives me a pitying look, "I think maybe you are reading too much into this babe." The endearment should have made me feel all jellylike, instead it gets my hackles up a bit.

We make our way through the streets of central Manchester towards a bar in the business district that Ben had introduced me to a few weeks earlier. I reach the entrance to the bar and reach out to pull the door open, trying to be gentlemanly when a hand closes around mine. A surge of electricity zaps up my arm making me jump back in surprise. A deep baritone voice to my left mumbles, "Oh I'm sorry, after you."

I turn towards the familiar voice, the one that has all my engines firing, the voice that caresses my ears as if it were stroking my dick. I don't want to look, but I am helpless. *Stupid eyes!*

"Lukas?" I gasp, then what sounds like a small sob breaks from my throat, and I cough to disguise it somewhat. Lukas's eyes shoot up to meet mine; he obviously hasn't been looking where he was going either. He pulls his hand back and retreats into a surprised Dawn, who is taking up the space behind him.

"Oof!" she grumbles as she reaches forward to steady Lukas. I can't stop my eyes from drinking him in, like a starving man confronted with prime rib. He is just as gorgeous as ever; my brain screams at me to shove my tongue in his mouth, to taste him again, to feel his tongue tangle with mine. I can't bear the effect he has on me: the desire that has me balling my hands at my sides to stop myself from reaching out for him, to run my fingers through his hair, grab his hand, snake my arm around his waist or anything that would give me the contact with him I craved.

Even though I can't think of him as anything else other than heartbreakingly beautiful, I'm a little taken aback by his appearance. I notice prominent dark circles under his eyes, his face is paler than normal, and he's lost what looks to be about 15 pounds. It doesn't impact his overall attractiveness, but it looks as if he hasn't been sleeping properly. My body is desperate to go to him, to wrap my arms around him and not let go.

"Tyler," he says simply, his voice hoarse and tired, his eyes heavy and lidded as if he has just woken from a long sleep. "Hey, how are you?" There's something really wrong here. I can feel something is off with him, I would have expected him to seem a bit happier to see me. The one thing I know about my Lukas more than anything else is that his eyes shine when he looks at me; now there is a dark hollowness that just isn't him. Wait, *my* Lukas? Not anymore. My heart sinks into my gut.

His appearance suggests he has taken the breakup harder than me… the thought *Narcissist Much?* runs through my head. He might be stressed from work, getting over the flu, any number of things. This is out of character for Lukas however.

"Yeah I'm doing well, hey Dawn." I wave over Lukas's shoulder at Dawn, who's smiling guardedly behind him. She gives me a quick wave of her hand and nods. "So how have you been?" Lukas's eyes narrow as he looks at something behind me.

I turn quickly to check if someone might have been coming up behind me. I'd completely forgotten Ben existed. "Oh my god, Ben! This is Dawn, and this is Lukas. We went to school together." I see the wince on Lukas's face, as if my description of him actually hurts. Just that fact alone makes me want to fall to my knees to ask for forgiveness. Then I remember why it is that we aren't an 'us' anymore and my anger peaks just slightly.

An awkward silence descends between the four of us; no one speaks for what seems like hours, but is more likely 30 seconds.

"So Tyler, what are you guys up to this evening?" Lukas barely manages to drag his eyes away from mine, glancing around to Ben.

"Just out and about really," Ben says, trying to break the awkwardness.

Dawn pipes up from behind Lukas, "Yeah us too, we are celebrating Lukas's first successful..." is all she gets out before Lukas breaks in quickly.

"Test score... from uni... did well you know."

Dawn bites her lip and looks at something behind her, however I feel that she is just trying not to meet my eyeline.

Ben grins at Lukas, warm and genuine. "Congrats mate." Lukas dips his head, so slight that if you blinked you might have missed it. Ben puts his hand on my shoulder. "Listen, I'm gonna go on in and grab us a table, do you want anything to drink babe?"

I visibly shrink as if I've been caught doing something bad. I bite the inside of my cheek and smile faintly at him, telling him to get me whatever he's having. As he disappears through the doors of the bar, Dawn points to the door after him and tells Lukas she's going to do the same thing, leaving me and Lukas standing awkwardly side by side, leaning against the front window of the bar. Time seems to stretch like the distance between us, neither of us saying any words but the tension palpable in the air around us. I can't stand this atmosphere between us, there shouldn't be this awkwardness, we've known each other forever.

"So how have you been really?" I turn my head slightly to try and meet his gaze, my hands swinging aimlessly at my sides. I see him grimace a little and then shake his head as if deciding not to say what he wanted to say.

"I'm not going to say fine, but I don't want to go into it." His mouth presses into a tight line. "Tricky subject, next?"

I suck air in through pursed lips and try again, "So I haven't seen you about much. What have you been up to?"

He shrugs and presses his head back against the glass. "Not much you know, just this and that. Tried to keep myself to myself but Dawn was not having any of that." He smiles, the warm inviting smile giving me the butterflies in my stomach that I've been hoping would return with Ben at some point.

However, seeing the defined cut of his stubble-lined jaw around his full lips, I want nothing more in that moment than to push him hard against the glass and slam my mouth down on his. I want to feel the burn of his coarse hair as it grates against my flesh. I want him to mark me and to claim me as his again. And yet, I might be a lot of things, but a cheater I am not.

"How about you? I see you have got yourself a new... friend." He says the last word with a sneer, and again I want to be pissed off that he's throwing any negativity my way, but the fact that he's a bit jealous makes my heart ache and sing in equal measure.

"Yeah I guess," I start, "Listen I don't want things to be really weird between us, I can grab Ben and we can go somewhere else."

Lukas puts his hand up and rests it on my forearm, I suck in a breath and my eyes immediately fall to his lips. "Don't be silly, we can all be adults." He drops his hand away quickly as if on fire. "We should probably go inside," he continues, "never know what they might think we are getting up to." Heat flares behind his eyes as they traverse every inch of my body. *Fucking kiss him you fucking idiot, grab his face and kiss him. Take him home and bury yourself so deep inside him until he knows that he is yours and no one else's.*

I grind my teeth together, my jaw aching as I fight every natural instinct in my body. A horrible thought goes through me that he might go into that bar and meet someone, he might take them home and put his strong hands on them. He might put his mouth on someone who isn't me, someone else might get to see how beautiful he is when he falls apart. Someone else might get to feel the warm strength of him as he presses himself against their back and he might hold them instead of me as they fall asleep. I fight back and sob and clench my fists at my sides.

He opens the door to the bar and gestures for me to go ahead of him. I have to squeeze past him to get in through the door, my side pressing against his hard chest and groin. My whole body responds by heating, I feel like I'm on fire. *Oh God, how am I going to get through tonight?*

During the evening, I feel Lukas's eyes boring into me; I'm attuned to his presence like no one else's. It's like a magnet that's suddenly found its pair again and is being drawn by forces that I don't understand. Everything in my body is yelling at me to go to him.

Ben puts his hand on my shoulder, shocking me out of my reverie. I jump at his touch. He pulls his hand back slightly and gives me a concerned look. "I was just going to see if you wanted to dance with me." I feel like such a shit. I see the truth behind his eyes, he recognises there has been a history between me and Lukas, and my obvious interest is hurting him.

I turn and walk into his arms, resting my chin on his broad chest, looking up into his eyes. "I'd love to dance with you."

He looks down and beams a smile, and all I can think is that it would melt a million guys' hearts, tragically, just not mine. I take him by the hand and lead him through the crowd onto the dance floor.

As we reach the dance floor, the music changes to a deep pounding bass beat, a slow sensual rhythm designed to make people want to fuck. I turn my back to Ben, pulling his wrist around my waist and holding his flat palm against my stomach. His body, always so responsive to mine, he pushes his crotch against my ass so I can feel his hard length against me. I push back against him, hoping to give him some sort of friction to relieve some of the hot pressure I had helped put there. He presses his body along the expanse of my back, his lips trailing up the side of my neck, his tongue darting out to taste the sweat and dragging it way up till he finds the shell of my ear. He murmurs hot promises about what he is going to do to me later that night; a smile tugs at my mouth and I gently bite my bottom lip. I groan and push further back into him.

As suddenly as before, my senses come alive, I feel the stare. Panic rises and bile creeps into my throat. My eyes scan the edge of the dance floor until they meet Lukas's glassy gaze, tears threatening to fall, his face hard and impassive. His mouth tightening into a hard line, he turns slightly to slam his glass on the bar and moves to leave the club. I want to die right then.

Chapter 24.

Lukas

I am not going to cry! Not going to cry! Not going to! Who the fuck am I kidding, the tears are streaming down my face before I get to the doors of the bar. I push my way through the crowd out of the club and into the blessed fresh air, the coldness hitting my face, giving me the shock I need to try and pull myself together. I move across the road to the fences on the opposite side that stop pedestrians from falling into the canal below. I lean over slightly, trying to catch my breath.

It had taken everything in me not to barge my way across the dance floor and prise the dickhead's fingers off my man and tell him to fuck the fuck off. This was before I realised that he's no longer my man, he is Ben's man. That was when I could feel the overwhelming, *oh fuck I can't deal with this now*, emotions bubbling to the surface and I knew I had to get out of there. I might not have been able to put my hands over him like I want to, like I *need* to, but I certainly don't have to watch some fuckhead do it either.

A warm hand skims my skin underneath my shirt. "Lukas..." Tyler's voice is like honey, soft and warm against my ear.

I move quickly away and turn to face him. "What the fuck man! Get off me!"

Uncertainty flashes across Tyler's face and he lowers his eyes to the ground. "I'm sorry... I... I just wanted to make sure you were ok."

That should have been a sweet sentiment, it should have been something a friend would do for another friend that should be accepted with appreciation. However in this situation I take it as well as a red rag to a bull.

"Why do you fucking care? Oh wait... you don't! Why don't you just fuck off and go back to your boyfriend, rather than come out here bothering someone who doesn't give a shit!"

A look of confusion which quickly morphs into anger twists Tyler's face, until he closes the gap between us and fists his hands into my shirt, his face so close to mine I can smell the sweetness of the alcohol on his breath.

"Doesn't give a shit? Are you fucking kidding me right now? Am I not the one who forgot all about our shitty past to make something between us work? Am I not the one who spent every day with you for weeks after we got back from Newmarket to make sure you were ok? Am I not the one who was so fucking stupid he let himself fall in love with you only to have you fucking throw it back in his face and act like he was nothing in front of your friends? So, call me what the fuck you want but don't you dare say I don't give a shit. If I wasn't still fucking in love with you..." That is all he gets out before I can't take any distance between us anymore. He's said he loves me and that's all that matters right now.

I snake my hands into his hair and bring his mouth to mine. My tongue darts into his mouth to taste him. I have a few seconds before he comes to his senses and kicks my ass. I have to make this a memory that might just need to last a lifetime. His hands ball into fists, gripping my shirt between us. A small gasp escapes him before a deep groan creeps up his throat. Like he has no control he pulls me closer to him, until a molecule of air couldn't pass between us. Our mouths fight for dominance over the kiss, neither of us willing to give an inch. His breath comes hot and fast against my mouth.

"Oh fuck, yes, I need..." he mumbles before pushing his tongue back inside my mouth.

I pull away from him slightly, just to see the lust-filled haze that swims in his eyes. "What is it? What do you need, baby?"

He groans deeper than before. I reach down to palm my aching cock that is pushing against my jeans, fighting to get out. He pushes into me again, his own hard length pulsing against my own. His hands dig into the muscles on my back, sliding down and gripping my ass. His palms full of my butt, he ruts against me. He attacks my mouth again like a powerful magnet is drawing him to me.

A loud crash sounds near the entrance of the bar, and a girl stumbles out followed by two of her very drunk friends, trying in vain to keep each other upright. Whatever spell that has fallen over us has now officially passed. A look of confusion and guilt twists Tyler's face as he puts more space between us.

I put both my hands on my knees and bend slightly, the kiss having taken it out of me as if I've just run a mile in under three minutes. "I shouldn't have done that, I'm sorry, you have a boyfriend in there," I manage to get out.

His eyes shoot up to meet my gaze, his face changing to anger in the blink of an eye. "Seriously Lukas, be more of a dickhead!" He begins to turn away from me, and I dart out my hands and grip his wrist, turning him back to face me. His head moves around, eyes looking anywhere but at mine.

"I just meant I kind of jumped you, I just missed you so fucking much." His eyes take on that lust-addled haze again. A smile tugs at the corner of his mouth and he looks like he is about to say something, but I continue, "but you have a… well you have a Ben and I didn't really give you much of a choice. I know we are over and I apologise."

Whichever part of my rant has hurt him, it shows on his face like he's been speared. He pulls his arm away from mine and holds it to his chest as if he's been burned.

"Fine! Have a good night Lukas," he says before retreating into the club. Again I've somehow managed to fuck this up, without even knowing this time how I've managed to go about it. I slowly make my way back towards the club when I see Dawn heading towards me.

"Maybe we should go somewhere else?" she suggests. Count on Dawn to read my mind. I nod and she links her arms with mine. We make our way through Manchester in search of a less complicated night out.

*   *   *   *

Ok so nurses and doctors are basically angels walking the earth, I just want to get that out there. However, right now I wish they would all go and fucking throw themselves off a fucking cliff. Maybe I'm just in a bad mood, maybe I have a bad attitude. Maybe it's due to the fact I'm in my second hour of chemo and I can't throw up anymore due to the fact that I'm fairly sure the only thing I have left to throw up are my actual organs, and they have just given me more some anti-emetics which have basically curbed that impulse. Doesn't stop you from feeling like absolute hot garbage though! Surprise!

Dr Long – Kate – has written me this course of treatment. *Bitch... or when I finally start to feel better... goddess.* She'd sat me down and told me the best course of action would be to treat the cancer with chemotherapy and then go in surgically if the mass shrinks as they hope it will, and remove the entire thing. She'd said she was very hopeful and the tumour had great margins. I'm sure all of that meant something to someone; all I can feel though is my head splitting in two, my stomach and throat on fire and aches gnawing away at every part of my body. Other than that everything's fine.

I sit in a small bay with Dawn frantically tapping away on her phone, no doubt caught in some battle with a 15-year-old girl from Russia on whatever online Nintendo DS game she's addicted to this week. Dawn's become my chemo buddy, never letting me attend an appointment alone, get in my own head or become too depressed. When it came time to shave my head when the chemo had started to make my hair fall out, she had held me for the longest time, then picked up the razor for me and made everything a little bit better. I may not have had my family with me all this time, but Dawn is more than family.

"Managing to beat Katerina, or Valeria or whoever it is you're struggling to overcome?" I murmur across to her as I struggle to sit from my usual lying down, eyes closed position. Dawn puts her phone down and comes immediately to my side, supporting my elbow as I sit.

"No, little bitch keeps on killing me, I swear it's a conspiracy!" she scowls, and I manage to chuckle.

"Yeah I'm sure that's it, I'm sure it's the CIA, MI6 and Triads all plotting to keep you from beating a child at Mario Kart."

Dawn pulls her head back and looks at me with fake shock on her face. "Well hello snarky bitch, we haven't seen you in a while!" I laugh and wince as pain lances down my side of my face. "Are you ok... sorry I..." is all she gets out before the curtain is pulled back and Kate comes into the bay.

"Why is it every time I see you two, one of you is hurting the other somehow?" Kate laughs and I shrug.

"It's how we show our love for one another."

She beams a little, then shakes her head and moves around to the other side of the bay. "Strange people. Anyway Lukas I'm guessing as always it's ok for Dawn to be in here whilst we discuss your case?"

I nod and move aside so Dawn can take the space next to me. Her hand instinctively finds mine and settles on my thigh.

"So how have you been feeling Lukas?" Kate starts off, and I can already feel the lead collecting in my stomach. I hate it when they start off with pleasantries, rather than just getting to the detail of why they're actually there.

"Yeah I've been fine, what's up Kate?" I hope to steer her towards the crux of her visit. She dips her head slightly and flicks through her notes. My nerves buzz underneath my skin, right to the surface until I can feel every breath of air that passes over the fine hairs.

"Well we have done more scans since we started your course of chemo as you know and we now have the results. It appears that the tumor doesn't appear to be shrinking as we had expected." Dawn's hand grips mine more tightly; I can feel her eyes on me as she moves closer until she is pressed right up against my side. "Now it hasn't gotten any bigger either which is a good sign, but I think the best course of action now is to be quite aggressive with treatment and surgery. If we can go in and get the whole thing then we will be golden, but you must be aware that with the size of the tumor you have, there may be some irreparable damage." Kate does appear to be hopeful, she reaches out and puts her hand on top of where Dawn's met mine. "We have become a little team here guys, I don't want you to get too down about this; yes it's not what we wanted here, but we aren't done yet. You're going to keep on fighting alongside me right?" Kate squeezes our hands.

Dawn smiles and nudges me gently. "Of course we are," she says, her fingers lacing in mine.

"So what do we do now?" I croak out.

Kate moves back to her seat and opens the notes in front of her. "I think we need to get you booked into surgery, like yesterday.

I'm going to book a theatre in the next few days if we have the availability and get this done, obviously there are some consent forms you will need to sign and a pre-op assessment by the anaesthetists, but other than that I think we are good to go."

I shrug and smile, it's the best I can manage. "Thank you so much Kate."

Kate lets out a deep breath before smirking wickedly. She closes her notes and places them on my bedside table, leaning back she lifts her legs and crosses her ankles on the edge of my bed. "So, another important thing we need to talk about." Her doctor persona slips away, and friend Kate firmly takes centre stage, "Dawn was filling me in on this guy you were dating." I turn to face Dawn whose eyes had widened like the proverbial deer caught in the headlights. Kate continues, "Yeah we had a chat about it the other day."

Dawn shakes her head slightly in Kate's direction *"SECRET*... Chat Judas," she grits through her teeth.

Kate blanches and sucks in her cheeks. "Oooh sorry, was this like a no tell situation?"

I chuckle and shake my head. "You are about to have a full-on look at the inside of my cracked-open skull. I'm not sure there are any secrets between us anymore."

Kate belly-laughs and leans back into the chair once more. "So have you spoken to him since you guys saw him last?" She quirks her eyebrow at me.

Dawn makes a sound that reminds me of a comic book *'PFFFT'* and then shook her head violently. "Nope he has not, he has just let him continue this doomed relationship with this Ben nobody... who is actually quite lovely and hot." Dawn looks away dreamily until I punch her lightly in the thigh.

"Hey we are on my side here," I remind her.

"So why have you not tried to speak with him again? It seems he was just as into the kiss as you were."

I sigh because I know exactly why I haven't called him, but I don't want to say it out loud as it makes me sound really pathetic. "I just haven't, ok." I've actually been dying to call/text/email/send him smoke signals for weeks now, but I just can't. I'm in a very vulnerable situation at the moment, and I know if he were here, I'll just lean on him for everything, because that was how he makes me feel. Safe, comforted and happy. Right now, I need to focus on the upcoming battles and not make moony eyes at my non-boyfriend.

Tyler has scolded me for this very thing before. After we had gotten back from my father's funeral, I'd spent a lot of time plastering a fake smile on my face to show the world that I was ok. There was a morning when all that changed.

I was lying on my bed facing the window. The sunlight was burning my retinas but I did not want to look away. It was the only thing that was stopping the tears from falling down my face and making me cry like a baby. I felt a warm heat press along the entire length of my back. A nose pushed into the soft hair at the base of my neck, hot breath trailing down my spine. Arms wrapped around my waist, pulling me closer to the solid mass behind me.

"Morning baby," he rasped into my ear, pressing light kisses against my neck and earlobe. I smiled against the sadness threatening to consume me.

"Morning," I murmured, though my voice sounded thicker than normal.

"Everything ok?" Tyler whispered. I reached down and squeezed the hand splayed against my stomach.

"Yeah everything is fine, so what do you want to do for breakfast?" I asked cheerily, moving as though to get out of bed.

He pulled me back down until I was flat on my back and he was leaning over me, his elbows resting on either side of my face.

"Listen, this stops now ok!" he said with a grave expression on his face, "It's been a day since your father's funeral and you either act like everything is business as usual or you make some silly comment about how everyone now has someone to blame and make a joke out of it." I went to move again but I was caged in by his arms. "You don't have to do this with me Lukas," he began, "nothing you're going to say or do is going to scare me away," **Liar**, "I'm here for you. Now I know it can't be easy the way your family treated you, believe me I wanted to jump across the room and punch every one of those fuckers who made snide comments or gave you those awful looks, but you don't deserve that." He began peppering my face with light kisses. "You are a good person, you are kind, intelligent, honest, loyal and I wake up every morning counting my blessings that I get to wake up next to a man like you." Something in me broke and I felt the tears start to fall down my face. He pressed his forehead against mine, locking me in place with his stare, as if he was going to help me shoulder the burden of the sadness currently threatening to rock my core.

But then he is gone; yes it was me who had fucked everything up, but he had promised me he wouldn't leave, and where is he? Shacked up with some dickhead.

Who am I kidding?

I'm still the dickhead.

I close my eyes and mentally prepare myself.

The knife awaits.

Chapter 25.

Tyler

You know that feeling at the beginning of a relationship when you can't wait to see the other person? You get butterflies in your stomach when you hear them coming up the stairs. You can't stop looking at them and will find any excuse to touch them. You get that tingle in your jaw and cheeks as a smile is always hiding just under the surface. As I look across the table at Ben in the small breakfast nook in my kitchen, I catch him stealing glances at me over the newspaper he's reading, and I realise that the feelings I'm waiting to experience are just never going to happen for us.

"Ok babe?" Ben murmurs whilst sipping his black coffee. I don't know why it irritates me, but why drink coffee black? There are so many things you could put in it, cream, milk, sugar, sweetener or syrups. It shouldn't annoy me, but it does. I guess I'm trying to find reasons to pull further and further away from him, but he is just so goddamn perfect.

I guess that Ben has been feeling it more and more recently, that I'm not sharing a part of myself with him. His touches seem hesitant and there is a sadness, almost, when we have sex. Like he has resigned himself to the fact that it is what it is.

"Yeah I'm good. So what have you got on for today?" I don't really care, and that is part of the problem. I should want to spend all my time with him, I should wonder what he's doing when he isn't with me, I should be having that talk where I demand that he dates no one else but me, but none of that is happening. When he isn't around I enjoy my time with Max, I enjoy my time alone. That is until my mind strays and thinks about what Lukas might be doing, who he might be dating, whose lips he has his pressed against. I grit my teeth and ball my hands into fists under the table so tight that I think my nails might pierce my palm.

"Not much, I have to work this morning and then I'm free this evening. Why, did you want to come to my place, maybe go out for a few drinks and then come home with me and watch a movie?" I see the hopeful expression on his face. It was an expression I would have to crush unfortunately.

"Oh I'm really sorry!" I gasp, "I thought I told you, Max and I have made plans, we are supposed to be going to see her parents later today and we'll probably crash at their place overnight." I clock Max's head pop out from the bathroom, hair matted down to her scalp whilst she mouths *What the actual fuck* at me behind Ben's back. I try to communicate with widened eyes for her to shut the fuck up and go away, which she seems to get as she disappears back into the bathroom.

"Oh no worries then, I guess I should catch up on some work that I've been putting off. Gives me a reason to get it done." Ben folds his paper and puts it down on the table. Downing his coffee, he moves around the chair and plants a chaste kiss on my lips. "I'm going to get ready and hit the road." I smile against his mouth and nod.

A few minutes later I hear the front door click shut as Ben leaves the apartment and I let out a sigh of relief. I potter around the kitchen cleaning up the dishes from breakfast when a crack from the edge of a tea towel smacks my butt.

"What the fuck!" I jump and turn around to see a pissed-off Max holding a blue tea towel-turned-weapon.

"That's my line! What the fuck Ty! Why did you tell Ben we are going to my parents' tonight?" I shrug and turn around, and begin tentatively cleaning the countertops. "Don't brush me off like that, if he asks me, I now have to lie. So tell me, why the fuck am I now a potential liar?"

I turn to face her and lean back against the sink. "I just don't want to spend time with him if I don't have to." I bite my lower lip. "I know how that sounds but I like my time away from him as well. That's normal right, you don't have to spend all your time with the guy you're dating?"

Max moves forwards and puts her hands on my shoulders. "Usually at the start of a relationship you do want to spend all your time together. I don't mean to be a bitch for bringing this up, but do you remember when you were first with Lukas, I had to fight to spend time with you? Now I have to fight to spend time away from you two, it's like you don't want to be alone with him any longer than you have to." She's hit the nail on the head. It's something I'm acutely aware of, but something I do not want to put a name to.

"Max, it's just so frustrating. I mean what is there not to like! He is soooo hot! He has muscles where I didn't even know you could have muscles. He is hung like... like I don't know what, eye-wateringly hung if you catch my drift." Max waves me along as if to move on swiftly. "And the sex, I mean talk about making your toes curl!" Max coughs and barks out a laugh.

"You're such a dickhead," she chuckles, "So what's the problem then, that all seems great."

I sigh and rest my forehead against her shoulder. "He doesn't give me the feels you know. He turns me on, but he doesn't make me happy."

Max makes a sad face as if she understands the subtext of what I'm saying. "You mean he doesn't make you feel like *he* did?" I return the sad face and nod. "Well then you are not the type of person who is consciously unkind to anyone, so you know what you have to do don't you?" She gives me a sad pitying look.

I bury my head in my arms and mumble, "Can't you do it for me? Isn't that what best friends are supposed to do?"

She tuts, pushes me away and wags her finger at me, "Now Tyler you know that just isn't true, we are there to make you cookies when you break up, we are there to kick your ass out of bed when you're late for class, we are there to tell you when the leather pants just aren't doing it for you honey, we are even there to get the dried-up cum from your hair when you walk-of-shame right into the lecture hall with an embarrassing white smear on the back of your black t-shirt, but we do not break up with boyfriends for each other." She was disgusting but right.

*   *   *   *

Later that night after coming back from Ben's place and feeling both sadder and lighter than I had in a few weeks now, Max does exactly what she'd promised she would do as a best friend and makes me the double chocolate chip cookies she knows I crave.

"So how did he take it?" she questions between large bites of raw cookie dough.

I reflect on the evening and frown in frustration. He had taken it much better that I would have. He was so very sweet, he had asked what he had done to mess things up, he had asked if we could still be friends, he'd asked if I was ok quite a lot. It was infuriating. I wanted the china flung across the room – he didn't have any china, but I wanted it broken anyway – I wanted raised voices and accusations of infidelity, but it was all so civilized. Maybe he had not been feeling passion with me either but hadn't known what name to give the demon.

"Yeah he was fine, like too fine, asked could we go out for coffee next week as friends fine." I scowl and shove another cookie between my lips.

Max grimaces and nodded her head, "Yeah that is not the type of reaction you want from a breakup." She places the tip of her index finger on the cleft of her chin. "Maybe you're just terrible in the sack and he has a better offer lined up? Maybe he has been pining after *his* ex-boyfriend and didn't want to be the bad guy? Maybe you kiss like a fish!" I reach out and punch her in the shoulder. "Ouch!" she giggles.

I purse my lips and look to the sky as if in thought, rubbing my fingers against my chin and muse the way Max had. "So what do you think is the correct amount of time to wait after breaking up with one boyfriend before ringing an old boyfriend to see if he wants to grab coffee, or go for a drink, or ravage me or get married?"

Max claps her hands and jumps up to her knees on the sofa. "So you are actually ready to give it another go?"

I nod quickly and decisively. "I'm through with spending another minute away from him, every second I'm not with him I am crawling out of my skin, I need him, I... I love him." Max's eyes become glassy with tears.

"Ok so action plan, maybe wait like a couple of days before calling. If he ever found out that you had been in bed with your ex only hours before trying to get back with him it might not go over so well. Also it will give you time to make yourself look a bit more presentable because honey, you have been letting yourself go recently," she instructs whilst rubbing her fingers across the smooth moustache I had allowed to form.

I pull back away from her, "Hey face fuzz is back in! It's ok to have a moustache!" I scowl in fake outrage.

"Yeah if you're a 70's porn star named Dirk it's ok!" she laughs and shoves yet another cookie into her mouth, then frowns at the still half full plate. "Also maybe we both should lay off the cookies, I think we have reached our annual limit on the sugars." She places the plate on the coffee table and gives her belly a rub. "Come on, get your things, we are going to the gym to tone up that flabby belly you big fat bitch," she says whilst rubbing the layer of pudge that has developed along my midriff.

"Ben said it was cute!" I widen my eyes at her.

She tuts and shakes her head. "Ben was too nice for his own good, he was probably a feeder and wanted you like one of those big gals who requires a crane to get them out of bed, now get a move on!"

"So a few days huh," I pout, "this is gonna feel like a long two days."

And a long two days it was. I hit the gym obsessively, giving my mind something other than Lukas to be preoccupied with. I catch up on the reading that I promised I would do before the beginning of the new semester. My room has never looked so neat and organized.

I sit at the kitchen table, my phone facing upwards, staring at me between my downward-facing palms on the table. Max sits across from me waiting to see what I'm going to do next, like she has been for the past five minutes.

"If you are waiting for him to psychically connect to you and ring you instead then I think we may be here a while," Max says with a smile. She's aware how much this means to me, she's clearly trying to keep her usually bitchy self in check.

"I just don't know what I'm going to say, *help me!*" I groan and pout.

She laughs with me and reaches across placing a hand over mine. "I'm not sure what it is you think I can do, I managed to snag Peter by smiling widely, pushing my breast out and cocking my hip to one side." She frowns for a moment before giving a *meh* shrug and starts to push her breasts together and pouts. "Is this helping?" she says between pursed lips.

"I know! Can you please call Dawn and see if he is dating anyone else, or has developed an allergic reaction to me, or has a voodoo doll of me, or some reason why I wouldn't want to call him, you know?"

Max shakes her head, still pushing her tits together, and narrows her eyes at me. Releasing the breast pressure she huffs. "Fine, I'll do your dirty work, but I ain't doing it in front of you cause you will get me all flustered, so go sit down on the couch."

I jump off the dining room chair and I'm on the couch in two seconds flat, looking at her like an expectant puppy waiting for her to throw a ball. Realising I'm not going to be able to sit still, also like a puppy I decide to be productive. I run to my room, quickly getting changed into something that shows off my body in a way that I knew Lukas likes. I'm done with all this waiting bullshit. If I find out he is single still, I'm calling him and we are meeting up *now*. I pace my room as I hear Max's voice talking to presumably Dawn on the phone. After a few minutes the talking stops. I grab my keys and wallet and head back into the kitchen where Max is sitting at the table staring at her phone.

"He is dating someone else isn't he, I fucking knew it, why the fuck did I not just hold on to him outside the club, what the fuck was I thinking!" I almost yell across the room.

Max looks up. "Tyler sit down for a minute."

I pace around the living room and turn back to face her. "It's me isn't it, he isn't with anyone else, he just doesn't want me anymore, I knew when I saw him in the club that he looked hurt to see me with Ben, well if that fucker thinks he can get rid of me that easily then..."

Max stands up and yells, "Sit the fuck down Tyler!"

I stop in my tracks and look at Max properly for the first time since walking back into the room, her face dry but eyes clearly red-rimmed from crying. I move to join her at the kitchen table, a mountain of dread pooling in my gut.

I sit across from her and grip the edge of the table. "What's wrong?" Max reaches across and lays her hand over mine. "Tell me what the fuck is going on Max." Panic buzzes in every cell of my body.

"I just got off the phone with Dawn, she couldn't speak too long as they don't allow phones on the ward at the Christie." The last word hits me like a ton of bricks.

"The Christie? What the hell is she doing there, isn't that a cancer specialist hospital? Oh my god is Dawn ok?" My throat starts to constrict as I try to prepare myself for whatever she is about to say.

"Yeah Dawn is fine, she is there with Lukas." My world begins to implode around me. "Tyler, Lukas has cancer. He had surgery a few days ago and is still in the hospital for observation, it's serious." Before she can get any more words out I throw myself off the chair, grab my coat, keys and wallet and run out the door.

Chapter 26.

Lukas

Well I can officially, from personal experience, say brain surgery sucks: not only does it leave you with quite a nasty scar if you're as bald as I currently am, but the pain is something to be marveled at, like fire ants have crawled across my scalp biting and burning as they traverse the now-hairless landscape.

The medical staff have given me a whole host of painkillers and anti-seizure medications. The pain however manages to break through whatever miracle medicine Kate has promised would 'take the edge off'. Dawn has insisted I try to sleep through it if I could manage, but I may have snapped at her and told her, *'You try getting holes drilled in your skull and having your body filled with poison and see if you can sleep through it!'*. I remember seeing her face crumple, and I'd thrown my arms around her and sobbed into her neck, the tears bringing some form of relief and validation to the agony racking my body. I had laid down after and promised to try and get some rest. That had been about half an hour ago.

I hear a commotion in the hall and my eyes fly open. I hear Dawn's loud whisper, "Maybe it just isn't the right time, if he wanted you to know, I guess you would know, sorry."

Who the fuck is she talking to? It can't be my mother because she knows exactly where I am, and aside from the nice bouquet of flowers currently gracing my bedside table, she has not made the effort to come and see her son.

"Fuck that!" comes a familiar voice that has my heart catching in my throat. My curtain is suddenly pulled aside violently, Tyler's face is flushed and distraught. His gaze finds mine and his expression melts into one of relief. I realise how different I must look and start to cover myself with a blanket. I'm around 20 pounds lighter than when he last saw me, I have no hair on my head or eyebrows for that matter and I'm currently sporting quite a nasty scar across my scalp. I almost apologize to him for having to look at me like this, but before I could say anything, he's pushing himself into my arms. If I feel any pain at all it's nothing compared to the joy coursing through my body right now.

"Thank god!" he sobs into my neck. I feel the warm tears against my cheek; I know they can't be mine because I'm so dehydrated that I'm not sure if I had any moisture left in my tear ducts.

"You're here," I murmur, more of an incredulous statement than a question.

He pulls back and gives me a stupidly quizzical grin. "Of course I'm here!" he says, peppering my cheeks and forehead with light kisses, "I'm always going to be here!" He pulls back again, his eyes meeting mine, and then he presses the gentlest of kisses against my mouth. A small sigh escapes my lips as if the breath has been waiting all this time to be released. In a way it kind of had.

I settle my hand on his waist and move it slowly up his side until I'm cupping his jaw gently. My fingertips trace the smooth outline of his jaw, the familiar current crackling along the surface of my skin, lighting me up in a way that I hadn't felt in a long time. He moves back from the kiss and I let out a small groan of displeasure. A grin blooms on his face as the smug fucker realises the effect he still had on me.

His face changes, his brow furrowing as irritation takes over his expression. "So do I kick your ass now or later?" is the question he asks whilst giving me a pointed look.

I grin and settle back on the bed, my arms outstretched over my head. "What? The bald, cut up, slim look not doing it for you?"

The internalized fear that he will not find me attractive anymore must show on my face, despite trying to mask it under arrogant bravado. He reaches across and settles his hand on top of mine and squeezes gently. "Baby there isn't a look on you that I would not be totally into." That fucker knows exactly what to say and when to say it to completely floor me. The heat in his gaze tells me he's not exaggerating either. "But that's not what I am here for."

I pout quite dramatically and then sigh. "So who told you?" Whomever it was, I made a mental note to kiss the shit out of them before killing them.

"Max found out through Dawn, don't be too harsh on her though." I make a mental note to destroy her later before smiling back at him once more. It feels like he is almost a mirage, and I hope this is not just a side effect from having my skull cracked open. I hope for a moment that maybe it's just my heart not accepting the fact that he is actually here, although my heart is hoping to god that my brain is dead wrong. Right then my brain decides to open my fucking stupid mouth and break me out of whatever spell his presence has cast over me.

"Hang on, where is Brian?" I know his name is Ben, but I hear that if you consistently call an ex's new boyfriend the wrong name it'll undermine their confidence in the new guy's worth. Evil? Maybe, but I'm not taking any chances here. It's probably bullshit but I'm only working at half power with the gaping skull wound.

I see the playfulness in Tyler's eyes, he can see right through me and smirks, interlocking his fingers with mine. "*Ben* and I are no longer an item. There is and *has* never been anyone else." I want to call him out on this as I clearly saw him openly fucking, for all intents and purposes, on the dance floor not that long ago, but something about the heat in his eyes has me stopping in my tracks and trying to catch my breath.

The bay door opens, Dawn and Dr Kate make their way into the room chattering amongst themselves about some nurse drama going on that I'm vaguely aware of. Dawn gives me an apologetic look, I can't say that I'm even remotely mad at her and I smile; however we will be having words later about the bro code and how it still applies to her and her vagina. She grimaces and comes to the other side of the bed collapsing in a huff in the plastic armchair. Kate smiles at Tyler and raises her eyebrows in question.

"Kate, this is a friend of ours Tyler. Tyler is this Kate." I can almost see Kate's brain buffering as she tries to place the familiar name. The hourglass stops as the name sinks in. "OH! Tyler! As in…"

I cut her off sharply, "As in yeah as I said, a friend of ours Tyler." I give her a sharp look that is basically a full-on hand wave and a loud *SHHHH*!.

She bites her bottom lip, holding in a laugh and comes to stand at the foot of the bed. "As we have a newbie in the room, I have to ask again, do you want people to leave the room while we discuss your case?"

I shake my head and tighten my grip on Tyler's hand. Kate has her stack of charts in her arms again, most times Kate comes into my room with those damn charts, it's usually to tell me that things weren't progressing as we have hoped, and that we'll be getting more aggressive with treatment. I'm not exactly sure how much more aggressive treatment I can take. "It's ok, you can talk."

Tyler winks at me and I feel my cock twitch. I glower at him playfully. Totally not an appropriate time to turn the doomed patient on. I wonder if there will ever be a time when he doesn't have complete command over my entire being, whether I'll ever be able to look at him without wanting to cry, throw myself at him, tear his clothes off and bury myself inside him, or what I have really wanted recently, for him to bury himself inside me, to claim me as his in a way we haven't done since the first time we'd had sex, to make sure that no matter what happened, I would only ever be his.

"Well as you know, I cracked open your noggin earlier last week." Dawn and I nod respectively whilst Tyler lets out a disbelieving laugh and mutters something I can't quite make out.

I chuckle and lean in to whisper in his ear, "You will get used to her." He visibly shudders as my breath skims across his neck.

Dawn barks out a laugh, "Wow I would say you two need to get a room, but then I'm realising we are in your room." I throw a pen from the bedside table at her which she dodges, but she continues to laugh.

"Ahem! Professionalism please children," Kate scolds. "Getting back to where I was, so I sliced open your melon, and shock of all shocks, you actually do have a brain."

I throw my arms up in the air. "Thank the lord, I wondered what that rattling sound was in there, guess that explains it."

"I know right!" Kate nodded emphatically. "Well since I got that out of the way, I might as well get to the results part." I nod and gesture towards her to finish. "So as you are aware, we completed a round of chemotherapy prior to your surgery, which didn't go as well as we had hoped. The cancer didn't shrink as much as I had expected it to, especially with how aggressively we treated it." I feel Tyler completely tense, I'd forgotten that this was all new to him, the big C word. I rub slow circles with my thumb against his palm. He looks down at our joined hands and pulls me to him with a sniff, wrapping an arm around my shoulder and tightening his grip till it borders on painful.

"Oh sorry, continue," he says to Kate.

"That's perfectly ok. We then all agreed it was best to attack this thing surgically because it had clear margins, I felt that I could remove the entire thing as I am... well for want of a better phrase, the dog's bollocks." Dawn nods along as if this is absolutely normal, whilst Tyler still has a very clear 'what the fuck' expression plastered over his face. "We took some biopsies a few days ago and a further MRI scan and I now have all the results with me." She opens her notes on her lap and moves the glasses which have been perched on top of her head down to the bridge of her nose.

I don't realise I am still holding my breath until Tyler whispers, "Breathe baby, it'll all be fine, we're together now, I can take care of you," into my ear. That small statement both fills my heart and makes it sink into sadness all at once. The knowledge of what I have to do cripples me.

"Well it looks as if the surgery was a total success. I got all of it, the biopsy and the scan came back clear. We did it! Now you will have to come back every few months for the next few years for more scans to make sure it stays gone, but as of now I think you're gonna be ok."

For a second I don't move. Tingling in my fingertips tells me I'm excited about something, but my brain takes a second to process.

I'm going to be ok.

I'm going to be ok?

I take a second to let that thought fully take hold. All at once emotions crash into me, I'm about to jump at Kate and throw my arms around her for essentially saving my life, but Dawn beats me to it, sobbing gently into Kate's neck and saying thank you over and over. I'm not sure who I have to thank for having a friend like Dawn, but I know for sure I'll never be able to say thank you enough.

Tyler pulls me to him and crushes me against him, his mouth pressed firmly in a long kiss to my shoulder. I revel in his warmth and the feeling of perfection that he brings just by being there with me. I know this will have to last me for a while at least, as I have to tell him that I can't be in a relationship with him right now.

A short while later, after I spend some time thanking Kate for giving me my life back and basically becoming one of my new best friends, she and Dawn thankfully read the tension rolling off me in waves and guess that I am desperate to spend some time alone with Tyler. They're right, but not for the reason they have undoubtedly assumed. I move to the door of the room, closing it and turning the small lock at the back of the door. Tyler lies back on my hospital bed, his jacket and shoes discarded underneath the bed, his head resting on his arms which were stretched up behind him. Why does he have to look so fucking good?

A small strip of smooth skin is deliciously visible where his T-shirt pulls up and taut against his stomach. He smiles at me and motions his head in a c'mere motion. I'm helpless around him and he knows it. I move to the bed, kneeling at the end, resting my hands against his calves. The thick layer of hair brushes under my hands, his shorts riding up high and pulled tight against his thighs. It takes every bit of my willpower not to run my nose or tongue up his leg and press my face into his crotch. I need him so badly it makes my jaw ache. He scoots down the bed, back flat against the mattress, pulling me up and on top of him. I lean down and press my mouth to his. The warm flavour of him coats my tongue as he slides his own into my mouth. He moans on contact, which fires all of my engines. He deepens the kiss at the same time as he pushes his hips up to meet mine, his arousal obvious as it presses against my stomach.

I need to figure out a way to make my brain put a stop to this; I know I have something to do, but his presence overwhelms me. He does it for me however when he moans, "Oh my god Lukas, I've missed you so much. I'm gonna take care of you now."

His words startle me and have me pulling myself up and resting back on my legs. "Listen we really have to talk, I'm sorry I let it get this far. But we have to discuss a few things." I cough, hoping I can muster enough courage to get through this without crying or giving in to what I really want to do, which is to let him hold me and take me home.

Tyler moves back off the bed and settles into the chair next to me, his face marred with concern. Part of me is screaming, *Shut up you idiot, you have everything you have wanted for months sitting inches away from you! Shut the fuck up!* I sit forward, my legs dangling off the edge of the bed. "Thank you so much for coming today, you have no idea what it means to me." He moves as if to respond to what I'm saying; I hold up my hand to let him know I'm not done. "For months all I have thought about is what I would do if I got the chance to be with you again, to repair some of the damage I caused months ago and to apologise for kissing you outside that club when you were with someone else. Not once in any of the fantasies I had about that would I ever be saying that this," I motion between us, "can't happen."

It takes him a moment for what I'm saying to sink in. Then he's standing up from his chair pacing the floor in front of me. "What do you mean? Like you don't want to be with me anymore?" His voice cracks slightly, his brow furrowed deeply.

"No you don't understand, there is nothing I want more than to be with you!"

He stops walking and comes to stand in front of me, his hands on my shoulders. "So what then! Is there someone else?"

Anger starts to bubble within me. "When would I have had a chance to meet someone new Tyler, huh? Through which round of chemo do you think I had a chance to meet the man of my dreams? Between the last round which made me feel like I was on fire and cold all at the same time and throwing up until I felt like I was turning inside out, or just before the surgery in which I had my skull cracked open?"

He stops then; looking at me, he bites his lips. His fingers tremble as if he is stopping himself from reaching for me. I know the feeling well. "I'm saying I want us to be together, but we can't." I drop my head, eyes trained to the floor.

"Why the hell not?" His voice rises to match the panic in his eyes.

"Because we just can't, ok?" My resolve wants to weaken. I want to wrap my arms around his waist and pull him to me.

"No that's not good enough, you don't get to tell me you want me as much as I want you, that you need me as much as I need you, but that we can't be together!" He drops to his knees at my feet, his head resting against my thighs. "I need to know why baby. Please I need you to be mine."

I know what I'm going to say probably isn't going to go down well, but it's something I know I will be hung up upon. "Because I want you to be with me for me," I admit. He looks up confused. I don't blame him. I'm confused also, but I just know this is the right thing to do. "I want you to be with me because you want to be with me. I don't want to spend the rest of my life wondering if you came back because you found out I was sick, and I don't know, maybe you felt guilt or some type of obligation."

He pushes back away from me sharply, the look on his face as if I'd struck him with more than my words. "Are you fucking kidding me right now Lukas? Do you honestly think I'm the type of man to be with you out of what? Pity? Obligation? Are you actually fucking saying that's the person you know me to be?"

I move off the bed and close the distance between us. I grab his wrist, but he pulls it away like it burns. I back away and hold up my hands. "I just need some time, ok? I need time to get through this and to make sense of what's happened. I just don't think I can do that whilst worrying that you're only with me because I could have died." My truth hurts me just as much as I think it hurts him.

His face changes from hurt and confusion to one of understanding. He moves towards me once more and wraps his arms around my waist. I give in to my desire then and rest my head against his chest. His mouth moves gently against my scalp as he whispers, "I understand, but don't for one minute think I'm going to stop trying to win you back. You're mine baby whether you want to believe it or not."

My heart begins to sing, and I hope to god he keeps that promise.

Chapter 27.

Tyler

I imagine that this is what hell is like, having the proverbial carrot dangle in front of your face only to be told the carrot doesn't want you to take a bite. Ok, maybe that isn't how the saying goes. Lukas has made good on his promise that he wanted us to be friends. I get the feeling this is more for my benefit than it is for him, or so he thought. Max, Dawn and Lukas sit in one of the booths at the coffee shop, chatting amongst themselves during my shift. There's a crazy Saturday noon rush happening, which doesn't leave me much time to sneak away to spend time pressed up obscenely close to Lukas. Instead I'm forced to sit off on the sidelines, watching as guy after guy sidles up to their table to hit on the guy that I'm sure is mine, even if he hasn't completely figured it out yet.

I take in a sharp intake of breath as a tall demigod of a man, all thick golden blonde hair, tan and muscles for days sidles up to the booth, shakes Lukas's hand and leaves it there for a fraction of a second too long. I grind my teeth together and pull down a rag from one of the shelves underneath the counter and start to wipe the surfaces.

"What's the matter, angry puppy?" I look up to see Dawn, propped against the counter, peering at me with a shit-eating grin over her large cappuccino.

"Absolutely nothing," I stare past her to watch the greek god fucking puff up his muscular chest to epic proportions, Max drooling whilst Lukas giggles at something the man mountain says. "I'm fan-fucking-tastic."

Dawn looks around to see the reason for my glare and chuckles, "You're not seriously worried about that little display over there are you?"

"No, I have no reason to be worried, Lukas is a single guy who can do what he wants, right?" I bite my bottom lip and go back to wiping the counter, the shine on the surface telling me it was likely already clean to begin with. I huff out a sigh and return the cloth to its shelf.

"You're an idiot," Dawn laughs.

"Erm excuse me," I stare at her eyes wide, "what's that supposed to mean?"

"I mean you're an idiot if you think that the boner-worthy guy standing at that table right now has any chance at all with *him*," She gives me a pitying look, "You're all he sees."

I look around her and catch Lukas looking back at me with a worried expression. He gives me a quick wink and then goes back to his conversation. My heart stutters in my chest as I whine. "So why are we not together right now?" I wait for her with a hopeful expression.

"You just have to wait." I sag a little. "I know that sucks, and I know he told you that he needed to be sure that you were with him for the right reasons, but that's not it."

I gape a little. "But he said..."

She holds up her hand. "I know what he said, but it's not him that needs to be sure, he wants you to be sure. He doesn't want you to feel trapped, to feel like maybe you missed out on something cause you were stuck with the sick guy. Just give him time ok?"

I smile at her, sadness welling up within me. He should know that he is all I see too. He's all I've ever seen.

*   *   *   *

A few weeks later, after our classes let out one evening, we all decide since Lukas has now finished his medication, we should go out and celebrate, and let him have his first alcoholic drink since 'rejoining civilized society', as Dawn has put it. The last few months have been taken up with rehabilitation, recovering from surgery and countless pills that needed to be taken with a variety of instructions – some before food, some on a full stomach, some while standing on your hands when the clock struck twelve. Lukas had been a walking, talking pharmacy for a while there.

He had come back to classes not long after the semester had started, after he had had a heart to heart with a teacher to whom he said he owed an apology. I'd walked with him to her office and stood from afar as he got out a few mumbled words before she threw her arms around him. They had stood there for a while until he had pulled back from the embrace, wiped his eyes and she had waved him on.

We've all kept in regular contact with Dr Kate, who has told him he can return to his normal life but to take it easy. She's agreed to join us tonight on our little excursion to the night life of the City. I'm secretly glad, as if he starts to overdo it, it can be her getting the stink eye and not me. We end up crammed in a booth in a larger-than-average gay club on the outskirts of the city. Lukas is surrounded by our friends and an ungodly number of hot young men who have made it their mission to come over to our booth and make my blood boil by finding any excuse to touch him, to congratulate him on making it through the hard times. I blame Dawn personally for having the DJ announce the good news shortly after we got there.

Max slides in next to me and wraps a protective arm around my shoulder. "You ok there buddy?"

I turn my head and narrow my eyes at her. "I'm fine," I seethe through clenched teeth as I spot yet another handsome guy lean across the booth, whisper something into Lukas's ear which makes him blush and then plant a kiss against his cheek. That's MY fucking blush.

I have to turn away to stop myself from jumping across the table and ripping the guy's head from his body, showing Lukas that he's not supposed to be letting other men kiss his cheek. That is *my* cheek to kiss and no one else's.

Max laughs and pats my shoulder. "Cheer up, you look like someone just shoved a hot poker up your ass."

Again I grit through my teeth, "I said I'm fine!" which only makes her laugh more.

"Yeah you keep telling yourself that fella, why are you over here anyway? Why aren't you over there peeing on his leg, that's how you gays mark your territory right? It's still with pee?" She looks at me with a quizzical expression.

I give her a withering look, sag my body and sigh. "I'm giving him space, he said he needed space to figure himself out, so that's what I'm doing, I'm giving him space, space to have other men pressed up against him, space to have men's lips pressed against his ears, space to..." is all I gst out before the plastic water bottle in my hand crumples, spilling water everywhere. I mumble embarrassed apologies to those around me who are in the process of shaking their heads and giving me 'fuck you' looks before turning my back on Lukas and facing Max. She looks at me like I'm afraid she's going to look at me, with sympathy and pity.

I move out of the booth and start towards the bathroom when I feel a hand tug on my bicep. I turn to see Max standing there, her face resolute. "He has had space Ty, don't you think that's enough now? You can't wait around forever. Go get what's yours."

"I'm not going to force him into anything he doesn't want." I shake my head, trying to control the need to cause chaos in the bar.

Max comes up behind me and puts both her hands on either side of my head, turning it in the direction of Lukas. "That boy has not stopped staring at you all night. If you don't do something soon, then someone else will." As she says this, another guy comes out of nowhere as if fulfilling a prophecy, sliding in around the booth to sit next to my not-boyfriend.

"Fuck this!" I mutter and storm across the room to where Lukas is holding court. I lean across the table and shout, "Can we please go somewhere to talk?" Lukas looks up from his drink, sees me and shakes his head, pointing at his ears. "I said can we go somewhere..." Once again he put up his hands in an *I don't know* gesture and mouths the word 'what'. "Oh for god's sake!" I reach out and grab his hand, dragging him from the booth and out of the reach of the Jared Leto look-alike/wannabe pawing at him.

We make our way through the bar, leaving from the back entrance through the cloud of noxious smoke courtesy of the few party revelers expelled to the outside of the club. Moving across the seating area, I position us on a bench facing out over the river. I see a slight tremble leave his shoulders and realise I've dragged him outside in the middle of October and haven't even given him a chance to grab his coat. I take off my jacket and wrap it around his shoulders, shrugging off his mild protest. I love the feeling of his body pressed up against mine, trying to seek out additional warmth. I put my arm gently on the back of the bench, allowing my fingers to fall and play gently with the edge of his shoulder.

"Nice night huh?" he mumbles. The couple of drinks he's had this evening, after not drinking for so long, are obviously having a calming effect on him. I look out at the calm waters of the River Mersey and the lights of the Wirral across the other side and follow the water as it stretches out into the cold Irish sea. The water is calm, without a breath of wind anywhere.

"Yeah, beautiful," I say, turning to look at him; he must feel my eyes graze over him as a smile plays at the corner of his mouth. Over the past few months he has gained back a lot of the weight he'd lost though treatment and he now has a decent amount of hair on his head. It has never mattered to me though; I think he's beautiful every minute of every day.

"So what did you want to talk to me about?" he asks, turning his head, his chin resting gently on my shoulder, his breath sliding down onto my chest. I feel my cock punch against the zip of my trousers, straining for some type of relief. Only he can have an instantaneous effect on me doing something so totally innocuous, only this time I have to show some form of restraint.

"Are you having fun tonight?" It's such a lame opening line, but I can't quite find the exact words I want to say.

Lukas laughs, then frowns. "Did you really drag me outside the warm club into the cold night to ask me *How's things*?"

No, I dragged you outside to stop myself from going psychotic every time another man dares to put his hands on you, before I bump you on your already sore head and drag you back to my apartment caveman style and fuck you senseless, but of course I don't say that. I'm not sure I'll ever have the balls to do... I catch Lukas looking at me open-mouthed and scandalized. I look around to see what he's gawking at when he says:

"Well it'll be very hard to stop you from doing that, I mean I'm all weak and helpless." He pouts playfully. Holy shit, have I been talking out loud? I seriously need to get control over my faculties around this guy. I feel the heat spreading up my neck to my ears, I know I'm blushing crimson right now and have to look away to gather myself. Lukas reaches up and turns my head to face him, pulling my gaze down; my eyes take him in, settling on his full lips.

His eyes are heavy and lust-filled, his breaths coming fast and sharp. I lower my head and press my lips gently against his. I breathe out a sigh and reach up to rest my hand against his jaw, the stubble there grazing against my knuckles and sending a tingling sensation down my arm. Lukas's tongue slides against my lower lip, trying to gain entry. My hand travels down and rests flat against his chest. I feel his heart racing, hammering against his chest. I push back against him, breaking our kiss. Slightly irritated, he looks at me with a questioning glare.

"Feeling a little needy baby?" I laugh, pressing a small kiss against his mouth. Like a cat pouncing on a ball of string, he turns and mounts my lap with the agility of a Russian acrobat. Slamming my body back against the seat, Lukas writhes in my lap, my cock pushing forcefully against him, as if it and him were in cahoots and I'm the only thing keeping them apart. Lukas groans, feeling the effect he's having on my dick, and pushes down hard until I can feel my length nestled in the cleft of his ass. His hands wrap around the back of my neck, he pushes his tongue deep into my mouth, his flavor consuming the inside of my mouth and eliciting small keening noises from me.

Finally realising that we are still in public I try again to push Lukas back off me. "Babe, I think we have an audience."

He slams his mouth against mine once more. "I don't care, let them watch," he groans and reaches down cupping my hard cock through my jeans. I chuckle and lift him off me, sitting him down beside me. "You're no fun," he laughs, adjusting himself through his trousers.

"Hey, there is nothing on this earth that I want more right now than to get naked with you, but I think I need to make myself clear on a few things first." He stiffens a bit as if I might be about to break some bad news. "I love you, always have and always will. I know you said that you needed space, and I have tried, I really have, but enough is enough. I can't wake up every day not having you wake up next to me. I tried and it sucks. I can't stand watching you with anyone else and I'm fairly sure you can't stand watching me with anyone else." He gives me a sideways eye roll and mutters something about Brian. "I only want you, the biggest mistake I ever made was walking out on you that day with Caleb. I let my feelings from the past influence me. Of course you would have been a bit freaked out being confronted by someone from your past."

Lukas puts his hand on mine and shakes his head. "Tyler you don't have to do this, I..."

"No I do have to do this, we definitely had a rough start all those years ago, but I saw something in you then that I still see in you now. Through all the darkness and violence there is a light in you that just calls to me. I'm not ok unless you're with me. Please say you'll forgive me and give me another chance." I turn to him and sink off the bench to my knees in front of him. "If I have to beg you for another shot I will."

 Lukas, quick as a flash, joins me on the ground and lifts my face to his with both hands, his breath on my face making the hairs on my neck stand up straight and a shudder run the length of my body.

"You will never have to beg for a shot with me, I've been yours from that first moment in Art class. I remember that day clearly as crystal. The second I saw you I knew you were something special, and it scared the ever-loving shit out of me. I obviously didn't handle it well."

I laugh a bit at that, I feel a small tear escape my eye and travel down my face.

Lukas leans forward and kisses the tear, stopping it in its tracks. "You know, the whole time I was going through treatment, the one thing I kept on thinking and the one thought that made me fight through everything was the fear that you didn't know how much I love you. I was scared I was going to die without you ever realising that you're the other part of me. I love you Tyler. I'm never going to stop loving you."

I lean my forehead against his, part of my self-sabotaging mind waiting for the other shoe to drop, waiting for the cameras to appear and someone to thrust a microphone in my face and ask me how much of a fool I felt. But none of that happens, instead Lukas whispers his love for me quietly in my ear over and over until I let out a breath and allow myself to fall.

Chapter 28.

Lukas

TEN YEARS LATER

"I swear to god Tyler you'd best not still be in bed, we have a long drive ahead and I am not driving the whole way this time!" This man is going to make me go grey far earlier than I ever thought possible.

"Slow your roll there husband! I'm up and dressed!" he says, peeking his head over the top of the stairs. I can't see his body so I call him on his bullshit. "Really, then come to the top of the stairs so I can see what you're wearing?"

He gives me a sheepish look and shrugs, "I can describe to you what I'm wearing, I don't want to move. I'm lazy?"

I give him a pointed look as he rolls his eyes and emerges from around the top stair. That man can still take my breath away. In the ten years we have been together and the five we have been married, not one day has gone by that he doesn't make me count my lucky stars that I have perfect 20/20 vision. There in all his tall, broad chested glory is my very naked husband. The smattering of hair on his chest is thick and full, leading down his stomach until it joins a well-trimmed nest of dark pubic hair, and my eyes travel lower to his thick long cock resting against his balls. My cock twitches at the sight. I'll yell at him next time. In long strides up the stairs I'm on him, forcing him back into our bedroom. The back of his legs hit the end of the bed, making him fall backwards onto the mattress.

"Well hello there!" he mumbles as my mouth attacks his, a groan escaping my lips as my cock hardens to steel in 3 seconds flat. "Maybe I should be more lazy in future," he smiles at me.

"Less talking, more sucking," I moan and I kneel up, bringing him with me. I smile, putting my hand on the back of his head, forcing it gently down onto my increasingly solid dick. As always like a champ he takes it all in one swallow. My hand fist the base of my cock to stop myself from cumming down his throat straight away. I have other plans for this man. He pushes me until I'm on my back, my head resting against the pillow and hands gripping the headboard behind me. Tyler lets my dick pop out of his closed lips and lifts it again, licking a fat stripe along the underside of the shaft. Moving further down the bed, he trails hot kisses down the inside of my thigh. "No fucking around Ty!" I moan.

He grins up at me. "Someone's being a little impatient this morning! Maybe I should teach you a lesson and get myself dressed and let you think about your actions," he admonishes playfully.

I reach forward pulling him down on top of me. "I don't fucking think so, I want your cock deep in my ass in the next ten seconds." I feel his cock swell in between us, pushing against my stomach. "Oh someone likes the sound of that huh," I beam at him, he reaches down to adjust himself and scrunches his face which makes me belly laugh.

Pulling me up into a seated position he straddles my lap, grabbing my face between his palms. "Have I told you how much I fucking love you?" His voice is filled with the same kind of awe that I feel on a daily basis.

"Only every other day, although I could stand to hear it more." He giggles and pushes me back down onto the bed. Sliding down my body, he ghosts kisses across my skin, goosebumps rising wherever his lips meet. He hooks his arms under my knees and lifts my legs until my thighs are pressed back against my chest, exposing me to him in the most deliciously vulnerable way. Each time we are together like this I feel sexier than the last.

I catch his smile as his head darts down and I feel the warmth of his tongue circling my hole. I gasp and reach down to put my hand on top of his head, forcing him a little deeper into me, his warm tongue exploring, sucking and licking. I think I might just come out of my skin with the need I have to be filled by him right now. He moves his head away slightly only for him to replace his tongue with his spit-slick finger. The familiar burn appears as he begins to probe into me, stretching me wider and wider with one finger only to be joined by another. Crooking his finger inside me he lands against my prostate, pushing hard against the small walnut-sized bundle of nerves, making my back arch and my fingers bunch the sheets against the mattress. The lascivious grin on his face pulls me to new heights, I already feel the beginnings of my orgasm starting to build in my core. I am not going to cum like this!

"Seriously Tyler, you have to fuck me, like right now!" My voice is heated and makes me sound like a total slut, which I know he really enjoys. Reaching across the side of the bed he pulls a bottle of lube from the nightstand and pours a good amount in his hand, working some along the length of his heavy cock, the glisten making the veins bulge along its length stand out even more. He works some of the lube into me with his fingers and then lines up the head of his cock with my hole.

"You ready for me baby?" I moan and arch my back again, the need slowly starting to become unbearable.

I feel the push of him, as he thrusts past the tight ring of muscle, the head of his dick sliding inside me. "Oh fuck yes!" I cry out, reaching up to push the tips of my fingers into his hard pectoral muscles and wind them into his chest hair. "Please fuck me baby! Fuck me hard!"

That's all the permission he needs as he starts to piston in and out of me, his heavy balls slapping against the skin of my ass as he rockets forward. I love watching him fall apart as he fills me up, the feeling of skin on skin as the heat of his dick meshes with the heat of my tight hole. Grabbing one of my ankles he pulls my leg across him until I am lying on my side, allowing him to get a much deeper angle into me, pegging my prostate on every pass and thrust. I know I'm not going to last long, but by the looks of him, neither is he.

"Please cum for me Ty!" I moan, I hear the wanton need and desire in my voice. Like I have any control of it was laughable. He places his elbows on either side of my head and picks up the pace even more, sending shooting white lights exploding behind my eyelids. I squeeze my eyes closed, the sensation bordering on pain but landing firmly in extreme pleasure. His balls tighten up against me, he screams my name and releases load after load of his hot seed inside me. I have seconds left before I join him in his release, I pull off him and flip him onto his back, straddling his chest, I let my dick rest against his lower lip as I quickly jack out my release. I gasp as my cum coats his tongue. He lifts his head forward, taking my length in his mouth and cleans the rest from it. He pulls off my dick and releases it with an audible pop.

"Well good morning to you too!" he smiles up at me.

"We are going to be late. Ask me if I care now," I laugh. "But we really should be hitting the road soon. Why on earth did Max decide to renew her vows so soon? Haven't she and Peter been married for all of five minutes?" The irritation creeping back into my voice.

"Well four years, but yes still fairly soon I have to agree. But I am the man of honor once more and she is a stickler for tradition and repeating the fuck out of things, so down to London we go." I push off the bed and make a move toward the bedroom door. "Everything is by the front door, all we need now is your lazy ass to get dressed and we can hit the road." I feel his release still inside me, but I have no intention of getting rid of that anytime soon. Twenty minutes later we are on the road, making the long drive down to London.

Chapter 29.

Tyler

As usual, any event planned by Max goes off like a military operation. Planned to tiniest detail with precision that would have made a covert spy operation look like a bumbling plan by a group of schoolchildren. I had given what she said was the perfect speech with just the right balance of love and scathing hurtful comments, which was just my style. We had barely gotten through drinks after dinner when Lukas and I had made a quick exit back to the hotel room.

I stare at my husband as he makes his way towards the hotel elevators, I watch as his suit hugs all his taut muscles. Yes I love to see that, but I also love taking it off. I can only stand other people ogling my man for so long before my complete wacko jealous side takes over and I have to mark my territory in the best way I know how. By claiming him in the bedroom, over and over until he falls asleep and can't notice anyone else but me.

The next morning I wake without the usual human furnace pressing alongside the entire length of my back. Instead I feel the dip in the bed as Lukas sits perched with his legs over the side of the mattress, looking wistfully out of the window into the gardens below our hotel suite. I sit up, concerned, and run my hand down his spine, causing him to shudder which gives me a twinge of pride. "Everything ok?"

He turns to face me and smiles at me with sadness in his eyes. "Yeah I'm ok, just thinking is all."

I move to sit next to him and wrap the duvet around his shoulders. The frost on the windows casts a seasonal glow in the room, the cold clinging to the January air. The room is warm, but still not warm enough to be sitting out naked as he is. I have to remind myself that he is obviously upset about something as my dick twitches at the sight. "Thinking about what?"

"It's been over ten years since my dad died, over nine years since I spoke to my mother last or my sister. It took me a long time to get over the fact that none of them came to support me when I was going through treatment or even bothered to phone when I was five years free. I know I shouldn't, but I just miss them. Is that stupid? To miss people who obviously couldn't give a shit if I'm alive?" He hangs his head and takes in a deep breath, the pain evident on his face gutting me. Whenever I see him hurt, I want to either kill the thing that hurt him or move the entire earth and the entire universe until I can find a way to make him smile again.

"Why don't we go and see them, like now?" I say, an idea beginning to form in my head. He whips his head around to look at me like I have just lost the whole plot.

"Don't be silly, we are here for Max, she has yet another lunch today, she'll go ballistic if we just up and leave." He places his head on my shoulder and resumes looking outside. Lunch or not, I am not going to let another second go by without trying to make him feel better. Max will understand anyway, she loves Lukas like a brother. Our small group has become our chosen family, protecting each other fiercely when anyone or anything tries to harm us.

"You leave Max to me, we can book a hotel in Cambridge and drive to see your mum. You need closure one way or another Lukas." He dips his head and smiles at me, leaning over to place a sweet chaste kiss on my lips and mumbling 'thank you' against me. My heart hurts for him.

Lukas has become such a part of my family over the last decade. It had taken my family a minute to understand what the hell I was doing with a former bully and the person they knew had beaten me up in high school on more than one occasion, but today he is closer to my family than I'd ever hoped. They call him son just like they did me, he's been part of our Christmases and special celebrations even before we got married. My mum had made a big deal about walking me down the aisle which had made me sniffle a bit, Max and Dawn had both beamed a wide smile and said, "Great! That means we both get to walk our Lukas down the aisle!" Lukas had been overwhelmed and I had had to leave the room before I made a blubbering scene in the family room.

"Whatever happens with your mum, just know that I'm here for you ok? It's me and you forever right?"

He smiles and kisses me softly before starting to pack our things.

I send up a silent prayer to anyone who would listen to please not break his heart.

I make our apologies to Max and we make the short drive to Newmarket.

Chapter 30.

Lukas

Pulling up outside my family home gives me a weird dual feeling of both nostalgia and complete bewilderment as it seems completely foreign to me. It has been so long since I have been back here that everything is new to me once more. The driveway has been repaved and the outside of the house has been repainted, but other than that everything has remained the same. Still, the feeling of familiarity escapes me.

We had decided not to call in advance, not giving my mother the chance to make up some incredibly polite middle-class excuse about why she couldn't receive guests and instead, maybe have a short conversation and leave. No matter how hard it might be, no matter how hard my mother might crush my spirits, it was important that I do this.

Tyler parks up the car, gets out and runs around the car to open my door for me, which always makes me chuckle, like I'm his date from the sixties or something. Taking my hand, he walks us up the drive to the front door and pushes the intercom button. I wait with bated breath as the static crackles over the speaker, waiting for the inevitable awkwardness that was sure to follow. I hear a familiar voice croak through, "The speaker is on the fritz, wait for a minute I'm just coming to the door."

I roll my eyes at Tyler; the intercom has been *on the fritz* since I was little, before we had packed up the house and left it gathering dust. A small commotion on the other side of the door cues the upsurge of anxiety and panic within me. Tyler squeezes my knuckles as he must sense my inner turmoil.

There is a bang on the other side of the door, and a voice shouts, "Hold on, I just need to get the key!" I smirk a bit; my mother was always locking the door from the inside and then misplacing the key somewhere in the bowl. It'll take her a good few minutes to rifle through its contents before finding the right one.

"It's ok, no rush," I call gently through the door.

"Lukas?" my mother's voice calls incredulously through the door, "Lukas is that you?" My heart begins to pound in my chest.

"Yes mum, it's me," I say tentatively.

"Oh my god Lukas! Please don't go, wait there... oh please... wait there, don't move ok... Oh my god Lukas are you still there?" I hear her voice cracking and the tell-tale sounds of her heavy breathing as she starts to sob, and a sound most likely of the bowl crashing to the floor.

An idea sparks in my mind, I kick a few stones in the flower bed and sure enough there is a dark grey stone with a glittery sheen in the centre of a rock pile. I crouch down and lift the cold stone, flipping it over to reveal the small clasp. Opening it up, my old key is nestled inside.

"It's ok, I'm not going anywhere." Hope in my chest starts to rise, Tyler's hand tightening around my own offering me the support I so dearly need right then. I slide my key into the small lock; before I have a chance to use it, the door flies open knocking into the small table I remember being behind the door.

My mother clearly doesn't care that one of her precious vases crashes onto the floor, smashing into countless pieces as she flings herself into my arms, sobbing into my neck, her arms circling me, clawing at my back as if trying to make sure that I'm really here and not a figment of her imagination. She repeats the same words on a loop like an incantation she is hoping will influence my next moves.

"I'm sorry, I'm sorry, I'm so fucking sorry," she says over and over.

My hand comes up to stroke her hair, trying to reassure her. All the anger, hurt and betrayal I feel towards this woman takes a back burner whilst I revel in the feeling of being in my mother's arms once again. She pulls back from me only to grip my face between her palms.

"Oh my god, let me look at you!" she gasps. "Look at the man you've become!" She looks to my side to see Tyler standing there looking somewhat sheepish, but clearly pleased for me and trying his best not to be awkward in the emotional reunion. She tries her best at a warm welcoming smile, and however much of a shift I'm seeing in my mother at the moment, warm and welcoming still does not come easy to her. So rather than a big beaming smile, she seems to show Tyler her teeth. I stifle a laugh as Tyler looks at me shocked over my mother's head mouthing *what the fuck*. I shrug and he winks at me. That man can settle me even in the most stressful situations.

"Tyler!" she exclaims, wrapping an arm around his waist in a strange display of social awkwardness. "Will you boys come in?" It's more of a hopeful question rather than a given welcome. She gestures for us to come inside, and we follow her into my old family home. Except right now, I feel like a guest. It's a feeling I hope will pass as soon as I cross the threshold. I stand strangely in the hallway waiting to be welcomed into whichever room my mother now uses to receive company.

"You boys come in!" my mother calls from the back lounge. Tyler smiles at me and motions for me to go forward. I'm so glad I have him with me. Although I have nothing to truly fear from coming home, having him with me gives me a sense of comfort that I would otherwise be lacking. We walk into the large lounge and my mother gestures for us to sit on an expansive comfortable looking two-seater couch facing the armchair where she sat.

"Can I get you boys a drink, a tea or coffee?" Ever the gracious host, she wouldn't be able to stand it if someone were in her home and felt uncomfortable in any way, unless she was related to them. We both shake our heads. "How about a sandwich, or I can make some lunch, I know it's a little after lunch time, but it's not exactly dinner time. I could run to the local deli and get some of that nice cheese and sourdough loaf you like. I haven't been there in a while, but I'm sure they will still have it. I mean Bill passed away, but his boy runs the deli now..." Her face gets a little red, as if she's struggling to draw breath.

"We're ok, really." I smile at her as warmly as I could muster. "We are not staying too far from here and they have a really nice buffet breakfast."

"Oh! What hotel are you staying at? Is it local?" She plays with the metal clasp of her bracelet on her wrist absentmindedly.

"We are staying at the Lisburn in Cambridge, a really nice place on the river." The banality of the back-and-forth between us is beginning to grate on me. This is not a natural state of being for either of us. Not much has changed in the ten years since I'd been here last. Something catches my eye however which has my eyes narrowing on the walls. The furniture may have been updated, but the same photos line the fireplace and side tables, the same artwork on the walls. The one thing I do notice however is that more photo frames have been added into the mix. Photos of me. Not just me, but photos of me and Tyler. Photos from our wedding. I stand up and move towards the group of photographs sitting next to her and pick up the most prominent one in front. It is a black and white portrait of Tyler and me in our wedding tuxedos standing under a huge arch, smiling as our friends throw confetti over us. I know this picture well as it hangs in our own hallway.

"Where did you get this?" I ask my mother, showing her the picture. She looks down at her hands which she is wringing violently. I squat down in front of her and place my hand over hers. "Mum? I asked where did you get this?" She sighs and looks up at me, guilt etched over her face.

"I asked your sister to see if she could get a few photos from your Facebook profile. I didn't have any of you recently and I wanted you close to me." The sadness in her voice floors me. I hate seeing my mother like this, so weak and defeated. However, a stronger emotion fights its way to the surface – anger. I stand up, placing the photo back where I'd found it.

"You know a good way of keeping me close to you mum, is not to abandon me in the first place." As I expect, her head falls forward, her eyes glued to the floor whilst she quietly nods, which only serves to infuriate me further. I want her to yell at me, I want her to tell me to have more respect for her in her own home, something that she would have done all those years ago.

"Lukas…" Tyler begins.

"Fuck no Ty! I have some shit to say, and she is going to listen to me." My voice is starting to become uneasy, my breaths coming quick and fast, and I know I have to get myself under control before I break out into a full-blown panic attack.

"It's ok Tyler, he has a right to say what he wants to say." She turns to me and gestures for me to go on.

"Do you have any idea how many times I needed you over the last few years mum, like when I *really* needed you? Like when I graduated from university and everyone else had their families there to show them how proud they were? I was looking into the crowd just hoping that you would show up and be there for me, but you didn't. I waited for you mum." I track a tear sliding down her cheek as it lands on her hands, she gently wipes it away. My heart is lurching but I don't want to stop, I can't. "How about when I married the man I love? The happiest day of my life and my friends had to walk me down the aisle. Those people have been more of a family to me over the past ten years than my own fucking family! Yet you still blame me for *his* death." My mother makes a move to speak, and I raise a hand to let her know I'm not done. "Finally do you have *any* idea how scared I was all those years ago, in the hospital, not knowing whether I was going to live or die. I was *so fucking scared* mum." I realise too late I've started to cry. "I tried to be strong, be brave, be a man, just like dad taught me, but I couldn't. I thought I was the reason dad died and that the cancer was my punishment. Do you have any idea how humiliating it is, not to know if you will wake up tomorrow and to cry like a baby for your mother, only to know deep down she didn't give a shit and wouldn't show up."

Tyler bolts from his seat and wraps his arms around me, pulling me down onto the seat next to him. My mother shifts uncomfortably in her chair, bringing the sleeve of her yellow blouse up to wipe at the tears streaming down her face. I turn my head away from the heartbreaking sight and press my face into my husband's neck. It's time for us to leave. Maybe this is why she has never reached out in all these years, as she knew how much it would upset her. That I would show up unannounced and ruin her life. Just as I am about to tell her goodbye, her small voice sounds from across the room.

"314." Her voice is weak and filled with sadness. "You were in room 314, before they moved you post-surgery and then you were in Bay 6." My head darts up and I catch her red-rimmed eyes before her gaze drops to the floor once more.

"What are you talking about?" I whisper, lead filling my stomach.

"I found out through a friend of a friend that you weren't well. I knew you wouldn't want to see me after how I treated you when your dad died." She moves forward, sitting on the edge of her seat, "But I couldn't just sit back and do nothing, so I drove up north and I waited in the hospital. I knew I couldn't sit with you, but I sometimes waited in the cafeteria, or the coffee shop downstairs. Sometimes when you were asleep, I would sit in the relatives' room next to where you slept. There was once when you were very ill and you were drowsy and not aware of everything around you, so I sat by your bed for hours. It was both the hardest thing I've ever done and the best day for me in a long time as I got to hold your hand, kiss your forehead and just be with you. You started to come round, so I had to leave." I sit there in absolute shock; of all the things I had expected her to say, that was not one of them.

"I thought I had dreamt you being in my room," I say, shock still clearly audible in my voice, "You were really there? When I woke up there were a bunch of flowers in my room and I thought I remembered a nurse saying they were from my mother."

"Yes I was there for about 3 weeks I think until I had to come back here, but by that time you were being discharged anyway." She stands up and comes to sit down on the other side of me. "There is something else that you *have* to know! You were not the only one who was subject to your father's violence. I just loved him, he would always tell me how sorry he was, how that time would be the last time."

"I didn't know!" My eyes widen and I feel the bile creep up my throat.

"This is not why I'm telling you." She places her hand on mine. "I am so very sorry for how I treated you after your dad died, but in no way do I blame you for that man's death. He was responsible for his own actions. If he had been a better father to you and accepted you for the wonderful boy you were and for the exceptional man you would become then maybe he would still be here with us today. But he wasn't, he was a son of a bitch." She squeezes my hand like her life depended on it. "So don't you for one minute think that I don't love you, I was selfish and scared for all these years that you would reject me, so I wanted to keep a small amount of hope in my heart that you were still my son. I thought if I didn't reach out then you couldn't take that piece away from me."

She reaches across me and lays her hand on Tyler's. "I want to thank you for loving my son and thank your family for being his family when his own wasn't. There is nothing I can do to repay their kindness but if you will both let me," she stares both of us in the eye in turn, "I will spend the rest of my life trying to make it up to both of you."

Hope springs from my chest and wraps me in a kind of warmth I hadn't known was possible anymore. There's hope for a family that I hadn't dared to dream would be there for me again. I'll hold on to that hope for all I'm worth.

Chapter 31.

Lukas

I stare at the walls of the gallery, my face unable to hold back the disdain and confusion that was obviously etched on it for all to see.

"Can you at least pretend to look like you don't hate the art and everyone in the room babe?" Tyler says, hip-checking me lightly as he continues to take copious notes on the small leather pad I'd bought him a few weeks earlier. "I'll do my thing here and then we can go get fucked up at whatever bar it is that you're dreaming about right now."

I put my hands over my chest and make moony eyes at him. "Be still my heart, my man knows just what to say to brighten my day," I say flatly. Tyler chuckles at me and then goes back to his work. I mill around the gallery, hoping to find something that doesn't inspire an eye roll. So far, I'm coming up empty. So far I've seen a wicker chair flipped on its side, and I'd received a stern talking-to from a security guard when I'd tried to be helpful and stand it up. He caught me just in time to tell me it was an exhibit. Fuck this place.

I'm here for Tyler though, a few years earlier after graduating with a Bachelor's and then a Master's degree in Journalism and English Literature, he had worked his way up through various gigs of online website writing, blogs and local press to his current role as an international fashion editor at Verdux, a glossy magazine for a global brand. Why we are in an art museum for a fashion piece I have no fucking idea, but here we are. I'd been told in a very snooty accent, "Fashion and art are one and the same Lukas, it's like you don't know anything about fashion!" I have to agree with him there, as long as clothes fit me in all the right places and still make my guy wanna rip them off me, then I am one hundred percent fine with that level of expertise.

I had completely pivoted on my career plans thanks to Max's meddling: she had introduced me one Christmas to the joys of homebrewing my own beer. Like the obsessive freak I am, this small gift turned into a full-on obsession until I started my own business two years ago, which now has a small factory and a growing number of staff making locally brewed ales. We'd never imagined the success that we both have in our lives, but it's most certainly the complete faith and support we have in one another that has given us both the strength to succeed.

I catch myself staring across the room at my man's tight ass in his suit pants, enjoying the way they cling to him like a second skin. I even enjoy some of the obvious attention he's getting from a couple of women just off to his left. I shake my head and smile. Tyler's head turns towards me and he spots me gazing at him. Heat flares in his eyes as it normally does when he catches me ogling him. I ball my fists at my sides to stop myself from marching over to him and dragging him to the nearest restroom. I have to remind myself repeatedly that he's here in a professional capacity... stupid work.

"Lukas Ford! Holy hell what are you doing here?" a voice to my left exclaims, "Long time no see man!" I quickly turn my head to see a smiling Caleb Irwin standing with a toddler propped on his head, her small face round and cherub-like, surrounded by tight ringlets of blonde hair. I can only assume this is Caleb's daughter as she bears a striking resemblance to her father.

"Caleb! What the fuck man!" I exclaim, seeing his face wince and him raising a hand to press gently over his daughter's ear and a slight shake of his head I mouth *Sorry*. "Hey, it's been a long time. I would say how have you been, but I can see you've been quite well!" Caleb has put on a small amount of weight; he's not the chiseled guy he had been in high school, but somehow he looks impossibly happy, his grin stretching from ear to ear.

"Yeah this is my little girl Melody; Lydia, my wife should be around here somewhere."

I put my hand on his arm and shake my head smiling. "You seem so different, like in a good way, you seem happy dude."

He nods his head emphatically. "Hard not to be!" He looks around. "So how about you Ford, how have you been keeping?"

"Dane actually," I say smiling.

His mouth parts slightly in obvious shock, shaking his head fast and then facing me again. "Say that again?" he laughs.

"Yeah, Lukas Dane." Just as I finish saying this, my man sidles up to me and kisses me briefly on the cheek.

"I don't think I'm ever going to get tired of hearing you say that name." I turn to him, the same heat in his eyes has returned, making my pulse kick up a notch, my tongue darts out to lick my lower lip, his eyes tracking immediately down to my mouth. I see his breath catch.

"Woah, you guys are in public. No F-U-C-K-I-N-G in the open please, not in front of innocent eyes." Caleb motions to his daughter.

"Wow, Caleb hi!" Tyler says, leaning in to give him a genuine hug, making sure not to squash the little girl. "And who is this little angel?" making funny faces until she giggles and reaches out to stroke his face. I'm always amazed by my husband's remarkable talent for leaving the past in the past. Here he is standing between the two people who had made his life a misery in high school for years and he's behaving as if we are all old friends. My heart aches to hold him and never let go. I plan to do that later.

"This is my Melody, say hi Melody." She does a small wave before getting embarrassed and hiding her face in the crook of her dad's neck. "I hear congratulations are in order!" Tyler nods, the happiness evident on his face. I tug him to my side, wrapping my arm around his waist; his hand reaches down to rest over mine.

"Thanks! Listen I'm about done here, I think I saw your wife over there looking at the Gauman exhibit, but if you want to grab lunch, we are free right now?"

Caleb nods enthusiastically and motions over to his wife. "I'll just go and grab her, be right back." Caleb moves through the crowd towards his wife.

"Thanks baby, are you sure you want to spend an afternoon with the two of us though?"

He smiles and places his hand on my chest over my heart, the heart that belonged to him. "He is your friend, and you're mine. So, let's go." He reaches down and interlocks our fingers. I never want to let go. So I don't.

Epilogue.

Tyler - JANUARY 2021

"It's your turn! It's so your turn," I moan into Lukas's ear, "It was my turn last time baby."

"Eurgh! Fuck you and fuck everyone else as well!" he moans back, swinging his legs off the bed, making his way down the hall to our son's room.

All the while I hear the small voice shouting, "Daddy! Daddy!" through the house. I love that boy more than life itself, but those people who say that you will never get sick of hearing your children call your name are either saying that under duress or have been tortured until they're suffering some form of sick Stockholm syndrome.

It's been an eventful year. In 2020, Lukas's mum finally made the big move and sold her house down south, and bought a very nice property on the seafront in Formby. She had become somewhat of an unofficial resident in the north the year before that, spending a lot of time staying with us when she came to visit. That was until we had a family dinner with my parents and my mother suddenly discovered her soulmate, which was an upsetting revelation for my mum's long-term boyfriend who had always assumed it was him. After that, both our mums had become inseparable. Travelling together, book clubs, Vegas holidays and eventually helping her secure a property not a million miles from their own.

Lukas has rebuilt somewhat of a relationship with his sister, she has stayed down south but spends a lot of her holidays with us and the rest of our family, her husband and two children in tow.

Around the same time Lukas and I decided we were ready to expand our family. We hadn't thought we could be any happier than we already were. We were actually very very wrong. Both Max and Dawn volunteered to be surrogates for us. It had been an awkward conversation with both of them when we said thank you but no thanks. There were a lot of children out there who needed homes, and we knew that we could be good parents for a little one already born.

Early last spring we were introduced to our son Gideon, a one-year-old boy. It had been a difficult transition but things are finally starting to settle down and we are becoming a real family. The door to our room opens up and in walks my stunning husband with our equally stunning now two-year-old son. "Someone woke up very early and now wants to say good morning." Lukas says through sleepy eyes.

He plonks Gideon down on the pillow next to me. His little face looks up at me, he reaches up to stroke my face. "Good morning," he says in a small voice that completely melts my heart. I lean over him and kiss him on the forehead.

"Good morning! Someone's up early!" He giggles and stretches out on the bed.

"Shush Daddy, I'm trying to sleep!" he smiles, turning over and facing Lukas who has climbed back into bed and has already begun the very quick process of getting back to sleep. Gideon scoots over until he is pressed up against Lukas's back, resting his small cheek against the large wall of muscle. I turn and sit cross-legged on the bed, looking at the two most important men in my life and knowing right there and then that I am exactly where I'm supposed to be.

THE END

About The Author

J S Grey lives in Warrington, North West England with his husband, son and Black Labrador. Having always wanted to write M/M romance novels, he spends his time reading M/M romance novels and watching awful TV shows he secretly loves. *Moony eyes over Arrow*

He loves going to the gym and then eating too much food and regretting it after. He once convinced his son it was still nighttime by keeping the curtains closed so he could get another hour in bed to read. Father of the year ladies and gentleman!

To learn more visit:

Facebook - https://www.facebook.com/AuthorJSGrey/

Instagram - https://www.instagram.com/thejsgrey/?hl=en

Website - http://www.thejsgrey.com

Whilst this is the end of Tyler & Lukas's story, they make a re-appearance in the second book in the series.

☐ Best Friends Brother

☐☐☐☐☐ High School Bully / Enemy to Lover

☐ Mistaken Identity

☐Cheating Lover

☐☐Best Friend Side Kick

☐Heart Break / Betrayal

"So, you might be wondering how I'd come to be sitting on the floor of my apartment, surrounded by clothes strewn all about the place with tears running down my face and a torn T-shirt wrapped around my palm to stem a steady flow of blood. I know I would be asking that question. How about we start from the beginning."

Raven's Way

Love in the South

Chapter One

Davis

NOVEMBER 2008

I press the ornate steel grey buzzer which adorns the ten foot high walls strewn with dark green ivy. The crackling of the buzzer makes me jump as the call goes through. I look down the long road on either side of me, noticing that this wall seems to stretch the full length of the country lane. It feels a whole other world away from my last high school.

"Hello!" a voice crackles over the line, the sound coming through but distorted as if someone were crinkling a bag of chips in front of the mouthpiece. "Hello is anyone there? I swear these little shithead locals keep messing with this good-for-nothing buzzer."

I suddenly realise that I'm just listening to this play out and I should probably speak before the person gets any angrier. I really don't need a member of faculty hating me on my first day.

"Oh sorry! Yeah I'm Davis Kennedy, I'm new here; I was told to come to this gate but it's locked." I pull the lapels of my hunter green peacoat up around my cheeks to try and stave off the biting November wind whipping around my head, no doubt messing up my hair which I had spent a long time perfecting before I left the house this morning.

"Well of course it's locked young man, we don't want just anyone walking around the grounds," the clipped voice retorts through static. I frown and look through the bars of the tall, intricately decorated wrought iron fence to see a long driveway lined on either side with what I had learned from my welcome pack, in the section on wildlife, were holm oak trees. I had rolled my eyes pretty hard when I read that the school prided itself on its pristine lawns and impeccably managed woodlands. At my old high school the boys used the bushes that lined the playground to take a piss. Not exactly the pride of St Albans High.

"So yeah it's my first day, I'm supposed to meet someone at the admin office for registration," I call back, hoping that the person hears my teeth chattering, takes pity and lets me in.

"Very well, welcome to Melwood Academy," the voice chirps before hanging up. A loud buzzer sounds, followed by the cranking of gears as the heavy gates slowly open, allowing me entry into my new high school. I take a deep breath and walk through.

*   *   *   *

Walking down the long tree-lined driveway, I notice that running through the trees are thick rails of fairy lights wrapped around each of the branches, connecting each tree as far down as I can see. I imagine at night when they are all lit up, this place is beautiful.

I stop my thoughts right in their tracks; I'd resolved to completely despise this place and the posh twats who came here. My parents could force me to attend school here, but they could not make me like it, no sir!

After walking for what feels like an eternity, the wind doing irreparable damage to any hairstyle that had been crafted onto my head that morning, I finally reach the end of the driveway. The path opens wide onto a huge lawn, which had been meticulously mowed into rows so neat that it looked like you might be able to slice your finger open at the end. Down the centre of the lawn runs a white stone path, not a patch of dirt on it from what I can see. I look down at my scuffed and muddy high tops and shrug. Those white stones won't know what hit them.

At the head of the path and surrounding the lawn stands an impressive old Georgian Gothic school building, the tall, high-arched doorways holding what appeared to be original heavy wooden doors with iron hinges and metal plates riveted to them to strengthen the joints. The windows decorating all sides of the building loom large over the lawns. High up on what might be the fourth or fifth floor is a giant circular window which stands central to the structure. Inside the aperture is a large detailed stained glass display. What it is displaying I cannot be sure, as it is so high up and I'm still fairly far away.

I realise I am still standing at the foot of the path and gawking, like someone who has just taken a donkey kick to the head. I look around to empty lawns; thankfully everyone must already be in class, saving me from standing out as the *weird kid who stares*.

I make my way towards the main entrance through the middle of three arches and push open the heavy doors. The entrance leads into a large, similarly Gothic atrium with a modern built-in mezzanine floor. Students are littered about the open plan space, some looking up from their conversations to take note of me as I walk into their space, a gazelle walking amongst a pack of well-dressed lions.

The space seems to be sectioned off into places for people to sit and read, with a small breakout space holding two rather dated vending machines. Off to the right, small banks of desks with racing green felt dividers hold groups of students just shooting the shit. My eyes snag on one particular group, who look as if they had just wandered off the pages of 'Hot Jock Fantasy'.

My roaming gaze halts on one guy in particular. Embarrassingly enough, drool starts to collect at the corners of my mouth; reaching up, I wipe away the offending liquid with the back of my hand. The immediate adjective that springs to mind as soon as I lay eyes on this guy is *beautiful* - the absolute personification of male beauty.

I watch as he laughs with his friends. His Adam's apple bobs in his throat, dark shaggy chestnut brown hair heavy on his face, messy strands falling across his forehead over his eyes. His full lips curve up into a grin as one of his other friends elbows the other. I have no idea what they are fighting over as my attention is unable to tear itself from this boy who has completely captivated me the moment I looked at him. He ticks all my boxes: the square dark stubble-lined jaw, the wide-set shoulders that imply that he either lifts a lot of weights and spends loads of time at the gym, or that he plays rugby. I guess, by the thick tree-trunk thighs straining against his jeans, that rugby is his game.

I move slowly down the corridor, keeping the group of jocks in my eyeline. The guy's warm olive skin, which stretches over his thick neck and down to the bit of his chest which just peeks out above his polo shirt, calls to me. I have an intense desire to lick down his neck and taste what I imagine is salty goodness there. *I'm so gross.*

Again I realise I'm auditioning for the role of *weird kid who stares* and decide to make my way to the administrator's office, when Hot Guy decides to look my way.

Our eyes lock.

Something in his stare has me unable to move, like a deer caught in some sexy as fuck headlights.

I notice a small flare of interest in his eyes, before he schools his features and blows me a big kiss, which cracks the rest of his friends up. He winks at me and then laughs, turning back to his friends. Heat flares up my neck and I bolt for the nearest hallway. Thankfully I notice a sign for the boys' bathrooms and duck inside.

Standing at a sink, I look into the mirror and immediately notice the flush creeping up my neck towards my face. Well, now not only will I have the reputation of a boy who stares, but also that of a creep who pervs. Absolutely fantastic.

It had definitely not been my idea to move here. I'd grown up in a small village in the cathedral city of St Albans. I'd loved my life, I loved my friends, my school and our small three bedroom house with a huge garden at the back. It had been perfect. I had made friends almost immediately in primary school and become lifelong friends with nearly everyone in my class. Now just because my dad had been made partner in a firm of solicitors in Surrey, we all had to up sticks and move here.

"It'll be delightful darling, just you wait and see," my mother had promised me. Yet she isn't the one who has been plucked from a perfect existence and plonked into Downton Abbey High. In my old school I was basically a big fish in a bigger pond, here I'm gonna be like cheap tilapia in a pristine lake filled with Beluga whales filled with caviar.

I had been right in my previous estimation that my hair would look insane. I run my hands through my shoulder length sandy blonde hair. I've been quite proud of my hair since the summer, when I'd spent a lot of time helping my father out in the garden and caught what can only be described as sun-bleached highlights. My hair makes me look like some beach bum surfer dude, just without the ability to surf.

I appraise myself in the mirror. I know that I might be considered more than averagely attractive. My high, wide cheekbones have been described by my best friend (potentially former best friend now I've moved several towns away) as the envy of a lot of the girls on her hockey team. My ex-boyfriend Mark had repeatedly told me that he could get lost in my eyes, which were the colour of warm caramel. I run my fingers along my jaw, the tip of my index finger reaching up to snag on my lower lip, plumping it up a little more than usual, imagining the hot guy pulling on my mouth before pressing his lips to mine. I shake my head and after splashing some water on my face, I pull myself together and leave the bathroom.